The Third Squad

Praise for the Book

'A melancholy cop's obsessions are just the tip of the iceberg as he leads a two-fisted team determined to clean up Mumbai's mean streets . . . Kumar's style, blunt but often by turns poetic and droll, is arresting . . . As unusual as it is compelling, this entry lays the groundwork for an entertaining series.' *Kirkus Reviews*

'Kumar evokes [Mumbai] with lyrical prose.' *Publishers Weekly* (Included in a *Publishers Weekly* feature on Crime Fiction focused on police corruption and brutality)

'[A] gripping thriller . . . Kumar has created some thoroughly intriguing characters . . . but the most fascinating of Kumar's characters is Mumbai itself – enormous, crowded, hyperactive, roiling, stunningly rich and grindingly poor, and teeming with almost unfathomable energy. International-crime fans should flock to this one.' *Booklist*

'*The Third Squad* ends with an emotional wallop, making it stand out among crime novels. It has the chiaroscuro effects of classic noir, but also the philosophical depth of highbrow literary fiction . . . Mumbai teems with lurid intrigue in this smart and affecting work of postmodern noir.' *Shelf Awareness*, starred review

'Kumar does a masterful job building the story's tension level as Karan draws closer and closer to his final confrontation with his superiors in the Indian Police Service.' *Book Chase*

The Third Squad

V. Sanjay Kumar

juggernaut

JUGGERNAUT BOOKS
KS House, 118 Shahpur Jat, New Delhi 110049, India

First published in India by Juggernaut Books 2017

10 9 8 7 6 5 4 3 2 1

ISBN 9789386228314

For sale in the Indian Subcontinent only

Printed at Replika Press Pvt. Ltd, India

Dedicated to my parents Sumedha and Vijay,
my siblings Ashok and Rajiv, and the idea that
willy-nilly you can get caught in the middle.

Once upon a time, a woman was picking up firewood. She came upon a poisonous snake frozen in the snow. She took the snake home and nursed it back to health. One day the snake bit her on the cheek. As she lay dying, she asked the snake, "Why have you done this to me?" And the snake answered, "Look, bitch, you knew I was a snake."

—*Natural Born Killers*, 1994

Somewhere Outside Pune, India
Police Headquarters: Special Training Unit

"You don't have to strip a man to see his face," says the controller. "But it helps."

I examine myself closely in the handheld mirror. The first rays slant through the wooden slats in the dark barracks. The sun rises between two peaks of the Sahyadri Hills, a range that shelters our training camp. In the last year we have grown to hate this valley. It has been a rigorous incarceration. Today it is all over and done with, and one way or another we will be freed. I am anxious; I feel like I have never seen myself before.

I get dressed quickly. The summons comes and the four of us soon file down a narrow corridor, shuffling and stumbling and smelling of sweat. We duck through a low door and emerge into bright sunshine and we arrange ourselves as we always do, forming a straight line with the tips of our polished boots. The roll call is poignant; one of us is missing.

He keeps us waiting as he examines each of us. I hold my breath.

"Spell discipline," he says.

I begin spelling the world and am cut off.

"*Chutiya*, define it!"

I glance around at the three others who are staring

straight ahead. Munna, Tapas, and Kumaran. It suits them to behave like three monkeys. I start again.

"Discipline: training expected to produce a specific character or pattern of behavior."

The controller nods. He holds a polished stick in his hand that he raps on his thigh.

The fleshy sound brings back memories and I wince. He has his back turned toward us. His worn brown belt has a tear and sweat is building under his armpits. He talks to the wall.

"And how do we go about achieving this?"

I look to my colleagues and they are still motionless, backs ramrod straight and showing no signs that they are about to respond. It is up to me again.

"Discipline is instilled by a combination of repetition, physical and mental challenges, and punishment for failing to meet certain standards." I could rephrase that. I could use *sister this* and *mother that* and tell you more succinctly that we were taught to follow fucking orders, or else.

In truth, there was no real need to teach us discipline; it was something that came naturally to each of us. We hardly spoke to one other and none of us made friends. And we busied ourselves in routine. Like taking apart and assembling our firearms every day. The whole day was lived by the clock, the week was lived by the calendar, and changing seasons made no difference to us. In the worst of rains we would still be out on our run every morning. We would still go to the range and shoot our socks off.

The controller nods again, gripping the cane firmly in the palm of his other hand, and a rap follows. He pivots on the toes of his left leg. He regards each of us in turn with bulging eyes and a hint of distaste around his mouth. Somebody needs to clean his spectacles.

"Why have you been called here, gentlemen?" he barks. He speaks without pausing and his phrasing is confusing—nobody has ever called us *gentlemen* before.

None of us wants to say why we are here. We all know it but are loath to speak. I sense his irritation and I crack first; I always do.

"To learn from those who have passed on?"

He clucks his tongue. "Why do you talk like this, Karan? Vague, roundabout, and always with a question. Say it as it is. One of you has died, has fallen, has failed. It is a failure."

I breathe deeply. One of us had taken a bullet between the eyes. The rest of us were asked to inform the family.

"He did not die in vain," I say. I sound like a schoolboy.

After a moment of silence the controller shrugs. "We need to learn. If you men learn from this incident, then what you say is true." And then he speaks in French: "*Dans ce pays-ci, il est bon de tuer de temps en temps un amiral pour encourager les autres.*"

I alone understand what he is saying. He looks toward me expectantly.

"Karan, you seem upset. If you know the meaning of this expression, why don't you translate it for the others?"

I rephrase it to make him seem less heartless than he is: "It is strange how it is good that from time to time someone dies so others don't have to."

Ranvir Pratap looks at me. He is surprised and there is a hint of respect as he nods slightly in my direction. They do not expect us to think, and they get worried when our gray cells start working, because thinking is their job and doing is ours.

"You may be feeling raw right now but I will not lecture you. Get used to death. I have operated in its realm long enough to respect it. It is extreme, and its finality is hard to stomach. You guys are not meant to respond like the rest of humanity. That's not your nature. Right, Karan?"

He wheels around and glares at me because I am a known weak link, someone who occasionally gets muddled and hesitates. I am in the squad only because I topped every shooting test, busting their all-time records. They could not dump me on paper. But I was on the case that claimed my friend and colleague. I was the backup and the sod who was slow to pull the trigger, who gave benefit of doubt to his target, and my colleague paid for it with his life. I did make amends. I finished the target, made him pay. A rage I never knew I had ruled me for a few minutes. The controller had arrived at the scene and was speechless at my handiwork. I guessed then that I had lost my chances of qualifying and they would post me back to a desk job in that morass of clerkdom from which we were pulled out. Rage is not good in this business because it's unpredictable.

Summing-up time, and Ranvir Pratap is brief. I expect the worst.

"We experienced a live situation and, despite your training, you came up short. None of us know how we will respond in a moment of extreme stress, when a split second decides life and death. We try to train you for it but that is only half the job. The other half comes from who you are, your genetic code. As trainers, our job is to choose correctly." He looks at each of us and settles his gaze on me. "Karan, you have barely survived this program. But I have decided to back you—I was the deciding vote. You will be under my direct command, so if anybody has to hold the can it will be me."

Later he pulls me to the side. "What I said there was for the others. Do you know why we chose you despite your mistake?"

"Sir?"

"All trainers look for just one thing and you have it. You have something that cannot be taught."

We entered Mumbai by road; there was no welcome committee. The four of us were in an unmarked jeep and as instructed we were in plainclothes. We hardly spoke during the winding journey through the hills. I felt a tingling sensation as we approached Special Branch which I chalked up to pins and needles. Ranvir Pratap's words still rang in my head. *You will lead a simple life*, he said. *There will be no statistics in the Third Squad, not if I can help it. There will be no presentations, no bar charts, and no medals. You will clean your guns, mark your ammunition, and do God's work.*

Arriving at Special Branch I caught myself smiling as we stepped out of the jeep. Kumaran had a pronounced limp, Munna the "lookout" was bumping into objects animate and inanimate, and Tapas was memorizing all the signs including one that said, *No paan chewing, no spitting, and no loitering*.

The four of us walked up to a drab building with a low entrance on the side. At the door we turned, stood with our backs to it, and clicked our heels.

"Stand down!" barked Munna, imitating Ranvir Pratap.

"Gentlemen," said Tapas, sotto voce.

We flipped open our minicameras, raised our hands in unison, and took selfies.

Book 1

The First Encounter

Some Months Later

The priests lit a fire in his house and fed it some cow fat. Flames leapt and the smoke licked the ceiling before spreading to the corners of the large hall. The small group of guests coughed and sneezed as the chanting reached a crescendo and tapered with, "*Om Shanti, Shanti, Shanti.*" They looked around the hall for Swamy, their host. Swamy was seated on the floor in a hidden chamber, head bowed, his legs folded beneath him. He was breathing deeply. "*Shanti, Shanti, Shanti,*" chanted the priest corps. Swamy scowled. It wasn't working. What was the point of having priests on his payroll?

He left quietly, a thief in his own house. Three bodyguards checked for any signs of trouble, ushered him into a black SUV, and then got in behind him. Swamy jockeyed for space to breathe. "All clear," said the driver. They pulled away. The vehicle weaved its way through lanes and alleys before arriving at a nondescript building. Inside was Swamy's lifeline. A doctor escorted him up some stairs and they entered a white-tiled room where Swamy rolled up his sleeves, exposed his veins, and submitted himself to the machine. A middle-aged man who was already waiting in the room shuffled over and sat beside him. It was a practiced routine. They spoke occasionally, cracked some jokes over the next three hours before their heads dropped and they dozed. Swamy's phone rang, breaking his stupor. He peered at the number absently.

"Would you like to live longer, Swamy?" asked the caller.

"What?" Swamy stared at his phone in horror. The SIM card was half a day old and they had traced him already.

"Take a deep breath, Swamy Anna."

He took one. He wanted to kill the call. The tainted SIM would give away his location very soon.

"You need blood, Swamy Anna, good clean blood. Stand up now, go take a piss."

He couldn't and they knew it. "How much longer?" he asked the nurse.

"We are done," she said. She massaged his wrists and his feet.

He stood up abruptly and his head swam.

"Go see your granddaughter, Swamy. She is traveling soon."

He rubbed his temples as he grew furious. He slumped on the bed, opened the back cover of the phone, and pulled out the SIM card. His hands shook as he broke it in two.

"They are threatening me." He pointed at himself. "Me." The bodyguards who stood near the door snorted in unison.

The middle-aged man spoke softly: "That is their job, Anna. They wouldn't dare take on someone as important as you."

Swamy wanted to get up and leave. He half rose before falling back, his head hitting the backrest. This new police encounter team bothered him. It was headed by Ranvir

Pratap, a name that brought bile to Swamy's lips. He coughed and almost retched.

"Get me a damn towel—you, quickly!"

A burly guard brought a white towel. In his hurry he dropped his automatic weapon and it clattered on the floor. The doctor jumped first and the nurse jumped next as the weapon's snout raked the room and came to rest pointing at their feet. Swamy glanced at the ceiling and then slowly lowered his gaze. His outburst was preempted by a pinging sound. The middle-aged man pulled out his phone and he read the message aloud. "*A week from now is an inauspicious date.* Message from Mumbai police."

"That would be the eleventh," said Swamy, his voice down to a whisper. "They have even declared a bloody date." He ruefully examined the veins in his hands. What had they done to him?

They left the makeshift dialysis clinic. It was night in this obscure middle-class neighborhood with its crowded streets, where the local population worshipped the Don of Wadala, who now sat in his SUV and allowed himself some filtered coffee. He took a couple of sips and his body relaxed, relieved to be away from the stern gaze of Mrs. Swamy. They headed to a small temple where a bare-chested priest was waiting impatiently, watching the clock reach the appointed hour. The priest lit some camphor as Swamy crossed the threshold, right foot first, head bare, hands folded. He then rang a small bell and made three circles with the flame chanting a Sanskrit *shloka*. The priest would often offer some fruits and flowers to the deity on Swamy's behalf. The stone deity was small and black and the sanctum was dimly lit. Roaches and rats scurried in the dark reaches.

In the first floor of his chawl Karan flung off the covers, brushed his hair, and threw on his uniform. He slammed the door behind him, took the stairs two at a time, and ran across the quadrangle down a narrow lane into a small nook where he parked his dented car with one wobbly wheel. His Fiat had bucket seats and a floor-shift and it rattled as he drove down the western arterial. When he exited at the office blocks near Haji Ali and headed toward the sea, he saw another version of the chawl. The chawls came in various shapes and sizes and this one was built on common land. The roadside here was a public convenience. Power was available on tap and water came in tankers paid for by the brotherhood. Everything (his car, the chawl) seemed makeshift and temporary and rightly so, because in Mumbai poverty was considered a temporary affliction. This was the faith, the one illusion that kept the murky reality at bay.

A single command before the voice on the other end of the line hung up: "Head to the seaface."

After a while the Worli Seaface turned genteel. Karan parked his car, locked it, and got down to his favorite pastime: watching. A rain-bearing cloud hung over the sea, thinking about landfall. The tide was low and the rocks jutted out of the water near the shore, where two men completed their morning ablutions.

"Don't get out of your car yet."

In a holster near his midriff, Karan carried an American pistol, a Ruger, just like his infamous predecessor, Inspector Pradeep Sharma—Karan admired his senior because of how he stood, hands folded across his chest, the matter-of-fact way he spoke, and above all the uncommon reputation he left behind him. Pradeep Sharma was from the Class of 1983, a Mumbai police class that eliminated hundreds of gangsters but subsequently did not age well.

At the stroke of nine, just as the second hand of his watch aligned with the hour, his phone rang again. Karan waited for three rings, flipping the cover open as he took it to his ear. After a small pause someone spoke.

"I hope you are not wearing your uniform."

"I am," he replied. He thought the uniform would help.

"Have you lost your mind?" shouted the caller. "Is that how you meet an informer?" There was a murmur in the background. "Well, because of your stupidity we'll have to change the location. Start the car and drive slowly past the Worli Dairy. There will be a traffic signal up ahead." The caller spoke again to someone who was with him: "Yes, that light will turn red when you approach. Don't worry, it will. Someone will come up to your window selling magazines. Keep your window down. You will buy a magazine from him. Inside there will be a message that will tell you when and where to go. Got it?"

"Why all this drama?" asked Karan.

"You do your job, I'll do mine. I have to keep the informer alive."

Karan looked to see if there was anybody around. The seaface was deserted. He did as he was told.

That night he reread Swamy's bulky folder. It was incredible how someone like Swamy had survived for so long despite the attention shown by the police and the judiciary. The court case against him began twelve years ago. Two witnesses were dead, one had gone missing, and fourteen had turned hostile. A decision was due next month and the file said it was likely the prosecution would lose.

Swamy began his career as a porter in a railway station. Tired of small change, he began to loot goods from trains that passed through it. In all he killed three people as he rose to the top of the heap in the railway yards. Each of the deceased was tied to the tracks and left to the vagaries of the overnight express train. Soon his leadership was undisputed. He granted people favors and in return he adjudicated their lives. His gang collected a daily or weekly fee from most commercial establishments in Wadala. He had the traders by the balls. Even Muruga, the ruling deity, was a lesser entity than Swamy in Wadala, a god with a weaker sovereignty. Swamy's followers knew that while Muruga might be a superior being above, in this life they'd have to reckon with this bloody goon.

Swamy was a Tamilian from the south of the country and built up his fearsome network between 1975 and 1985. A phone call from Swamy was a dagger to the heart. People who answered his call died twice. Every year Swamy would conduct a show killing and the press built his mythology by going into a feeding frenzy every time, making him out to be the most fearsome don since Haji Mastan and Karim Lala.

Meanwhile, nobody dared search Swamy's pockets, and for some decades they swelled with ill-gotten gains. Some of it went to cops and some to magistrates. The rest was naturally seen with a blind eye. Who the fuck cared?

"I do," said Ranvir Pratap.

A couple of years back a reputed astrologer told Swamy he was past his due date. Swamy disappeared and went underground. Nobody had seen him since, though it was rumored he came out at night in an SUV with tinted windows and that he visited temples where he prayed for his own longevity.

He had reason to feel threatened. The Bombay police had taken out a contract on Swamy, after all. That was just how it was done. The local term for this practice among the crime gangs was *supari*. No one in the police force wanted this particular *supari*, and so it landed in the lap of a greenhorn, a relative newcomer in a new squad who had a reputation for never missing in target practice. His name was Karan and he was reported to be a little mental. He had agreed on one condition—the encounter would not happen in Wadala. There was no question of challenging Swamy on his own turf.

"Do we have a date?" asked Karan.

"Yes," said Desai, his controller. "The eleventh. Boss likes the eleventh."

"Why?"

Because on January 11 Surve died. He died, man. They were waiting for him and they waylaid him. He lay in an ambulance and cursed till the moment he went. Karan saw the body and the grimace in a grainy photograph. Surve was a burly figure with a chestful of hair. They trapped him when he emerged from a taxi near the Ambedkar College junction. The police had been tipped off and two cops got him. Surve was armed; it seems he fired first, but he missed. Raja Tambat and Isaque Bagwan entered history books by firing a clip of bullets into Surve's chest and shoulder. This was history, the first encounter killing carried out by Mumbai police. And it happened in Wadala on January 11, 1982.

It was said of Karan that he seemed like a "decent" person when he joined the force. The fact that he would kill people would color his résumé somewhat but that was a departmental thing—a job description—and something he had to do to get a salary and a promotion. His boss Ranvir Pratap had ground to make up. Too many hoods who had practiced mayhem for so long had lived well into their eighties and nineties. It felt unnatural, almost a failure for cops like him that so many of them died from natural causes.

Karan was an unlikely specialist. He was prone to stand for hours on the roadside, an uneaten dish in front of him, speaking in a monotone to either his wife Nandini or to his controller, a disembodied voice named Desai. And this would happen in the midst of an assignment. It was scary that he could still execute successfully.

"What was in the magazine?" asked Desai later that night.

"A list of two things: the temple he will visit tomorrow; and his preferred seat inside his car."

"Is that enough for you?" asked Desai. He sounded skeptical. "Do you need backup? Should we get you a semiautomatic weapon?"

"No, it will be too obvious. His people will spot me." There was no point in telling Desai that he had never used an automatic weapon.

"Who was that?" asked Nandini when he returned to the table. They were having dinner.

"No one important," said Karan. He sat down heavily and stared at his plate.

"Then eat."

He couldn't. He poked at the food. "I'm not hungry."

"Then go to sleep," his wife said.

The night was too quiet and the chawl was full of furtive sounds. In bed, he couldn't toss and turn as he wished because Nandini was a light sleeper. He stared at his phone in the dark and watched time pass slowly.

"Why aren't you asleep?" she asked at one point.

He found an excuse to walk into the outside corridor where he could glimpse the city lights. Beyond the chawl Bombay was shape-shifting. The factory worker and the trade unionist had walked into the sunset, pulling down the curtain on the era of local manufacturing. The militant political party had thrived using jingoism and strong-arm tactics. Spiffy office-goers arrived, and they too thrived thanks to liberalization and the opening up of the economy. A certain licentiousness had seeped into the city, a rowdy good nature exemplified in its cuisine and its festivity. Then, with the arrival of immigrants, Bombay retired, its suburban identity prevailed, and the city called Mumbai found its voice. Mumbai turned its back on Bombay, then dropped its pants and showed its rump. One survivor in this transformation was the chawl. It was a distinctively Bombay creation, and a hardy piece of architecture that was now a curious remnant in Mumbai.

The next morning Karan stood in the shower and let the hot water burn his back and his arms till they reddened. He toweled himself down slowly and deliberately. This would be his first kill. It was a strange assignment and he had been told if he had a clear shot he should take it, even if it was fleeting. He knew that it would happen near his home, too close, but still . . . it would be public and brazen.

"Aren't you going to the office today? It is raining, Karan, so you better leave early."

What should he tell her, that he was waiting to find an auspicious time for a kill? She left for work after packing his lunch. He stood by for a call that never came, and finally at noon he sat at his dining table and ate his lunch. And later, he snuck out like a thief.

It was raining hard on his chawl in Parel. The chawl was covered with blue plastic sheets held down by bricks. Beneath them was a tarpaulin cover and the few cracks in the tiled roof were filled with black tar. Karan waited under an awning but water still found a way to drip onto his head. From his vantage it seemed parts of the city were literally going down the drains.

His thoughts traveled back to a time when the city bled. It wasn't long ago when Bombay was divided on religious lines. The Mumbai riots were terrible and right here in this gully there was arson and looting. Today no signs remained; nothing except the figureheads and their sycophants. The *shakhas* were still around, and then there were the local *mukhyas* and *prajapatis*. These were the true *satraps* of this city. They sponsored the revelry on the streets. At festival time they would take money from the residents and fund their *pandals* and processions.

He was meticulous in his preparation. Karan had readied his weapon the night before but keeping it dry in the monsoon was a challenge. The roadside gutters had flooded into streams. A large, ungainly rat looked on as the swirl consumed its hideaway; a child gleefully watched the animal get carried away by the deluge.

Umbrellas formed herds at traffic junctions. The office workers waited impatiently for the traffic lights to change before heading to the new gleaming towers that had sprung up where the mills once stood. When he got tired of taking practice shots Karan joined them, walking with them for a couple of kilometers before returning, a black umbrella hiding his head. Another hour passed and still no news, so he zigzagged across the road, visited some shops, and returned to his spot once more. Occasionally he stood in the open, defying the driving rain.

A few vehicles clattered past the chawl, splashing water and making waves, a street vendor shouted in vain as his wares were sodden, and the gears of a double-decker bus clashed as it rounded a bend. This was getting tedious. The delay continued. He held his umbrella high and negotiated a crossing. When he tired of holding it he folded it, exposing his mop of soaking black hair.

He was just another tall man wearing a gray raincoat and plastic shoes.

The day departed and the rain mercifully eased. Nightlife arrived in a taxi, an old yellow-black Fiat, a braveheart that had seen three engine changes. The cab and the cabbie idled by the roadside, their engines ticking, keeping an eye out for cops. Their passenger was clearly a woman on the make.

"*Mangta kya*?" she asked passersby, thrusting a hip, parting her lips, and twirling a bag around her right wrist. She posed next to the Fiat, trying to entice. The interior of the taxi glowed and was playing a song from the film *Pakeezah*. A drunk leered at her. "*Chal phut!*" she shouted. Get lost.

"*Randi*," said the drunk. "*Raat ki raani*." In his stupor he was a connoisseur of women.

Across this tableau stood Karan, a silent observer, patient, still, black umbrella by his side, his hair wet and streaming. After four hours of waiting his phone finally rang. It was time.

"Where are you?" Nandini demanded, breaking his concentration. "You forgot your lunch box. Wait, it's empty."

He flexed his fingers, rotated his neck and shoulders, and blinked a few times. "Can you get off the line? I'm expecting a call."

"Are you at work? How long will you be?"

"I don't know." He hung up on her, then reached inside his coat, felt his holster, and pulled out his gun in a single smooth motion.

A black SUV came speeding below the overpass, turned, and swerved. Its dark windows were rolled up and its bright lights screamed momentarily into Karan's eyes. Two traffic lights turned green and the vehicle began to accelerate. Karan took aim at the green lights and fired. Two muffled thumps and then confusion as cars braked and skidded.

"*Thamba!*" shouted a nearby duty cop, waving his arms.

"Motherfucker!" cursed a driver as he braked, screeching into another car before hitting a pole. Glass shattered and pedestrians jumped out of the way. In the ensuing slowdown the SUV drew alongside Karan, blasting its horn, its tires crunching over the strewn glass. Its custom license plate glinted as Karan's gun sparked again; the bullet pierced through the windshield glass, spreading a small spiderweb. He waited for the telltale sign as the car swept past. He finally exhaled; there was red splatter on the rear windscreen.

The SUV jumped the red light and made a sharp U-turn, its tires squealing as the driver shifted gears and gunned the engine. Black smoke and diesel fumes spewed behind the SUV as it sped away. The duty cop futilely ran after it, then jumped onto his motorcycle and set off in chase. A couple of street urchins looked toward Karan wide-eyed. They had heard something but they weren't sure. He was standing erect and seemed to be brooding. Karan's gun felt warm in its holster. After a brief pause Karan opened his umbrella and moved toward the chawl, entering it without glancing back. Elongated shadows followed him home, stretching around the bends.

Soon, at half past twelve, the traffic lights were turned off and would flash orange till the sun rose again. Dogs settled back down on the pavement and in back alleys. The city dragged its feet for a while, its moral compass awry. Down south the famous Rajabai Tower stood tall between a university and a high court. Its clock chimed desolately into the night.

The day after the assignment Karan stayed home and counted sparrows. He had heard that sparrows got fried out of existence by electric towers, so seeing some of them buzz in and out of the sloping roof gave him a sense of hope. Nobody called him, which itself was eerie after yesterday. For some reason he remembered the church at the Don Bosco School in Matunga, where he had studied as a young boy, and how he once by chance attended an emotional memorial service there. He had to stare at a stained-glass window to distract himself from the outpouring of grief. An old man next to him kept smiling through the function.

"Are you a relative?"

"No." He shook his head. "I come here for all the memorials."

The chawl was customarily quiet at this midmorning hour. Nandini had seemed quizzical since waking up. She was relentless. "What's the matter?" she asked again as she ironed his uniform. The iron wove around his buttons.

"Nothing," he replied.

"What are you thinking?" He was midway through brushing his teeth.

"Nothing."

She sighed and smiled gently. "Don't worry, I'll eventually get used to you and your moods."

When she left he removed his uniform and changed into his pajamas. He slunk on a chair and waited for a call that might not come. At the chawl domestic life proceeded at its own pace; he was the interloper.

"Karan *bhai*, you are at home?"

He nodded. Wasn't it obvious?

"*Su* Karan *bhai*?" asked a Gujarati neighbor. "*Majama*?"

"*Majama*," he echoed, managing a smile.

"Karan *kaka*, all well?" asked a maid.

The inquiries were polite, his replies were tart, and the air was pungent with the smell of spices that were seasoning lunch. He sneezed often. He detected the scent of detergent and the slapping sound of clothes being hand-washed. He snoozed for a while and awakened to find the sun in his eyes. He had to retreat further into his small abode and there he rediscovered the small things that made this place home. He puttered about, discovering Nandini in her absence. Her taste showed up in the carefully placed bric-a-brac, her mauve Kashmiri shawl, the two-layered curtains filtering light through the windows, casting shapes on crowded stacks of books that spoke of their shared love of cities. He settled down for a while with a coffee table book called *Bombay: The Cities Within,* and found that its observations spoke to him. Finally, he sat at the one item that truly belonged to him: his writing desk.

You are not a writer, he said to himself. He really wasn't, though he had tried. *Your attempts are surreptitious and your thoughts are clandestine.* He read aloud from passages he liked, taking care to pronounce each word correctly. And he often sat with a thesaurus, sometimes attempting an original composition with esoteric equivalents of commonly used words. He envied his boss Ranvir Pratap, a man with a mordant wit and a quicksilver tongue. What did he look like? He was stocky and unathletic with no six-pack to boast of.

After lunch, time passed slowly in his head as he tired of checking his phone for messages. He lay listlessly on the sofa. He felt like he was seated in a railway waiting room or at a doctor's clinic. He twirled a blue paperweight and rapped it against a table, admiring its sound. He watched TV, flipping channels and hoping to get lucky. For a while he slept again. And he dreamed of his city, of its various parts that assembled before him like an archive of the quotidian, an everyday life that he could write about lucidly when he slept.

Words are easy on the tongue but work is hard to find in Mumbai. Old men vie with chokra boys, and sisters vie with mothers. All day they climb up and down the rickety stairs of the chawl doing odd jobs. The city scrimps in its daily life. Chai from a tumbler is shared in groups. Car cleaning pays but only in small change. Elevator attendants, security guards, and peons are proof that vocations trap you for life.

Every chawl is a bunch of kolis, *small rooms that house the middle class. During the day they run* kiraana *shops, tailoring shops, coaching classes, and crèches right out of their homes. There are doctors too who practice where they live.*

My Parel chawl has good proportions. It has a family life. You flirt in the landing, get engaged in the corridor, your marriage takes place in the quadrangle outside, and your honeymoon is in the cupboard.

Dust is unhurried in this city. It never settles. Summer brings clichés and the measles, and rain brings the thundering clap. Men wander at this time for nightly visits with painted folk.

"Don't be fooled by the bright saris, the kohl eyes, and painted lips," warn our elders. "Before you flirt with streetwalkers take our hands and check the gender."

Chawl life is intimate. The men lean on railings with feet apart, wearing tight pants. The women sit on the floor with feet apart, wearing nightgowns. The neighbors are second rate and the amenities are third class. The scenery is underwear, displayed like newspapers in a kiosk. Every clothesline speaks.

This is our theater, our darling middle-class Center for Performing Arts. Life is a truthful bore so a little acting helps us all. We know we are God's rejects but at home we pretend we are Mama's favored infants. The elders keep telling us that we matter. You are the inner city, they say. This is the soul of the city that resides in chawls everywhere; even in pretentious South Mumbai. Look out for a U-shaped two-storied structure around a quadrangle, with corridors and rooms in a row. Here you will find no entitlement. If we need subsidy we are told to go out and beg.

In the chawl we roll up our sleeves, hang our shirt on a wall, and really examine ourselves. Can you? Good. See here, two arms are all it takes. Both hands now. Submit. Remember, power is hungry.

Late in the evening Desai called, finally. Karan grabbed at the phone like it was a life raft.

"Yes?" He breathed deeply, shutting his eyes.

"Yes," replied Desai in his lackluster manner.

"What?"

After what seemed an eternity Desai spoke again: "You are unbelievable. You shot through glass into a dark cave but you got your man."

"He is dead?"

"Yes. Internal bleeding killed him, luckily. Go to sleep, you are now officially an encounter specialist."

There was a big splash in the newspapers the next day but it was the location of the incident that gave him away.

"Karan, where were you the night before last?"

He sat her down and told her that he had been assigned to an encounter squad.

"What did you do? I mean, were you assisting someone?"

He coughed. "I shot him." He tried telling her it was a prestigious posting, one that any officer would want. "I am lucky. Do you know my predecessors have appeared on national television?" He even had a recording of a field interview which she insisted on seeing, so they sat next to each other and watched. The people who were being interviewed were his seniors. The anchor was stout, bespectacled, and he was behaving like a fanboy. He spoke animatedly (was that a smile?), aware that this *Walk the Talk* episode on the NDTV channel was the best-rating material he would ever have. Two men with black, well-groomed hair and mustaches walked alongside him. They seemed casual, diffident, and their eyes buttonholed their neighborhood and never wavered. Behind them walked a lithe, uniformed security cover with an automatic weapon. This was a self-aware tableau that expected retaliation.

Inspector Pradeep Sharma and Subinspector Daya

Nayak were being questioned by the anchor, an admiring Shekhar Gupta. They remained expressionless through all of it and made no attempt to gloat. Gupta used the cricket analogy of a century score that ended up sounding frivolous and macabre. He spoke glowingly about Pradeep Sharma's scorecard of ninety-two hits ("nervous nineties," he called it) and wondered whether at seventy-eight hits Daya Nayak felt the competitive pressure.

The cops conveyed what they felt; nothing deep but a quiet satisfaction. They said they shot only in retaliation. A rooster crowed loudly in the background. They complained about their silly portrayal in Hindi cinema where the cops did nothing and always arrived late. The threesome walked through a slum along a narrow path that had low shanties on both sides, disturbing a boy in shorts and a woman in a doorway. Another rooster flew up to Daya Nayak's side and flapped its wings at him. Talk of killing continued with what happened on New Year's Eve 1996, going back to 1992, touching on their feelings before an encounter and after, seeking out how they felt (if they did) doing God's work and dispensing death.

They passed a tattered signpost that said, *Welcome to Seaface*. People trailed behind them, curious about the cameras and the gun-toting. A small child sat with one leg crossed over the other, ignoring them. The talk veered to the film actors and producers who were the soft targets for extortionists, who lacked bravery in real life when confronted with the filmic tactics of the underworld.

"Injuries? Did you ever get attacked?"

"Bullet through the thigh," said Daya Nayak, breaking stride and showing his leg. It still hurt sometimes but no longer in the leg.

The Mumbai Dairy soon appeared on their right and they walked past it discussing calls from known gangsters who tried to threaten them personally. "The crime lords called us and cursed us and we cursed them back in their own language," he said.

Pradeep Sharma waved his hands in front of him and spoke up, dismissing these gangsters as loudmouths and humble *vada pao* eaters who now ate chili chicken, a superior cuisine for those wanting to move up the social ladder, as if that gave them the right to talk big. They were local goons without the organization and skill sets to qualify for the tag *Mafia*, he felt.

"This is morbid," she said. "In a few years you will be just like them."

He wasn't sure why she was disturbed by that thought. He wasn't very good at divining what went on in her head.

"I need to get some fresh air."

"Shall we go for a drive?" It was nine a.m.

They walked to his car, quietly, with pieces of a puzzle in their heads. He squeezed his tall frame in, started the engine, and reversed. A sleeping dog underneath the vehicle yelped and got away just in time. They rolled down the front windows to let in the breeze, then rolled them back up as they passed the shanties, smelling what the city had digested from yesterday's takeout.

Near Prabhadevi they ran into revelers carrying a huge idol on a cart, loud music blaring from speakers. Some danced in front of them, some knocked on the car's windows and pressed their faces against the glass, leaving lip marks and spittle behind. Then they moved slowly aside, staring as they let the car through. The sound was deafening and the revelry seemed frenetic. "Is this God in our midst?" Nandini asked as they moved past the idol. No, not this; this was just the bully pulpit.

Back at home it hit Karan with surprising clarity as to how cinematic this city truly was—it was also the uncut version of a civic nightmare.

"So what did you learn from that interview?" she asked him.

"Nothing," he replied. What was there to learn from those who had done it so many times and yet survived? He would rather study those who failed.

"Smart-ass," she said, clearly irritated.

"I need to remember that targets actually shoot back. Not everything is staged."

"I see. I feel better suddenly," she deadpanned.

That night he went to the Jasmine Parlor, really just a small shed. The barber broke a new shaving blade in two, set one piece in a holder, and gave him a close shave. He had his hair oiled and neatly combed and then had his mustache trimmed. He patted some Old Spice onto his cheeks, enjoying the smart stinging sensation. Outside on the sidewalk a man sat on his haunches and spoke softly to him as he cleaned his ears, collecting the wax in his palm. Below the overpass Karan parted with some change to two kids who were playing a game with stones. They thanked him in Tamil. He returned home, fresh and renewed. He headed to his small private den where he took out some creased press clippings, smoothed them out, and read them once again. It was important that he read and reread about those who had faltered. This was the 1983 puzzle, the surprising decline of a hugely successful batch of encounter specialists who had themselves committed crimes. Karan belonged to a different breed, or so he hoped.

The next day dawned and the chawl stirred with signs of life. An old man in a singlet walked into his view, scratched his balls, and waited for the sun. At first light the man closed his eyes, folded his hands, and murmured a prayer. He then looked around blankly, noticing nothing, not even the black umbrella that Karan left out to dry that had tumbled across the corridor to his door.

Karan yawned and did some stretches. He had walked for an hour in the middle of the night and returned agitated. Half the time the city spat and half the time its pants were around its ankles. After returning he laid on his back and stared at the ceiling, waiting for his wife to awaken. He had things to tell her about Mumbaikars. Nandini's smooth forehead was furrowed. Her thoughts were writing the worry lines of the city.

Whole sentences felt out of place in Mumbai, Karan thought. Nothing simmered and foreplay was missing. Gone were the days when you could have an uninterrupted view of the setting sun as it dipped into the sea. As the lights went out the men around him changed, they turned predatory or just behaved badly, blurring the line between man and beast. The chawl resembled a pigsty in the morning. There was no room in it for nicety, and barely enough space for intimacy.

Later, after dinner had been ingested and the television serials were winding down, the age-old Chawl Symphony began nearby. He would first hear the rustle and then imagine the quiet moves. Family after family retreated into a common room, a six-by-eight-foot intimate space in which people took turns. The lucky ones had their lovers tonight and a private space, but the lonely ones like Takia Khan the pillow hugger and Chadder Master the restless sheet spoiler were denied; they listened to those who made out and just fucked the bed. It was quick and it was furtive. The tumescent *chokras* bit their lips and read Savita Bhabhi. She kept her porn columns simple; she knew that syndromes couldn't hide under the sheets.

Should I wake her up like I used to? wondered Karan. Snuggling up to Nandini was a signal they both knew. Not this time. He felt deflated and the moment passed.

The next day brought strange tidings. A boy who did odd jobs for them had taken to crime and submitted himself to a warlord a few weeks ago. He had now gone missing and his mother showed up at their door pleading for help. "Do something!" Nandini shouted at Karan. "You are a policeman!"

"I'm not that type of cop," he said, feeling helpless. What could he possibly do? "Wrong department," he added by way of explanation.

What they needed was a fixer, someone like that Tiwari, the bête noir of his boss Ranvir Pratap.

Encounter Twenty-Five: Gonzales

The neighborhood of Mahim had an old church and a green mosque and roadside eateries where tied goats stood outside and chomped grass. Inside, large cooking *handis* were being stirred. Fat was on the boil and aromatic spices in the mix awaited fresh meat. Soon the throats of the goats would be slit. Despite its narrow lanes and its heavy traffic this suburb found space for festivities. The one thing that cast a pall over Mahim was the smell: it was putrid. A car of doctors traversing a road through Mahim would immediately think of an endoscopy camera journeying through an intestine. There is a creek in Mahim that no one has ever seen because most people who drive by roll up their windows. Those who walk through the place know the creek well enough to ignore it like people do in Mumbai—ignore what is clearly inhuman and not to be put up with. How else could the place survive? In a place like this the question of Mumbai or Bombay loses meaning.

Karan saw the coffin being loaded. He did not accompany it to the cemetery because Gonzales was a don and Karan was the reason he was in it. And he was there against his best judgment because he had followed his wife. He spotted Nandini standing by the side observing the ceremony, and the pall of grief that surrounded her was visible on her face. Tomorrow the welts would appear on him. She held the ends of her sari between her teeth. She turned suddenly in his direction and he had to duck. Her lips were pursed and her eyes held back something akin to guilt. Was she trying to atone for him? The crowd headed toward the cemetery at Bandra and she melted away.

She left behind a question that nagged him: was Nandini the weak link in the family chain, or was it he?

Two days earlier his boss Ranvir had given him a lecture on social niceties and handed him another folder. Karan had no time to waste on decorum. Deep into the night he sat at his table and read about his next target. *Name: Gonzales.* Gonzales was a warlord with an army of mercenaries available for hire. He functioned as a recruiting agent for other gangs. His bulky file was slow reading, and it contained many pictures. He seemed friendly, with a smooth face and an amiable smile. It was hard to imagine him as a target. He had killed no one personally but his recruiting skills made him a potent force, so the police were desperate to get rid of him. Gonzales funded many charities and asked for nothing in return. He was a family man with two daughters and three sons, all of whom kept clear of their father's business. There was a photograph of his wife as well. She was a school teacher.

Karan needed something to motivate himself, but in this case it wasn't happening.

"Need anything else, Karan?" asked Ranvir.

He needed a date, a place, and a time. Each was

important. After forty-eight hours of nosing about, he finally had it. He had a plausible scenario.

He would catch him at a time when he was meant to be alone. Gonzales would look surprised. Life and death would meet in a long second with many fractions. Karan would deliver. His hair stood on end when he visualized it. He felt these people would know him when they saw him. They would recognize the moment.

"This is unreal," said his handler Desai. He called sounding concerned after reading Karan's one-page plan.

"It will happen," Karan insisted. "I guarantee it."

"What about contingencies?" asked Desai.

"There's no time for contingencies."

He had no second thoughts and he did not want to develop a backup plan. All he had to do was wait for the green light. This time they called him at the last moment. Desai rang him from an unregistered number. There was no introduction, only a cryptic order and an urgent tone. He had just five minutes to get ready. He walked quickly to his cupboard in the rear room and opened the drawer. The Ruger was ready for action, fully loaded and heavy. He held it in his right palm, used his left hand to form an armature under his right wrist, and took aim in the mirror. He imagined the Gonzales eye; dark brown it was, with one rogue eyelash and a red fleck in the iris. Outside the rain was pelting down. Karan pulled on his gray raincoat, slipped the hood over his head, and ducked out into the street.

He told himself he was dreaming in fast motion; this was his degree of separation.

Look down and your feet take steps. Your hands stay dry in the raincoat. You walk with no purpose till it is time. On days like this every child on the street bears your name. You can hear their laughter and innocent purpose. You cross the road and voices follow in your wake. Nobody is supposed to know you today. You are anonymous. You are Brahman.

He was wearing a dark shirt, black trousers, a belt without a buckle, and dull suede shoes. He wove a path through some lanes, made sure his tracks were clean, then headed past the Mahim Causeway, taking a left onto Hill Road in Bandra. He crossed the road twice and paused under a lone tree, looking around as if seeking directions. He then walked up to the end of Hill Road and vaulted a fence behind some trees, landing softly, darting his eyes left and right, fearing movement. He crept under the cover of a hedge, keeping his eyes peeled. He had reached the designated spot.

Gonzales was there kneeling before his mother's grave. Alone. It was four a.m. in this Christian graveyard in Bandra. It was Purnima, a full-moon night. Most of the graves were covered with thick weeds but Mrs. Gonzales's tombstone shimmered. Her caring offspring, a respected son of Mahim, was down on his knees with tears in his eyes. He was wearing white. His three-man guard remained at the cemetery gate to ward off trouble. Karan rose from behind the gravestone. Was there a breeze? Yes. Gonzales's wispy hair swayed, his *kurta* flapped open, and moonlight bounced off the cross he wore.

He loved his mother, this common hoodlum—it was a poignant moment and Karan was hard-pressed to pull the trigger.

Karan must have drifted momentarily because the quarry nodded at him and was about to ask him a question. The marksman gathered himself, his left hand rose, the armature set, the gun took aim and sent a bullet into that brown eye with a rogue eyelash and a flicker of red. His quarry slumped in disbelief. There was a flurry at the gate and Karan should have left in a hurry but couldn't. *What have I done?* he asked himself. His feet were curiously leaden, as if held by the soggy ground, and when he moved his gait was confused. He stumbled down a pathway he shouldn't have taken, one that led him toward the henchmen. Unsurprisingly, there were flashes and the sound of gunshots. He climbed over the fence and stumbled, hurting his knees in the fall; later, he felt his side where a bullet had grazed and drawn blood, six inches from his heart.

Karan had left his shell behind again. The gangs knew what caliber he used. Ranvir was livid; he banished Karan to Lonavla for a week. It was a dry spell in the *ghats* and he sat for hours thinking, unable to sleep. He walked to the railway station every morning and sat on the platform, expecting trouble. If the gangs sent somebody for him, Karan wanted to see him first. But nothing happened.

When he returned home he thought he would sneak in quietly. Nandini was waiting for him and she met him at the door. "Done with your Silver Jubilee celebrations?" she asked. "So many days to celebrate your twenty-fifth?"

That was grossly unfair but it was true that each number was significant in the encounter units, and twenty-five was a real milestone. He wanted to explain his absence but he couldn't reveal where he'd been these last few days.

"Is this fellow Karan a mental case?"

It was frustrating. Karan was not meant to take chances in his job. He had been repeatedly told that he'd often have just one shot, so there was no margin for error. But he usually needed just one shot.

Whether he was standing, sitting, prostrate on a terrace, or leaning into the wind and fidgeting, when the moment came he was cold, motionless, and—to use a cliché—deadly. Statistically, he had a 0 percent failure rate, but more than once he had taken a leap of faith. How else could you describe shooting into an opaque door? "I could sense my quarry," Karan had replied when questioned. Remarkably, he had gotten it right. He always faced the target when he took his shot, even if that exposed him somewhat. Was he being polite, fair, or even-handed? Yet of late he seemed to be hesitating when the moment came.

They decided to step inside his mind. People were asked to try to get close to.Karan, to try to understand and influence him. They reported a *lack*. A deficiency. He had a fixed smile and a noncommittal manner and most times he lacked an opinion. But he wasn't a junkie.

They consulted a psychologist who suggested someone should talk to his wife. A counselor was sent under the pretext of department routine. Her name was Ms. Daftary. She was from Bombay, a little old-school. Aware that she was visiting a chawl (she could not understand why someone would forsake the comfortable police quarters and choose to live in a place like that), she dressed down for the occasion and as she entered—squeezing past a Slimline fridge, a sofa bed, and other space-saving devices—the splendid aesthetic hit her (her own words) and she suddenly felt dowdy sitting across from Nandini, who it seems made a simple *salwar kameez* come alive and elegantly carried a couple of accessories that could best be described as bling. She offered her guest sweet orange *jalebis* and crisp salty *khakhra* from Swati snacks, and a green-colored drink made from *khas*, if you please. It was not the kind of presentation Ms. Daftary had expected in a chawl.

She filed a quirky first-person report of what had happened in their meeting:

> *"Do you have any idea what he actually does?" I asked Nandini.*
>
> *"He tells me stories about encounters," she said. "They sound like bad dreams. I cannot imagine him hurting anyone."*
>
> *"Have you seen his weapon?"*
>
> *She nodded. "I've tried to hide it," she said.*
>
> *"Why?"*
>
> *"What do you mean? Shouldn't I?"*
>
> *I was stumped and then I saw her smiling. "So what did you do?" I asked her.*
>
> *"What do you people make him do?"*
>
> *"Nothing extraordinary."*
>
> *She seemed exasperated. "Should I be like him and just pretend everything is normal?"*
>
> *"Yes, isn't it?" was my reply.*
>
> *She walked into an inner room and returned with a pistol. "Have you ever held a gun that has killed people?" she asked.*
>
> *I could not tell if she was serious. She is a well-grounded person, talkative and candid. Theirs is a marriage of love, she told me. She does not like his job and constantly questions him about his assignments. I am sure they fight because she feels strongly about the police killing criminals without a judicial process. She lectured me on habeas corpus. I have a feeling Karan must be suffering because of a growing rift caused by his job.*

She said something in passing that I found significant. It sounded like a marital complaint but I think it is more than that. She said, "Karan has the attention span of a fish and most of our interactions are just that—a minute or two at most. After that he wanders off into something totally unconnected."

Karan dropped in as I left. He did not look toward me nor did he say hello. I experienced the well-documented diffidence firsthand. He saw the gun, looked at Nandini accusingly, and then picked it up, held it, and put it back in the inner room. It is clear that he has a first-person relationship with his weapon. When I spoke to him he always came back a little late, as if responding from a distance. But he was alert to his surroundings. Walking to the sink, I stumbled on a mat and dropped my teacup. Karan was nearby but looking elsewhere—I hardly saw him move but he somehow caught the cup before it hit the ground. He stared at me as he straightened, expressionless. It was eerie. I realized why he was so good at his job. If he ever killed me I would not know how. I recommend we administer some tests on Karan. Let him go through a physical examination again. We also need to check for stability and a few psychological issues. There is no one who is a natural-born killer, so there will be stress issues.

I sincerely wish they had a child. So often a child changes the narrative for the better in our families.

What Ms. Daftary did not tell them was that Karan spoke to her as she was leaving. "Ms. Daftary," he said, halting her in her tracks. He held her hand lightly, looking away. "Am I in trouble?"

"Of course not," she had replied.

Karan wasn't convinced. "I need this job," he told her. "Please try to understand. This is the only thing I am good at."

For a day or two she puzzled over his situation. What kind of a person would tell her that what he was good at was being an encounter specialist? And there were related questions that piqued her curiosity: Was it possible for Karan to take pride in a job well done? Was his self-worth linked to being extraordinarily good at killing people?

Someone followed Karan for a whole weekend on Ms. Daftary's instructions. Why? There was no good reason. After tailing him for two days all that the officer could report was that off-duty Karan was oblivious to his surroundings and unaware that he was standing in public places and getting in the way of people.

"He lacks something," said the officer. "He looks like he is posing. He stood outside a clothing store staring at the mannequins in the window for almost an hour."

"Is he posing because he knows he's being followed?" asked Ms. Daftary.

"Of course not. We were mostly in Dadar. In Dadar his friend Welkinkar runs a small photography shop that does passport shots. Behind a curtain he has a modest studio with white walls and some lighting equipment. I entered the shop and pretended to look at some cameras. Karan wanted a family portrait. That's what he told his friend. *Where is the family?* asked Welkinkar. Karan brought in three random shoppers from the street outside. A mother, a father, and a younger brother; they completed the picture. They posed happily, laughing, and when the camera was ready they said, *Cheese*, and showed their teeth. Karan liked the photograph. *Thank God it isn't sentimental,* he said."

"You spent the whole weekend in Dadar?"

"Yes. He was window-shopping. You know Dadar—it isn't posh but then again neither is a policeman. I think he likes the suburb. He looked comfortable standing outside places like the Bedekar Condiment House watching these middle-class Maharashtrian families. He walked into a restaurant that serves coastal gravies. I ate whatever he ate. He really knows his food and he's a hearty eater. I could hardly get up after all that crab, fish, and prawns in *kokum* and coconut. After that he stood outside a textile showroom that displayed saris and *churidaars* and watched women going in and trying things on. Weird. Then he stood outside a jewelry store next to a guard who had an old rifle. Finally the guard chased him away."

"Let me guess: all Karan did was observe families?"

"Yes. It made a lot of people uncomfortable. He kept staring. I don't think he means anything by it though."

"I'm not surprised that you don't understand," said Ms. Daftary. "People like you are lucky that parents come to you by birth. You are born and you are part of a family tree. Not so for Karan."

Within the department Karan was described as a *slack jaw*—not a slacker or a lazy sort, but someone who promoted that impression by looking as if he had been rescued midway through a stroke. Yet that picture did not fit in with the reality of the police encounters he handled.

Ms. Daftary made a prescient note in his file: *While a possible explanation for Karan's recent setbacks can be the result of him slowing down, another plausible one is that he is increasingly confused and disoriented in life-and-death scenarios. This can come from a need to place himself at the very edge, taking an inordinate risk as a form of atonement.*

Encounter Twenty-Six

"Casual sex," remarks Ranvir Pratap. "Do not treat a kill like casual sex." He picks up the used cartridge from the floor and hands it to me. "Here, you dropped your sheath."

My sheath looks empty and misshapen. I slip it into my pocket.

"Always pick up your DNA," says my boss. It is a mild reprimand delivered with a wink.

The room is strewn with dirty clothes, stale food, and the DNA of a man who had hunkered down for the final standoff. We called him Churi Ram. He lies spread-eagled and his eyes have rolled.

Ranvir does a walkabout. He is piecing together how I carried this one out. He is forensic, unsparing, and clinical, looking for chinks, for that one small fissure in my mind.

Churi Ram had no idea it was someone like me but he was still careful. I knocked on the door and quickly side-stepped to the open window. I could not see him but I heard him creep up to the door; he would have his knife in his hand. We held our breath and waited—till he knew. The legendary killer and serial rapist sensing danger. At that very moment he whirled, his knife glistening, and charged my way. I believe at moments like these a second has fractions. Within one long second I aimed where his head should have been and fired; his knife took air and lost speed, clattering to the ground; he came into view and started to fall. Churi Ram had three eyes, one in the middle of his forehead. The other two eyes flickered as he saw me before he went down. His fall was silent. We lost touch with each other as he collapsed.

"You shoot blindly and yet you spill his brains. Either you are gifted or you're a fool," concludes Ranvir, standing at the exact spot where I took my shot not so long ago. He examines the hole in the door, then turns to me, and I look at my trigger finger.

It was a strange moment and it brought me no joy. I had taken down a fellow marksman, a man who could split hair with a knife from fifteen feet. The chap was on our hit list for two long years and had survived our three previous attempts.

"Karuna," chides Ranvir in a singsong voice. He is measuring how far the knife had traveled toward where I stood. "You gave him a chance, did you not?"

Had I really run it this close? I had no bloody idea. All I know is Churi Ram's last living act was the throw of his *churi*. And that should never have happened.

They have turned me into a killing machine and I make Captain Fantastic—Ranvir Pratap—proud. Initially the rest of Special Branch worried at my clinical efficiency and monitored me very closely. They sent Ms. Daftary. Now they worry I might be softening and slowing down. So they pack me off on forced leave to a lodge in Lonavla, a rainy haven where clouds drift into my living room like ghosts. I sit in a chair all day and worry that they must be sitting somewhere in a meeting and deciding my fate. Every other day the rain seeks me out by beating down on the windows. The water trickles in and puddles collect around my feet. My socks get wet and I feel miserable and cold. I call Nandini and then don't know what to say. "Are you hiding?" she asks.

After a week I am recalled. "Come back, son," says Desai.

"How do you feel now?" they ask. They search my face to see if I've been drinking and drowning in that open shower called Lonavla.

"Cold," I say, looking down at my feet.

"Cold-hearted?" asks one of them.

"Cold fish," mumbles another.

They want me to show some feeling.

"Cold feet," I reply.

"Karuna, twenty-six down, and you still have cold feet?"

They laugh; all of them find it funny. I do not join in and the laughter tapers. Somebody coughs.

"Err . . . Can I leave now?" I ask.

They glance at each other, shrug, and let me go.

And then I get called in for a formal debriefing. There is a room in a covert building just for this purpose. It has blue walls, fluorescent lights, and a cement floor. Ranvir prepared me for this, saying they would try to unsettle me. "Do not discuss details of any operation; simply say it's all there in the files." (The files are black holes.) "Don't explain your actions. You follow my orders and that's it. And one last thing: please don't share your thoughts."

"Step down, Karan."

They are seated in a semicircle and I'm placed under a spotlight. They examine me without expression, and the nagging feeling that I had when walking in won't go away—that of being a specimen in a lab. Parthasarathy is here as well. Should I be worried about that?

"What troubles you, Karan?" asks Ranvir as he examines the report on the clinical killing that I had carried out. "Is there anything you want to say?" It's unlike him to ask such questions, but I remember his warning.

"Umm . . . nothing, sir," I reply. It's true. The sum total of what worries me amounts to nothing.

Parthasarathy stirs. There's a fat file in front of him. He gazes from it to me. "You seem to be slowing down. In the last couple of cases it's almost like you've been asking for trouble, like you want to get yourself hurt. Are you aware of this?"

"I have no wish to be injured, sir," I reply. "As to slowing down, why would anyone question me when I am the last man standing?"

I feel breathless after that salvo. Someone snickers while the rest turn toward Parthasarathy.

There's a grain of truth in what he said. What caused me to pause at that very moment when I wasn't supposed to? But I'm not qualified to hazard a reason. I guess I pause a lot in most things I do; when I speak, when I walk, and sometimes people have stepped up to me to shake me. I realize I've paused again because Ranvir has asked something that I haven't heard. He rises from his chair and peers over the photographs that have been placed on the table. There are grainy black-and-white images of the last two encounters. He smiles at me and I nod in return.

"I asked if you have been seeing the counselor, Ms. Daftary," he repeats, echoing the question on everyone's mind.

I shake my head. "No sir."

"Are you are scared of meeting someone like her?" asks Parthasarathy. "You missed the last two appointments."

"I believe they're optional, sir," I blurt out.

"Do you doubt what you are doing? That is what she would have asked you."

I say nothing.

"Are you aware that your wife follows you occasionally? Do you know that she has anonymously visited the homes of some of your targets?"

I'm not prepared for this question—there's no point in looking toward Ranvir for help on this one. I nod absentmindedly.

"Why does she do it?"

Why not ask her? "I have no idea, sir."

"Can you stop her?" asks Parthasarathy.

"No sir," I reply, for once answering quickly. Should I have said I would try, that I would discuss it with her? Was this the end? Had I just finished my career with that one answer?

"Do you think she has anything to do with your slowing down, or your so-called hesitancy?"

"No sir," I say as firmly as I can. I should have denied any slowdown, and it hurts to know they consider that a given. Parthasarathy stares at me for some time and I know better than to meet his gaze.

"Why does she do it?" he repeats. It's not really a question directed at me; it's more of a puzzle that interests him. "What did she tell you after her Gonzales visit?"

It was obvious the two of us were being tailed by the department. I can't evade this direct question. I look toward my boss who in turn is staring at my shoes, as if urging them to get up and walk. Should I repeat what she told me? Nandini had been unusually quiet when she returned from Bandra after the Gonzales funeral. At the dinner table she had toyed with her food and finally said something I didn't understand: *I saw his wife and realized death has a human face. Don't you ever forget that.*

"You can leave now," I hear Ranvir tell me, though my mind is elsewhere.

As I walk out I catch him saying to Parthasarathy, "I am sure it's temporary."

And part of the reply: "He is going to get killed very soon. It's a question of when and not . . ."

I walk away and drive back to Special Branch. I head for the washroom to freshen up. This time I examine my face in the mirror. There are no worry lines on my forehead and no bags below my eyes. I trace my hand along my forehead and feel a cold glass sheet. Water drips from my palm down my reflected eyes and cheeks.

Tiwari walks in at that moment. He spits juice into a corner and loosens his belt. He looks toward me sympathetically. "I have information," he announces. His belt is undone and his pants begin to sag. I have to turn away.

"You always have information, sir," I reply.

He laughs and leans over the urinal, placing a hand on the wall. "The department has had enough of you and Ranvir."

A splashing sound comes in spurts. I glimpse his vast backside and settle upon a spot on his balding head. I know the caliber that I will use if I ever need to puncture that pumpkin.

"What about the others, sir?" I ask him.

He shrugs his shoulders and his pants sag farther. "The word is out on all of you."

"Why are you giving me this information, sir?" I ask.

"I could help you," he says. "I could help you if you help me. People like you burn out quickly. You should take a transfer immediately. We need a man who can use a gun. You see, I need protection. The information I carry in my head needs protection."

He cozies up to the urinal and shuts his eyes as he finishes. And then he turns around, hitches up his pants, and struggles with his belt. As he washes his hands in the basin, I meet his eye in the mirror and approach. He is wary as I walk up and whisper into his ear.

"Come with me, sir, to these places that I roam."

"What?" he says curiously. He leans away from me and his eyes widen. "Come where?"

I place my hand on his shoulder and I can feel him shudder. "Come with me to the shadow lands," I whisper.

The basin tap is open and the water is gushing hard. Drops are splashing onto his trousers but Tiwari doesn't notice. He is gaping at me. "Are you mad? You are truly mad!" he says. He wants to get away from me.

I place my other hand on his shoulder as well and I stare at a space a few inches above his head. He crouches and tries to get away.

"Sir, I do not kill friends," I tell him. "I may be mad but I am not crazy. I do not kill friends."

He retreats backward, looking at me the entire time. Then he stammers out, "I am not your friend."

We spend a few precious seconds doing nothing. He recovers, straightens himself, and points his fat finger at me. "You," he says. "You," he repeats. And he is gone.

I take the long way home that day. I have to muster up courage to confront the questions that will come at me from Nandini. She knows about the review, knows it was an untimely one, and really the first since I joined the police force. This to her is a harbinger of change in an already unsettled world.

Encounter Twenty-Seven

"Do streetlights bother you?" he asks me, shining a torch into each eye. It is a sharp, focused light.

I do the reading test. "*E F P . . . T O Z . . . L P E D . . .*" I am quick, way too quick and sounding as if I have memorized it, which I of course have.

"When were you here last?"

I could have told him the exact date and time. "It was raining, doctor, I remember. Sometime in August last year."

"Lean forward."

He fits a heavy, metallic spectacle frame on my nose bridge and places my chin on a cushioned holder. I lean forward not knowing, as always, what to do with my hands.

"Which is clearer, red or green?"

My head spins. Neither?

An assistant comes in.

"No prescription for him, no lenses either," he tells her.

Dr. Godbole is at a loss. "They told me you have slowed down and thought I might be able to find a reason." He scratches his head. "I can't see anything wrong with your vision. Why does it have to be your eyes?"

I realize we are done and I get up to leave. It seems a wasted effort. "Headlights bother me," I tell him. I really hate high beams and hate people who drive around shining bright lights into people's faces. "I hate headlights."

"Who doesn't?" says the doctor.

They call me that night, after the eye test report reaches them. "Karan," says my caller, with a degree of false affection, "how are you today?"

"Are you slouching, Desai?" I ask. I have an image of him in my mind, a ghoul bathed in green light. "You will choke, Desai. Your chin will choke you one day."

I hear him straightening. "You wish," he says. "Killjoy, you need a haircut tomorrow, first thing. There is a salon outside Churchgate Station called Aircool. As you approach the main entrance it will come up on your right."

I find that surprising. A haircut? I just had a trim a week ago. Then I realize. "The target—first tell me about him."

"A guy with long hair," he replies flippantly. "The rest will be e-mailed. Don't worry, once you read about him you will be happy to get rid of him."

The line disconnects.

"Karan, are you there?" Why does she shout from the bedroom when everything in this chawl is right next door? "Didn't you hear the doorbell ring?"

The neighbor's boy stands at the door peering in, his hand outstretched. He holds an empty cup before my groin. "Sugar," he says.

I let him in and walk over to the hallway. Outside, the chawl courtyard has a young fan club that looks up at me and cheers. I wave and shoot a mock bullet their way and they cower and run, their peals of laughter dry in the morning sun. And memories flood back of a picnic by Powai Lake where as schoolchildren we ran laughing into the water and one of us couldn't swim. I retreat to my place by the lamp in my den. I write the first few words without thinking.

Today was an unbelievable day. I met a man. He saw me once.

"Do you remember me?" he asked.

How could I forget? My memory never lets me go.

The godforsaken bell rings again, interrupting my reverie.

"Karan, are you just going to sit there all day?" asks Nandini.

I remember heading to Churchgate at five that very morning; the hour of the milkman, the *doodh-wallah* who roams Mumbai streets with his milk cans. The express train was late by two minutes and I was restless and jumpy, wanting to get off that platform. I caught a local train instead, comforted by the anonymous crowd. At the end of the journey I got pushed out into the chaos. The station announcements echoed in the vast hall and people hurried, spilling into the streets. Outside I had time to get my shoes polished. The shoeshine boy who sat on the pavement had a runny nose and his hair was unwashed and matted. He was skinny and he chattered as he polished, clicking his teeth.

"You use it as a mirror now, uncle," he said proudly as I looked down at my shiny black shoes. I suddenly remembered Nandini's tirade on child labor. I felt a pang of guilt as I placed a small fat coin in the boy's palm. His hand was so cold and that got me down.

I crossed the road and waited outside the salon's glass doors. The place had ten chairs in two rows of five, and they were mostly occupied. A magazine vendor had spread his wares on the pavement outside. I picked up a Marathi weekly with a shrill headline. "Hello Mumbai, this is Marathi speaking," I mumbled. The vendor smiled, displaying a large gap where two front teeth should have been.

My guy walked into the salon and they sat him down immediately. It was definitely him; as Desai said, he was alone. I heard the waiting customers click their disapproval at this preferential treatment as I entered through the door. The air was cool inside and the sounds were hushed. Click, spray, wash, and dry. This salon was like an assembly line.

"Be seated," a voice said.

The mirrors on the walls faced each other and all reflections retreated into infinity.

"Haircut?" asked another barber. "Shampoo?"

I walked up to the man who was busy explaining how he wanted his parting.

"Right side," he was stressing. "Not the left side."

I stood near him and was momentarily confused by his many reflections. Damn mirrors.

The two of us paused, a cop and a hood at the edge of a labyrinth. He had cloudy eyes. We exchanged glances.

"Do I know you?" he asked. I nodded into infinity.

This was a page that I had read before. This was a chapter that I had understood.

His eyes darted in sudden recognition. He knew this was the end of the line. I watched his hands under the white sheet that covered him. "Don't be brutal," he whispered.

I placed a hand on his shoulder, keeping faith as I took the shot. I recoiled, expecting shattered glass. The muffled sound traveled the length of that room, the blood falling short. I could see his exit wound.

I remember him now. I remember speaking to him as I left. What did I say?

"Are you going to sit there all day?"

"Karan, where did you go so early?"

"Haircut. I needed a haircut," I reply.

"Show me, chief." I like it when she calls me that.

She turns me around and feels the hair on the nape of my neck. It is a moment of intimacy till she sees the gash. Her fingers find the bandage under my collar, the blood seeping at the edges.

"What happened?"

"The barber. The barber got me good," I joke. Her breath turns shallow.

Desai calls just as Nandini is about to launch into a tirade. I wait for two rings before answering.

"Job done, Karan?" he asks loudly.

"Yes," I reply in a low voice, suddenly resenting his blasé manner. "Yes, it's done."

"Describe," he says. He sounds bored; perhaps he is tapping a pencil and doodling instead of making notes. Nandini stands next to me, watching me closely and making me very self-conscious. I turn away from her as I speak. Should I try to sound as if I cared, for her benefit?

"I couldn't see his hands," I begin. "The guy was sitting wrapped up to the neck in a white sheet on the salon chair. Only his head was visible."

"You had a clean shot?"

"Yes, and I took it. I was disoriented by the mirrors. I hate mirrors. It was disorienting but still I took it. And then . . ."

Desai taps his pencil against the receiver.

"The barber was his regular. He had a straight razor. He came at me from behind. I saw him in the mirror but by the time I turned he slashed me."

Desai has ceased tapping. I can almost feel his frown. "Karan, you need more tests. I can't imagine a barber getting his way with one of our best."

There's nothing wrong with my eyes. I'm physically all here. I'm thinking clearly and executing successfully. What I need is something they won't give me—a DNA test.

People have patron saints and in the state of Maharashtra many of the Hindu faith look toward Shirdi and its patron Sai Baba. They acquire small photographs of Baba, seated with one leg crossed over the other and a palm raised, offering you blessings. They frame them and hang them up and hope for benediction. Nobody took me to Shirdi. Nobody anointed my walls with Baba. Nandini for some reason has placed an incense stand in my small den and the smoke curls from it, looking for a place to get away. The smell of sandalwood seeps into the upholstery and ash blows on the floor. I sit in there with a burned match, not sure where to throw it.

The festival days are upon us. They batter my doors down with sound. A loudspeaker blares out a *bhajan* loop all day long. Then, at night, a procession march that never leaves. It takes them a week to rouse the idol. Finally they place the Ganesha idol on a pushcart and wheel him away, leaving behind an empty silence.

I'm feeling lucky so I decide to tiptoe to my shrine. I place my speakers on a pedestal and light another match. The strains of a *raga* hesitate. And then my gods take center stage. My patron saints are singers; music is my shrine.

"Karan, there's smoke coming from beneath your door." I hear footsteps. "Karan?" She twists the doorknob and enters. "What are you doing?"

"Searching. Can't you see? I'm searching."

"Searching for what? In the dark? Why are all the lights off anyway?"

"I don't know."

She leaves the room with a look that says, *I'll see you outside.* It is a Saturday and we have to go shopping. There is a sale in Big Bazaar. Nandini is serious about sales. She says it's the reason we're able to pay the rent and go on vacation.

I sit in the dark of my den with boarded windows and try to remember where I come from. There is no clarity. I remember a young man called Evam (a *mofussil* type and a scatterbrain with his heart in the right place) who took care of me and others like me. I remember what I told a sympathetic teacher at Don Bosco High School.

"I never got to know my mother. She left me when I was an infant. My father never even knew I existed."

I had a restless and febrile imagination.

"Why do they only test killers and rapists, madam?" I asked her. "I want to be tested."

"What test?" she asked.

"I want a DNA test."

I had some telltale signs. I was sure my fair skin and light eyes came from the Konkanastha Brahmin community. It wasn't a large community so surely I could trace my lineage there. My teacher told me nothing.

I did not rest easy. I was obsessed. As an orphan child I constantly searched for my parentage, hoping it would answer the burning question, *Who am I?*

"Studies show that a lack of knowledge of your origins inhibits your social skills. So you can keep searching," said my teacher, "but be aware that you may never be satisfied."

I remember Evam telling me, "There's a child inside that will never let go of you." He ran a place we called Evam's Ward. "This child inside you wants to make you whole. You should let him, but you are also scared. You are scared of the thought that who you are depends on what became of your parents."

It was complicated. I was tagged "special"—the word has dogged me ever since I learned to spell. Special care, special assistance, and specialty ward; but one day the veil lifted and it all went away. My friends were not so lucky and they remained at Evam's Ward, which was really more of a day care center. They made faces when they saw me leaving—that was the norm. They made faces all the time, as if they were unable to arrive at the same muscular presentation as regular people. But I had given up trying to speak to them in a form that was understood as conversation.

So my life accumulated day by day, leaf by leaf, till I was introduced to my future boss. Evam asked me to meet a police officer, a leader of men. He saw something in me. Ranvir Pratap was that police officer and he shaped my career.

"Why don't you have an idol or at least a framed photograph of one like everyone else?" Nandini sometimes asks.

She doesn't like the blank nature of my worship or the line that I have written on the wall of my den. In black marker I've written the words *AHAM BRAHMASMI*, which means, *That which cannot be abandoned, that which is whole and ever present*. To me this made a lot of sense, perhaps as a counter to those who gave me birth and then abandoned me in a place like Evam's Ward among those they considered worthy of "special" attention.

When Nandini saw the quote for the first time she translated it as, *I am Brahman.* She did not like it. "It sounds like you have a high opinion of yourself. Remember, there is nothing sacred about what you do."

I wouldn't let her erase it, so below the words she has written, *Your name is Karan. You kill for a living. Work like this must be so hard to find.*

Cast a Lazy Eye

A "special" like me has a girl like Nandini. I have an unknown past and she is most concerned about losing her identity. Mumbai, her fitful muse, nourishes her and also eats away her being. I get to hear a lot of what she thinks on the subject. Every day she bemoans a lost custom, a forgotten festival, a curtailed ritual, or even words that lost have utility and disappeared. She feels we are being reduced to a lowly herd by Navi Mumbai, the new Bombay.

"Cast a lazy eye on this city," she said once.

What?

"Or make love instead."

She has been reading poetry in the parlor while getting her legs waxed. Nandini was determined that she would not simply be a sufferance like her city. Every day she observed Mumbai and compared it to her Pune, the smaller metropolis just two hours from here, and in her dispassionate manner she stated that the *character of the city* would not endure. To endure was to die. To all those who glorified the ability of the city to bounce back from adversity she had this to say: Mumbai Devi is a selfish hag full of selfish people. Its known benefactors, the Parsis, were also selfish. They had selfish enclaves and selfish sperm.

Even the worms in the compost in their baugs were Parsi.

Roaming the city she felt for the small nooks, corners, parks, and temples—Gowalia Tank, Gamdevi, Teen Batti, Banganga, and Bhuleshwar. There were Christian precincts, Muslim gullies, Goan houses, the Lohar Chawl, Crawford Market, P D'Mello Road; the list was endless. She looked hard at the people in these places to see if they belonged. She wasn't so sure.

Mumbai has no sons and daughters. The city changes hands way too often, even as you speak. Belonging is hard to come by; even if you own a few square feet on the twentieth floor, one day your sea view might suddenly be obscured. The only upward graph the city has is one that shows property prices.

Nandini wants to disrupt Mumbaikars. I don't know what drives her or what causes her grief but her chief instigator is the city. Standing outside Churchgate Station in the morning, being part of the rushing hordes of office workers, she cannot believe the cops use a dirty rope to shepherd them through traffic. She rails at the inefficiency of the ticket counters and cannot understand the patience people have, standing endlessly in long lines. In town hall meetings, between heated arguments about parking and water conservation, she asks people to calm down and read the *Bhagwad Geetha*.

The rampant encroachments in the city disturb her, the illegal power-tapping, the water-hoarding, the *hafta* or bribe that is demanded by people doing jobs they are being paid for, the noise pollution—all of this gets to her every day.

Despite all this Nandini is proud of her city; she loves Mumbai. Love is too strong a word for me. I like Mumbai and I hide my liking behind a veneer of criticism. But it is a hard-working city and I fit in. I am thorough, diligent, and I do my job without delving into the "greater good" or the "higher purpose" which other encounter teams believe in or say they believe in.

Nandini leads Heritage Walks that are a mixture of fun and learning. Some days I follow her and hover in the periphery. Some days I mingle with the group. By now I know a lot about Bombay. Every building has character and every place has history. And every *chutiya* on the street is on the make. I say, *You want to see Mumbai? Look into their eyes.*

Today she is looking pretty in a red and yellow *salwar kameez*. I watch the others as they observe her. I can never get used to the sight of her. I am tailing her because Special Branch has information that a gang is out to hurt her for what I have done to one of their own. The intelligence is unconfirmed but we need to be careful. I had to tell Nandini about the report and for once she said nothing. But I'm sure the unsaid will surface later. (I can imagine her confronting me, saying, *One day it will come home to roost, this monster you're rearing.*)

"Art deco?" she questions the group, raising an eyebrow.

The group stares at the Regal Cinema. It is early on a Sunday morning and there is a slight haze in the sky. A breeze is coming in from the road that leads to the Gateway of India and the Arabian Sea behind it.

"Architect Charles Stevens; the theater opened in 1933," says a smart aleck. He's juggling a bunch of handwritten notes, a smartphone, and a large camera.

"Looks fairly ordinary," observes somebody else. "I prefer multiplexes."

The Regal Cinema had its moment in another era. It

was an era when every city in India had a Regal, an Odeon, and a Ritz, and the crème de la crème wore trousers and pressed shirts and watched Hollywood movies.

"This is a single-screen theater," says Nandini. "Somehow that sounds dated."

"Isn't that the Shantaram Road, the Colaba Causeway?" asks another, pointing toward a crowded lane.

There are ten of them in today's group. Four young couples from Bangalore and Chennai wanting to "know" Mumbai and two cheerful European backpackers. The latter perk up on hearing the S-word.

"Really?" says one of them. He pulls out the hallowed book and feels its dog-eared pages. "Can we go there now?"

"Later," says Nandini. She pirouettes on her feet and her *salwar* flows in a full circle behind her. The group follows her gaze and takes in an eclectic mix of buildings and roads.

They are standing at the center of a parking lot where six roads meet. On weekdays it becomes an island marooned in a sea of traffic. This is where Nandini begins her South Mumbai Walk, where the city for a moment reverts to Bombay. On Sunday mornings it is quiet, traffic is thin, and you find time and space to take shade under fully grown trees. Around you are buildings that have withstood the relent of time, and the air you breathe is testimony to bygone eras that have been erased inadequately.

A few deep sighs and they set forth into the road that leads to the Taj Mahal Hotel. I hang back for a while and peer into an antique store called Phillips.

"Watch your step," warns Nandini. "Careful not to walk over those drains with your noses open."

They tread carefully around the iron grates that dot the roadsides. The pavement is irregular and footwear tangles with broken stone. Visitors can never get used to the smells of Mumbai—around restaurants, on the train, near the docks, in the vicinity of street people, and from the sewage that courses through those ubiquitous drains. The smell of fish and saltwater, the dank smell of cloth and sweat, the fumes from vehicles, and sewage fill this place we call Mumbai.

At the gateway the shutterbugs get busy. The sea is calm and a few boats provide fodder for cameras. The Taj Mahal Hotel sits in profile against scattered clouds. A variety of merchants and opportunists accost them for trade and favor and Nandini waves them away weakly. And here her wandering eye comes into play. She spots the people at the margin, the ones sleeping on the pavement, the balloon seller who is puffing his cheeks and blowing his wares, and the *mofussil* group that has arrived by van at an early hour to capture the sunrise and then head for the Elephanta Caves. I find her glancing at me and I nod ever so slightly. I part with some loose change and grab a pink balloon.

She gathers the group for a brief history lesson. They listen patiently but their eyes cannot help but roam. "Look, there is Shivaji on a horse," says a middle-aged man, and a younger woman photographs pigeons taking flight.

She does the causeway next and that takes an hour. The group could easily spend a full day there lingering about.

"Come back here in the evening," she advises them. "Come back here to the streets of Colaba at night if you are adventurous."

"What kind of adventure?"

"Look around. People shuffle at night through smoky joints. You can find a place that serves cheap alcohol and fried *surmai* fish where they also play the music of Al

Stewart and Jethro Tull. Just remember to stay anonymous."

They head back to the six-road crossing. Nandini moves toward a nearby structure. The group is distracted by two beggar women holding infants, who they finally pay to move away. Nandini meanwhile stands and observes this building that has so captured her imagination.

"Made of stone, more than a hundred years ago," she begins.

"Architect Stevens," reads Smart Aleck from his notebook. "But wait, that doesn't make sense." He looks toward Nandini with confusion.

"It wasn't designed by Charles Stevens but by his illustrious father, Frederick W. Stevens."

The structure is very different from the nearby theater. It is made of chiseled stone blocks and there is no carving. Yet the architecture, the design, and the detailing come from a spare, compelling aesthetic. There are a series of arches across the facade and the detailing is inlaid with stones of varying colors and sizes.

"Damn, it's a beauty," someone from the group mutters.

And then they glimpse the sign out front that reads, *Maharashtra Police Headquarters*.

"Cops, in this building? I mean, why?"

"Why not?" replies Nandini.

He shrugs.

"Let me tell you something. The police of Mumbai have moved into buildings with character and history, and perhaps rightfully so. Think about it: the cops in Mumbai write its history. This city is big and in your face; crime is big, business is big, and so is the police force. And offense is taken and given."

The group glances around curiously and eyes a traffic

cop. He is a little overweight, wearing fashionable dark glasses and a gleaming belt. He is busy giving someone a ticket in Marathi.

"Mumbai police have developed a character that takes from the city," continues Nandini. "Every now and then, Mumbai throws up superstar actors, billionaire businessmen, and crime warlords. Cops get big on you too, so the police force has responded by rearing so-called supercops, or they at least like to propagate that rumor."

"The papers make such a big deal about encounter cops and shootouts," someone says.

Nandini laughs. She glances toward the lamppost where I am standing. As if on cue I release the balloon. It rises and tangles with a wire before bursting. Everyone turns in my direction. Some of them duck and others laugh nervously.

A little later they reach the Victoria Terminus Station. It is a remarkable structure with vertebrate arches and ribbed turrets. It has domes and there are figurines and gargoyles in the mix as well. The building could be a Victorian palace or a Gothic seminary. There is a more recent extension on the side that is ordinary and more down to earth, where the passing hordes don't bother looking up and merely climb aboard trains each day to lead them to suburban homes and factories.

"Architect Stevens," Smart Aleck announces again smugly.

Nandini walks them through an alley past another Gothic-looking structure. A sign outside says, *Mumbai Police Headquarters*. The building is marred by fat sewage pipes that crisscross its facade. There are Y joints, L joints, and gravity-defying U shapes. Finally she leads them to their minibus, gives a brief summary, and sends them on their way.

Some days Nandini follows me. She retraces my steps. How does she choose the days and how does she get them right? Simple. She reads about what's been happening around the city in the newspaper, stares hard at me, then reads my face. I ask her why she does this. She says she needs to know and she needs to understand. And sometimes she needs to set things right.

"I don't need a conscience," I tell her. "And please don't keep count."

She doesn't listen.

Later that evening Desai calls and says, "Rest easy; the information was spurious. No need to follow your wife around more than you already do."

Why does Nandini show the tourists these police buildings when there is so much else to see here? I am at least glad she stopped at the Mumbai police HQ because a few steps away there is a small nondescript structure whose architect is unknown. This is the Special Branch, an elite unit of Crime Branch, Mumbai. No one from this branch wears a uniform, even on field duty. No names are displayed and there is no roll call. The building is squat and square and it has no detailing. Nothing that happens here gets recorded and yet the stuff of myth and legend is cast in every stone.

The front portion of this building houses a small, secretive unit called the Third Squad. It is ruled by a taipan named Ranvir Pratap. He is a living legend. The rear of this building is operated by a unit informally known as the Khabari Squad, which deals in nuggets of information and billets of dirt. Heading this network is a King Rat called Tiwari. Both warlords have an unknown rank which is quite senior.

Both men also have one common trait: they are constantly talking. In the case of Ranvir, he simply assumes I am there and most times I in fact am. In the case of Tiwari there is nobody. The turd talks to himself.

The contrast between the two teams is remarkable. Members of the Third Squad are known to be quiet and antisocial. It seems we do not mingle and we have no opinions to share. Our boss approves of this framework. The Khabari Squad, on the other hand, makes a living by trafficking in rumor, opinion, and hearsay. According to my boss all are treated with the same brush and painted up as fact.

Ranvir Pratap and Tiwari report to a dry, dull suit named Parthasarathy. He is an IPS officer and a bookworm who has risen to great heights by some unknown accident. In meetings he echoes what people say and usually does nothing. At the last meeting held in his fabled office, Parthasarathy asked Ranvir Pratap to put his team through a series of medical tests, including home visits from a counselor. A lady (she was indeed a lady) named Ms. Daftary called on us and she immediately fixated on the three fat thesauruses sitting on my table. She asked me why three. I had never even thought about it before. Perhaps this went back some years, I told her, when in my school and college I was accused of being emotionless and cold. I was also called moody, sullen, withdrawn, and introverted. Words like these became my name if not my identity, and I had to look to these fat tomes for synonyms and meanings. And then suddenly Ms. Daftary, the kind lady, asked me if I felt any pain. Pain? I mean an ache, she said. I said no, other than some odd gym-related stress now and then. She said that wasn't what she was referring to. And then she spoke to me about phantom pain. She said people who lost limbs sometimes feel a pain from that very limb that no longer physically exists. This was a phantom pain but it was very real, and sometimes it was so acute that it wrecked people's lives. I was whole, hale, and hearty, I replied, but she did not laugh. Neither did Nandini, who by this time was paying complete attention. Do you miss not having a father or mother? asked the kind lady. Was this the ache, the phantom pain she was asking me about? Perhaps. Never having a parent, could that still qualify as—? Yes, she said. And thinking about this later, but not too hard, I felt that there might be something called a father figure who perhaps I'm unconsciously acknowledging. It wasn't such a big deal. I mean, I did respect Ranvir Pratap a lot and I did follow orders and we as a team obeyed. Above all we obeyed.

You need to see Ranvir Pratap in the evening of his life. He has a distinctive air, gray hair, and that word I found after much search: *erudition*. How do I describe him better? Perhaps in another time and place I will.

But I have to try to understand him to answer the question that Nandini poses now and then: "How can you trust a man who puts your life on the line?"

The easy answer is: "You have to."

City Happenings

What would you call the characters in these encounters? The media had names. They had invented a terminology, comfortable shorthand serving as a lazy guide. One paragraph of such stereotypes would be found in the "City Happenings" column of the newspaper every other day: *A* was either a gang member called Altaf or a cop called Athavle. *B* was a gang member called Bhansali or a cop called Bhosale. *C* stood for a term that was never used on paper but was practiced: Choreography. *D* was a Company, and the D Company was an infamous gang. *E* was for Encounter. And *F* was for Funnily Enough.

Most encounters took place in the suburbs, at night, and in lonely places. (There are many lonely places in Mumbai, it seems.) Officially, the hoods always fired first, and the cops only retaliated. Bullets came and went as fusillades and cartridges scattered themselves on the scene, providing evidence. Those who died were criminals and they conveniently carried IDs indicating their name, age, and gang affiliation. Funnily enough, people couldn't get enough of these reports. These cut-and-pastes were the literature of the underworld.

One reason Karan stuck to this occupation was Ranvir

Pratap, his boss and a stellar officer from the Indian Police Service who wore his disdain on his forehead. People from the city of Allahabad, at least those of a certain vintage, were learned and would look down once they were out of the state of Uttar Pradesh. Looking down in UP was inadvisable because its gentry had poor habits. If dirt had a retinue it was Uttar Pradesh, said Ranvir. Now comfortably outside UP, when Ranvir glanced down he would find a bloated corpuscle named Tiwari, a man who wasn't even an IPS officer but who instead came up the ranks and was thus naturally inferior. Tiwari outwardly resembles a lamb, donning this camouflage to hide his devious occupation. He is a sneak, a gatherer of information.

As a *khabari*, some people decry his being in the police force. Not that he cares what anyone thinks. Opinions are so tedious, he would say. Up there in his cranium deviance reigned and he let loose his manners. In Mumbai, Tiwari was the crude outpost of this new world, this Navjeevan society we call middle class.

By bringing two such people to loggerheads, Mumbai reinforced the view that the city is bipolar. In a strange way they exist because of each other. Their differences are many and yet they both serve the only altar in Mumbai that affords any respect: *nateeja*. Meaning: results.

Ranvir Pratap

People expect to glimpse the stately city of Lucknow in Ranvir. This capital city of Uttar Pradesh leaves an imprint that the poetic language Urdu describes as *mijaz*. Besides his style, demeanor, and diction, Ranvir has what is known as *andaz*. Off-duty he wears long white *kurtas* made of fine cotton or muslin. He chooses custom buttons made of silver. Crisp white pajamas complement his *kurta*. Ranvir's favored drink is tea and it is a finicky brew, otherwise he won't touch it. The water he drinks comes from his house in a flask, every day, as does his glass. He does not trust other people's hands. In a police station he would rather salute than shake them.

Ranvir is a private person and a well-read one. He has seen an India of small towns and villages where women fetch water from an open well and men till the soil with their bones. Where the farmers worship the sun that burns their backs and the land that breaks it. Where their meager surplus goes to the market, where money hides behind merchants. Most people would rather reside in cities than lead this simple life. The next generation migrates out of this modest existence to places like Mumbai because the city has a strong pull and offers newcomers a different trajectory. Some of these migrants give Ranvir reason to hold a gun. Mumbai's soil is fertile; moneymen flourish but crime has taken root as well. Crime is an industry in Mumbai whose recruits come from all communities and castes. There are hard-working gangsters here and hard-working cops. The work is alluring but sometimes deadly.

Ranvir has a leathery face with a few creases. A broad forehead greets you. His lips are pursed and above them a mustache dips at the ends. He has been known to smile at family functions. A smile makes him a different person. Or so it is rumored.

He is not actually from the city of Lucknow though he is fluent in Urdu. He quotes poetry and occasionally waxes eloquent about the fragrant preparation of *dum biryani*. And people cannot reconcile this with what he does. It would seem that the head of a unit that dispenses summary justice through a gun should in some sense be visibly a lesser mortal, perhaps from a place like Azamgarh, a district in Eastern UP where *khadi bhasha* was spoken and *lohars*, the local blacksmiths, made *kattas*, the local pistol. Azamgarh is an interesting place that has produced poets like Kaifi Azmi alongside dons like Abu Salem. This is a juxtaposition that makes perfect sense in Uttar Pradesh, a state where crude reality has been given a sort of poetic license.

Ranvir's narrative began in a place called Allahabad. In its time this was a town with *raunaq*, *tehzeeb*, and other nice-sounding epithets that describe its soul. He grew up in the neighborhood of Civil Lines. In its quarters Urdu was spoken and pure Hindi grew on its trees. Thoughts can make a city; sometimes words can save it. Allahabad had a fragrance despite its open drains.

He was the fifth of seven children. He lost two siblings when he was in his teens. They were a close-knit family and these partings were gut-wrenching. The family astrologer, Gopal Shastri, had made an interesting prediction for Ranvir. "He will choose a career where he risks his life, again and again," said Shastri-*ji*. "He will take lives as well."

Ranvir's father, a feared freedom fighter, laughed when he heard this. This fever-ridden, skinny fourteen-year-old son of his was not exactly the biggest threat he had ever seen.

Ranvir had an idyllic childhood in Civil Lines. The family bungalow had a mulberry tree in front that yielded delicious berries resembling centipedes. The branches of the neighbors' mango tree spread over their veranda. The neighbors were famous lawyers and some members of that family would become chief justices. Behind the house was a renowned poet whose son would become an iconic actor. Across the lane were freedom fighters and civil servants. The air was charged and Ranvir's father firmly believed that since his children breathed it, they would do well in life.

Yet a fertile land that nourished freedom fighters and threw up poets like Nirala, Mahadevi Varma, and Jaishankar Prasad is likely to mess with one's head. In this land of metaphor there was plenty of room for ambiguity. Ranvir left Allahabad with a confused sense of what was right and what was wrong. How was he to know?

The train journey to Mumbai prepares you for the worst. All along the railway tracks you see the backs of shanties and the backsides of people. The accumulation of dirt and detritus paints a bleak picture. It also smells. At the Bombay Central Station you encounter crowds in motion. That is the first thing you learn in the city—how to move in a moving crowd. The next thing you learn is how to speak as you walk past. Nobody pauses; they carry on and try to help you as they pass by. Directions come to you from the corners of mouths and half-turned faces. The taxi is a rattling death trap driven by someone from your home town. If you start him off he has a story to tell, just like everyone else.

Ranvir's first residence looked like it had been put in a compactor, and resembled an aged face with a hat for a roof.

"In Mumbai there is water, electricity, and a get-ahead sensibility that thrusts and competes with naked ambition. You realize very quickly that you have left your native place behind. Where you came from is a story nobody wants to hear."

So said his first landlord, Girdharilal, who pocketed the advance and gave him a piece of advice, something that Ranvir took to heart.

"Don't look for help in Mumbai," Girdharilal told him. "This is a self-service city. Everybody here is a *swayam sevak*."

"I just need a little luck," said Ranvir.

His landlord snorted. "Luck will not pay your rent."

They stood together briefly, sharing tea and a *ragda pattice*. They did not meet again for a year.

The street where Ranvir lived was a mirror image of every other street in Mumbai. This is a city of convenience in aesthetic but it is ambitious in its needs. Luckily, unlike the landscape, the people are nuanced.

There are no famous Ranvir-isms. His approach is simple and borrows from the animal kingdom: stay low during pursuit, keep beneath the radar, live in a nondescript building, wear plainclothes all the time. Second: lock horns, engage from the very start, deal with people directly. And third: go for the jugular. Follow the animal instinct that says, *No thought in action.*

The principle of natural selection works because someone pursues and someone else runs. That becomes instinct over centuries. The deer always run, the cats pursue. But there is no hand-me-down DNA for this among men, so the training has to be one-sided. Here is the drill: you are a cop, you are the hunter.

His team's groundwork was always thorough and the quarry was researched exhaustively. Ranvir never got personally involved. And he never pulled the trigger—except that first time. An incident at an interrogation set the tone. The quarry was a known killer and the questioning was hard—hard on everybody. The guy admitted to a spree of crimes, showed no remorse, and he was grinning when he died. He didn't see it coming. The other people in the room said it was a clean break, it was a bare-hand execution: Ranvir held his hair and broke his neck.

After Ranvir left they strung the guy up in his cell with his bedsheet. Another prison "suicide."

This incident saw him get a mild reprimand. They posted him out to a remote corner of UP for a couple of years, ostensibly to cool his heels. But incidents have a habit of following people like Ranvir. He was watched closely to see if he might measure up to be the head of the next encounter unit.

He was assigned to the town of Baraut in the Baghpat District, where he ran the station during this stretch. This small UP town had a polytechnic college, and students would come from all the nearby areas to enroll in the numerous vocational courses it offered. Being a small town in an unruly state, there was considerable political influence over the college. Policies and rules were subject to various external pressures. A year into his assignment Ranvir learned of a new principal who had joined the college. Chaubey came to Baraut from one of the city colleges. This was his first assignment in a politically charged atmosphere. It didn't take long for the sparks to fly and within a month of his arrival, word was out that the local community was already plotting his transfer.

Ranvir met him for the first time at a college function where they shared the podium. He liked the man's simple, crisp style and engaging manner. He could also see that this was one fish that would soon be out of water. They stood for a couple of minutes chatting after the event.

"So, officer, how has your posting been? Have you settled down well in these parts?"

Settling down was the last thing on Ranvir's mind. Baraut was a dull place and a punishment posting. The contrast to Mumbai was striking. "No, Mr. Chaubey," he replied. "In my line of work, if you settle down they transfer you out immediately. Honestly, I place no premium on being appreciated by the locals."

"So, what do you like about this place?" asked Chaubey.

It was a question Ranvir had asked of himself. He counted with his fingers as he spoke: "Let me see: community toilets on the terrace, sparrows getting killed by my bedroom fan, monkeys parading around in my underwear."

Chaubey laughed. "This is Uttar Pradesh, after all. And what do you dislike?"

Ranvir thought for a moment. "I guess the *kathor bhasha*.

The language is rough and immediate, like the people."

Chaubey reflected on the nature of curse words commonly used in Baraut. *Naali ka keeda* was the genteel opener. "I agree," he replied. "Words bristle on people's tongues out here. Even verbs sound coarse in Baghpat District."

To Ranvir, silences were a measure of a place. In Allahabad he treasured the silence. He could hear poets at work in those long hours when time stood still, usually in the afternoon. In Baraut he could sense an unruly quiet; he could feel lonely men hatching predictable plots. There was nothing commendable about the silence in Baraut.

The local police station was a crude outpost. They had a simple approach to dealing with suspects: bring them in, work them over; if that fails, do them in. The cops also relied heavily on local hoods to do most of their work and only bothered to show up when absolutely necessary. As a result, there was a parallel system of enforcement that had sprung up with the active connivance of the constabulary. Ranvir had to work hard to break this mold. The first thing he noticed was a complete absence of records. Many cases were not even filed, and those that were had hardly any paperwork. He made an honest attempt but after a few months he realized the futility of trying to change something that was ingrained in the very fabric of the place. Rather than Ranvir changing Baraut, the place changed him. When he returned to Mumbai he looked the same but he was amenable now to getting things done the way they did in small towns. In other words, he had the right disposition to head an encounter unit.

He arrived back in Mumbai unheralded. Nobody had noticed his absence in the first place, other than counterintelligence, which had been following him closely. Ranvir rose rapidly up the ranks.

His seniors called him Rana, which he liked. After a few years he was asked to study the Class of '83 and do better in assembling an encounter team of his own. Do better than *them*? They had an enviable track record at eliminating targets and were publicly acknowledged as heroes. In sum, this group of police officers had eliminated more than six hundred underworld gang members. One unfortunate side effect of this new dynamic had been lawlessness within the force itself; the spirit of the Wild West seemed to have emboldened most of these officers into making extracurricular money and exercising their power for private gain. The city was "cleansed" and extortion cases decreased, but while gangs felt the heat and their activities were severely curtailed, most of these specialists were soon involved in some misdemeanor or another. As they say, success is a perch that breeds entitlement.

It was eerie. One by one the batch had taken pieces of the law and broken them. It was almost as if they'd been told to pick their crimes from a catalog of vice.

But the department was unwilling to accept these misdemeanors as the necessary price of ridding the city of six hundred hoods. They wanted a different approach and a team that could be controlled better, a quiet team with a low profile. The deputy general of the Maharashtra police publicly said, "Socks. And corrupt officers. The Mumbai police needs to pull up both if they want to win back the respect they once commanded."

Ranvir's boss was part of the old guard, a tenured officer who asked him strange questions like, "Do philosophers make good omelets?"

Ranvir thought he was joking. He wasn't. His boss was a guilty man; at least he behaved like one. He was forever trying to justify the encounter approach to himself. He began quoting extensively from the *Bhagwad Geetha*, a text in which killing brothers in a war was arguably acceptable and philosophically tenable.

Thought has its place in the police hierarchy, but at lower levels it is preceded by action. That is how Ranvir trained his men. If someone were to ask Pradeep Sharma, *How do you get around to killing somebody?* he would describe in great detail exactly how he would do it. It wasn't complicated and it certainly wasn't a philosophical issue.

The targets were violent people who had taken lives. They could not be reined in or brought to custody easily, and many were beyond the pale of the justice system. The judicial process was multitiered; it was often infiltrated, witnesses were vulnerable, and they were either bought or they paid with their lives. The accused had the backing of gangs and they had the recklessness of cornered animals. The gangs employed lawyers who were trained in subverting the judicial process. On the one good day when the prosecution actually got a conviction, the system of appeals was endless and stretched beyond people's career timelines. The Swamy case was a prime example and it exhausted Ranvir. Moreover, when Swamy was gunned down, Ranvir got a stern lecture from the judge, a dressing down that he found hard to stomach.

The encounter teams were given the choicest bits, those that were truly beyond the purview of the best sociological minds. Their subjects' files were fat and juicy reading. Bring out the meat carver; this was blood that needed spilling.

"Ours will be a cool, collected operation and the

odds will be stacked in our favor. We depend on good information, which is why we will tolerate Tiwari."

But when the moment came someone still had to pull the trigger. It was tricky. There was no animosity or personal connection, but they still had to do it. Ranvir needed the right people to complete the task.

"I do not belong to this world. I don't think anybody does. What we do feels artificial, even if it isn't always staged."

And that posed a challenge.

"You lost your hold on reality after a while. I needed to be careful with my team and look for people who would be less affected. Sympathy and empathy were unwanted. I wished for a while that I had a genetically modified team to manage, one that spoke less, operated alone, was less social, did not feel for the targets or imagine what would happen to their families."

Mulling these qualities over in his head, Ranvir wrote out a job description for the team.

~

Ranvir and his wife settled into the comfortable police quarters behind Worli Seaface. It was on a private road and housed a large community, so she was happy. In the evenings, they would walk along the seafront and peer out over the water. Life felt precious in those days, to say nothing of the two gun-toting guards who walked behind them wearing black combat uniforms.

A lot was happening in his personal life back then.

His wife, a Brahmin from the south, was inbred, which was the norm in her community and by itself wasn't a bad thing. Except for the fact that cousins marrying each other, aunts wedding their nephews, and uncles getting hitched to their nieces sounded strange. But these were real people and the ages were right, with the men older than the women by a few years, as Brahmin society had so wished. The issue was that the human species hated this sameness and sought diversity; if it felt cloistered by blood that grew thicker, then its innate need for freedom tripped the neural wiring.

Their child (a son) was born with disabilities. The one bright moment was when the nurse came out of the delivery room. ("You have a son.") The rest they gradually delved into. The child turned out to be severely autistic, and all Ranvir could do was be courageous and support the mother. They did not weep. There were no tears at all. What followed was brief and intense.

They went to a young man named Evam Bhaskar, a "doctor" who they met by accident at a social function. He ran an obscure outfit in Gamdevi which they could not find at first. The entrance to the place was through a small gap between shops selling electrical wire and spare parts. The narrow entrance opened into a small courtyard graced by a lone tree. Three rooms surrounded the courtyard.

The first time Ranvir met Evam Bhaskar he was unimpressed. Intuition told him this was a person who was as strange as he looked.

"Dr. Evam, you are trained in which discipline?" He held Evam's business card by a corner and brought it close to his eyes. He flipped the card over and was disappointed to see the reverse was blank.

"Non-Freudian medicine," said Evam, watching Ranvir closely, aware of his disregard. "Psychology."

"You mean psychoanalysis?'"

"No sir," replied Evam. "We actually believe in chemo." He tried a laugh. It was a solitary sound that slinked away through the window.

"This place is your clinic?" asked Ranvir.

"Yes. I also have a consulting room near Dharavi. It is where I . . . keep my records."

He handed the card back to Evam, who looked surprised. Ranvir smiled and patted him on the shoulder. "I have always wondered how you deliver your cures. It must be a difficult practice. There is no eureka moment when your patient is suddenly cured and can simply walk away."

"There is no cure, sir," Evam said. "There is no disease either."

"And yet people come to you and they pay good money?" he asked, his dislike for Evam immediately apparent. Ranvir would soon gather that his patients never walked away either.

He would later reflect: "Evam ran a strange operation, and I for one was not convinced he was properly qualified. He didn't look like a psychologist or a psychoanalyst, but nevertheless he spoke to us about autism. He said boys are more likely to be autistic (so don't blame yourself), that more than one in a hundred children are statistically affected (I am not sure I'm stating it right), that we should be prepared for our child to not speak at all (some words might materialize but they go away), that a host of illnesses like allergies, bowel diseases, persistent viruses, and sensory-perception problems will follow him—and he stated all this in a calm, everyday manner, because this, it seems, was his everyday. I had to hand it to him. He lived with a bunch of these kids and their parents, day in and day out. I would have questioned the need long ago.

I only had one child, my own; Evam bore many. He had a homily up his sleeve at all times. (If science fails then homilies are the cure.) He told me, *When a normal child is born your windows open out. You breathe fresh air, hear new sounds, and you see a brave new world. When an autistic child is born you go knocking on doors.*"

Moments of love and affection were few but they were breathtaking. Half the time Ranvir looked at his son in wonder.

"He couldn't speak our language, so we invented words or expressions as a convenient shorthand. And then I kicked myself back into the present. When my son died of a severe infection we were barely there. To try to describe the feeling would be hollow. But it seemed then that someone had sent us this child as a sign. It was fleeting. It was a flare."

Nandini

The very sight of Nandini knocks people over and they compete for her attention, hoping that she'll notice them. Her gestures, her spirit, and her manner play havoc with common sensibilities. But she has more. She has insouciance and the charge of summer lightning. How could you blame them for falling in love with her?

Karan blamed his peripheral vision. She walked into it one day wearing a floral dress that swirled in the breeze. Things that swirled caught his attention. A faint hint of perfume teased his senses. He saw her and quickly looked away, then had no choice but to return his gaze to her. That was it for a while.

The next time he saw her she was wearing a purple T-shirt and white jeans. The jeans were embroidered with brass studs that glinted in the sun. He stared. Stuff that glinted got his attention. She caught him staring at her legs. That was it for a while.

They finally met. She was smoking a long, thin cigarette in the college canteen. And the smoke made him cough. The cough brought tears. Tears got her attention. She stubbed out the cigarette and walked up to him.

"Speak," she said.

He coughed again and he glanced around at his friends. They were busy watching him struggle. She sat next to him and wouldn't go away. He waited for words to form. The canteen emptied.

Karan was tall, good-looking, and a *chikna* who appeared lost all the time. He didn't have a bike like the other studs and he didn't wear brands, not even the cheap rip-offs. He wasn't part of any of the cliques on A, B, or C Road. The girls were wary but intrigued by his brooding eyes and loner disposition. Here were secrets to be found.

He landed the girl who all the boys chased. She breached his honeycomb. Nandini was the only one to walk up to him and hold his hand. She liked his long fingers, his fair complexion, and the feelings he evoked. When Nandini held his hand his demeanor changed. What was diffident became shy, what was distant became a hesitant proximity. He discovered he liked holding hands and thankfully she led him on; this is why the affair happened. It shocked the class but he wasn't thinking and she didn't notice. Their relationship moved rapidly and he had no experience but she knew what she wanted. For the first time in his life heaven was on earth. He shuffled around the city as if in a cocoon that obscured its common nature. Time was elastic and days stretched as weeks flew by.

Nandini was born to a Hindu father and Christian mother. Her father was in the army and his postings flirted with the perimeter of the Indian map. He was a valiant officer who had survived some challenging campaigns. But one morning the neighbors found him slumped over the steering wheel of his jeep, his dead body pushed against the horn.

Nandini took to poetry at a young age to deal with

heartache and taking care of her mother after his death. Yes sir, she took control. She had her father's disposition, his athletic flair, and his ability to kick ass. They lived in a small house on the outskirts of Pune with two bedrooms and a flower bed out front. It had a view of hills till a newly constructed apartment blocked their vista. Clothes fluttered where trees used to sway.

Soon Nandini won a sports scholarship to a college in downtown Mumbai. She packed a bag and took the highway straight there. Life changed when she saw Karan.

"Karan who?" asked Nandini's mother. "Tell me about him."

The answer was not forthcoming because Karan was not forthcoming. Nandini had a job at hand. So she decided to learn everything about this fellow she was to marry. Karan who?

One evening she sat him down and tried to get him talking. She chewed a freshly sharpened Nataraj HB pencil and prodded: "Start with school—everybody starts there."

"I attended an English middle school," he said, emphasizing the word *English*, the study of which was an early obsession for him. "Don Bosco School in Matunga. I was sent there for observation. A father was meant to watch over me, so he did and the children did too."

"Why? Because you were a strange kid?"

He pretended not to hear that. He had never before known that he was even capable of pretending. "Nobody would come up to me. Nobody would sit next to me," he said. "But all these nobodies would ask me questions, one after another."

"Like?"

"Like, *Where are you from? Do you have any brothers or*

sisters? Where do you live? Is that close by? Then why do you walk to school? And how come you always eat in the canteen?" He sat in silence for a moment.

"These are normal questions, Karan."

"Yes, perhaps," he replied. "But they always found my answers hard to believe."

"So let me ask them," she said, sitting up straight. "Where are you from, Karan?"

"I don't know."

"Do you have any brothers and sisters?"

"I don't know." She stared at him sharply and he repeated it. "I don't know."

"Where did you grow up?"

"In a home, a place for homeless kids."

"Was it close to the school?"

"Close? No."

"Then why did you walk to school?"

"I had to. I had no choice."

"Why did you eat every meal in the canteen?"

"Because it was free."

And then Karan spoke some more, all on his own, for the first time in his life. "After this, the more pointed questions and observations would follow: *Your clothes are a size too small. Why don't you get new ones? Your shoes are torn, have you noticed? Who cut your hair? Your stationery is wrinkled and your compass box is broken; have you noticed? Are you poor?* Yes, maybe there was poverty. Not just of the money kind. I had very few answers."

You could have asked questions too, Karan, wrote the pencil in Nandini's hand.

"But I never felt sorry for myself," he continued. "Why would anybody feel sorry for what they are?"

You don't react, that is your problem, wrote the pencil.

"People kept asking me what I was thinking. They wanted to know what I was feeling."

And the answer is nothing, wrote the worn-out pencil.

"Nothing. I wasn't feeling anything, I wasn't thinking."

"What subjects were you good at?" asked Nandini to change the topic.

That brightened him up. "I was good at math. I felt I never got tested in math. It was too easy. But I wasn't good at explaining it to my friends when they would come to me for help."

"How about sports?"

"I was good at chess. It was one game I could get obsessed with. I remember a grandmaster—a former student—who once played speed chess with ten of us kids. We all sat in a row and he walked to each table making moves at lightning speed. After a few moves he started spending a lot of time at my table. I noticed because people began to gather around us. In the end, the game was a draw. He beat everyone else and I *let* him draw. You are shaking your head but I'm telling the truth. I did let him draw, and he even acknowledged this afterward. He saw me hesitate over one move and he knew immediately. He asked me why I did it and I said nothing. You see, I didn't want the attention. Everybody would have stared at me and would have asked me more questions. I hate questions."

Next our genius will say he can bend a spoon, wrote Nataraj HB.

"What about early childhood?" Nandini tried instead.

He scratched his head. "I have very few memories of early childhood. I remember places and things, but not people."

"Are you violent?" Nandini slipped in that question; something had compelled her to ask.

"Violent?" He sounded surprised. "You mean, have I gotten into fights? Aside from police training, where we had exercises in combat, no. But I was good in hand-to-hand only—I would often miss, but when I hit it was extremely hard. I could break bones, even when wearing a glove."

"Did you ever apologize?"

Here he paused. Sorry? Should he have apologized? "No," he said.

"So you hurt someone and you felt nothing?" She glanced down at his rough, hardened knuckles.

"Well, it hurt, of course," he replied.

Big, lovable baboon, wrote Nataraj HB.

"But you didn't feel anything inside?" asked Nandini, only half jokingly.

He nodded and said, "A teacher also once asked me this question. I remember that and I will never forget. She made me stay after school and write on the blackboard hundred times, *I have feelings*. It was very difficult for me. I took two hours. The teacher saw me struggle and asked me if I'd ever cried. I don't remember ever crying. But when children would die at the home I'd feel ill sometimes, like I had a fever. Once I even vomited. I think it was because of the food."

"The vomiting?" asked Nandini.

"No, the deaths," replied Karan.

"You need to learn how to feel," she told him sharply. She had broken the point of her pencil and so the interview was over.

He smiled to himself at the end. He wasn't naive, nor was

he dumb. He had analyzed his childhood and understood his hesitancy: the fact was that he had no ethnic identity, and in a country like India where your caste, creed, and religion define you, he had no way of introducing himself.

Their wedding happened at the Defence Club in Pune. Karan invited Welkinkar, who doubled as photographer. He did not invite Evam. The absence of guests from the groom's side was noticeable, as just three tall and quiet young men stood in a corner and did not mingle with the rest. Most people thought they were undercover agents, but they were acquaintances from Evam's Ward who like Karan had managed to outgrow the place.

Karan and Nandini made a striking couple. "You are a handsome bastard," she had told him. "And you are killing it," he replied, and they kissed while the guests looked on. Her mother handled the proceedings jovially but shed some tears whenever she remembered her husband. The Defence community had turned up in all their finery, the men with some gray at the temples, the women fully dyed, and they held their glasses tight and traded regiment stories, and when the deed was done they raised a hurrah for the dead father and someone clinked a glass and paid a glowing tribute and then they all retired to the lawns. The army veterans closely scrutinized this young police officer in the making and some raised their eyebrows while others just shrugged their shoulders.

"Does he drink?" asked the mother-in-law, a good Christian. "I could offer him some wine." She had tried to break the ice with her son-in-law for a week after they first met and almost gave up.

Karan had no idea how to handle a mother-in-law.

He was extra polite and the idea of loosening him up with alcohol seemed to work. One evening they had a few glasses of red, treacly wine and Karan, perhaps under the influence, walked up to her abruptly and hugged her, holding her close. He wouldn't let go. She tried to step back but he held on. She was affected; she found this strange man of good heart.

"Hello, stranger," she said. It was a phrase she would keep using.

"Hello, Mother," said Karan. Strange words he thought he would never use.

Wasting no time after their marriage, Nandini soon announced, "I want a house with sloping roofs. Go find one."

In Mumbai this was a tall order. Karan could find sloping roofs only in chawls. These two-story structures had tiled roofs and a rough disposition. They were intimate dwellings where you walked out of your room into a common corridor and right into your neighbor's clothes that were hanging to dry. Chawl people borrowed sugar, salt, and each other's thoughts. You listened to your neighbors' radio and watched their lives play out like they did yours. Occasionally you fought and then pretended to make up. Everybody finally adjusted, burying their differences beneath a veneer of civility.

They bought three adjoining single-room units. They were in poor shape with cracked floors and exposed brick walls. No matter, said she. She had plans and all these plans worked well till the first rains came and then the flooding left the place in tatters.

"I should have married a *damberwala*," she wailed. "I would have had a dry home. If his *damber* worked we would have made love. If it didn't he would have held out a bucket."

Karan held a bucket. And then an open pressure cooker, and finally an oil drum. When the rains paused, the *damberwala* came and poured black tar on their roof. And after he left they clambered up there and poured buckets of water to test the repairs. Nandini stood below with an umbrella just in case. There was no leak.

When the next rains came Karan and Nandini made love through the monsoons. They were a noisy couple and the neighbors learned to live with the rhythm of their nights.

"What's happening?" asked someone that first time. They could hear whispers, immodest laughter, and then creaking furniture.

When they discovered that Karan was with the police force the chawl members got wary. All their transgressions stood out like beacons but he seemed to notice nothing. Soon life went back to the messy Indian way. Word of Karan's exploits in the force began to percolate and a legend would eventually form. The fellow had a third eye. He was incarnate of someone called Karna, didn't you know? The children wondered where he kept his gun. One boy who claimed to have seen it said it was black as a krait and had two barrels that resembled the exhaust of a car. Karan left for work every day with a trail of curious eyes following his jeep.

Every time he used the weapon in an assignment, Karan would ceremoniously clean it afterward. In the dead of night in the corridor outside his door, he would lay a white cloth on the floor, get down on his knees, and clean it. He was empty of feeling as he examined barrel, chamber, and snout.

"Can you break a sentence?" asked Nandini, startling Karan. She shook her newspaper and said, "This murderer wants a leave of absence from his jail term. No joke. Can you even do that? Can you break a sentence?"

Karan was back at school. His English teacher, Mrs. Rosario, was waving his test in front of the entire class.

"Broken English," she admonished. She seemed distraught. Karan tried not to look at her and also ignored his classmates who were staring at him.

Mrs. Rosario started to read from his exam: "I met a man. He asked, 'Do you remember me?' I tried to say, 'I do not forget.' He shook his head. 'Do you remember me?' he asked again. He held my hands. 'Please,' he said. 'Try to remember me.' He had forgotten. *Karan," said the teacher, "what is this? You have broken your sentences."*

Nandini offered Karan some tea and biscuits.

"Parole," he said. That was the word that broke prison sentences.

She folded the newspaper twice and buttonholed the crossword. She licked a pencil and filled in *parole*. "What would the victim's family think?" she asked.

Karan felt he was a victim at school. He could never finish a story.

His teacher was still waving his sheet. "What has he forgotten?" she asked. "What has the man forgotten?"

"His name," replied Karan.

The class laughed and the teacher tried not to smile.

"Why do you break your sentences?" she asked.

Nandini's eyes had strayed from the crossword. As Karan feared, she came across the news item. "Where did you go yesterday?" she asked him.

"I was at the Aarey Milk Colony." There was no point in lying.

"Did you . . . ?" she began. "Were you responsible . . . ?"

"No," he replied sharply. "No."

"Did he have a family?" she asked.

"How should I know?"

"What was his name?"

"Panduranga. Vithaldas Panduranga."

Encounter Twenty-Eight: Panduranga

Vithaldas Panduranga was a God-fearing foot soldier of Mumbai. He floated through life with the firm belief that someone up there in the heavens would take care of him. Bhagavan, the god above, put him to the test. Vithal ended up at age thirty in the Aarey Milk Colony in Goregaon squeezing teats. His hands smelled of foamed milk and his feet of auspicious dung.

Rectangles described his life. Home was a ten-by-twelve-foot room with a five-by-four shared bath. The building was a squat structure with two floors. Each floor had a long corridor that was flanked by twenty rooms, ten on each side. All the rooms were connected so even the slightest sound carried. In the dead of night you could hear your neighbor breathe. The residents shared their most private moments but the close proximity bred no friends. They shied away from each other.

"I know what you did last night, you horny Mastram."

"Yes, I know. I heard you listening."

The building was called Suryodaya. Vithal had chosen this place because the chawl faced east. Surya Devta, the

Sun god, came in through his two-by-three window, bright and early, every morning. God was also a rectangle that traversed his floor, climbed his wall, and dried his clothes.

Vithal's dilemmas came in circles. His every action was predicated on the movement of those around him: If someone crossed the road, he would too. If a bus overtook that car, he would wait. The aggressive traffic on the Western Express Highway was a nightmare. Three lanes of speeding maniacs to negotiate, then a low fence, and on the other side even more lunatics. In the ten minutes it took him to get across he would consider his peculiar assignment of the last year and his spine would tingle.

"I am Vithaldas Panduranga."

In truth he was a two-faced lowlife, a *bahurupi*.

"Blacken my face if you will."

Yes, if he was actually found to be an informer, that would be his fate.

"I rat on the criminal class even if they are my friends."

The police force thanked him for this.

"Tiwari-sir gives me money. *You are doing* punya, he tells me. In his presence I feel closer to God."

He was closer to God than he could have imagined.

The police will protect me, so this should be a safe job, thought Vithal. *Safer than crossing this road.*

Vithal ratted on his kin for more than a year and nobody knew other than the cops. Till one day he crossed a line. Some information that he passed on was leaked to the press and it came out that an encounter Ranvir had organized had been staged. It was an embarrassment that Ranvir could not stomach. He had someone send Vithal's phone records to Govardhan Bhai, the local don described as the *baap* of all *bhaiyas* in the western suburbs of Mumbai. Govardhan Bhai ruled Goregaon, Jogeshwari, and the community of migrants from the heartland states of Bihar and Uttar Pradesh who lived there. Bhai was by turns benevolent and violent. He grew livid when the details of Vithal's calls to Tiwari surfaced.

"Brothers, kindly take care of Vithal," he instructed his informal army. "He is a *bahurupi*. I want you to show me what's under his skin."

They took good care of him. They brought him to the *goshala* and gathered around him like hungry crows. They mashed his face black and blue, strung him from a clothesline, then slit his tongue. He rocked back and forth in pain but he couldn't scream. That was just the beginning. Did they really need to ask Mastan, the butcher from Sultanpur, to skin his hide?

Bhai saw Vithal before he died. He almost felt sorry—so much pink, so much blood mixed with milk. There was an uneasy silence among the group. A few of them gagged at the sight and most looked on in disbelief at what was left of Vithaldas.

"Where is his protector now?" asked Bhai. He circled the body with a sickle in hand.

Nobody responded to this question.

"Where are his loved ones?" shouted Bhai. He searched their faces and they all glanced away.

They stood in silence. It was a learning experience for those migrant workers who lived far from the villages they came from. Each had moved here alone, and out here they had only one other—and Bhai.

Who is this Tiwari? wondered Bhai. He grabbed Panduranga's cell phone and tried Tiwari's number. He needed to deliver the news and send a message, and do so in front of his army. The number was busy but Bhai needn't have bothered—word had already spread like wildfire. The *khabari* network was intricate and incestuous and bad news moved quickly. It started with the status *Khabari in trouble* and evolved quickly into *Khabari down*. The informer network waited for Tiwari's reaction. Tiwari had to do something. He calmly considered how Vithal's phone records might have been accessed. Perhaps the telephone company had released them to the police under pressure. And there was one person with possible motive. Tiwari decided to call a fixer who thrived on dirty work.

"Where is Atmaram Bhosle?"

"Somewhere in Andheri."

"I have an assignment for him if he can reach Aarey Colony in half an hour with his bazooka."

He could. Bhosle was an alleged cop-killer in hiding. He was an expert shot with a scope rifle, and had the mentality of a seasoned sniper. He was promised immunity and a hefty sum from Tiwari's slush fund.

While this was happening, Ranvir and Karan were also en route to the site per their orders. And Ranvir was on the phone with Tiwari.

"Everybody here looks like a *bhaiya* from Uttar Pradesh," said Ranvir. "But I don't feel at home."

I was there, two steps behind him, trailing him like a heartland wife with her bowed head covered by the end of her sari. We were traipsing alongside fields of long green grass that would feed black buffaloes and yield creamy, foamy, and slightly warm white milk.

"Are you speaking to me, sir?" I asked.

He shook his head. A white earpiece buzzed loud enough for me to hear.

"Well, if not UP then from Bihar," he continued. "There are only two types of *bhaiyas* in India."

We waited as a herd of buffalo crossed our path, leaving behind a variety of black mounds. Their droppings resembled coiled snakes.

"What do you *bhaiyas* do in Mumbai? Either you drive a taxi or you milk a cow. You are an exception, sir-*ji*. You even have a title." Ranvir paused to swat at a horsefly bothering his exposed neck. We had finally reached the Aarey Milk Colony in Goregaon. "How do I know so much? *Bhaiyas* give themselves away when they speak. They are *sher-mukhs* with big mouths and small brains."

Ranvir chuckled and spotted a buffalo wading through the grass. Despite rushing here it seemed my boss was in no hurry to get to the scene. More squawks came from his earpiece. He turned around and looked at me.

"Karan? You'll never guess where he is. But why do you want to know? Am I in trouble?"

We spotted a crowd ahead of us.

"Do you have an informer in Aarey Colony? You can tell me in confidence."

Ranvir was bluffing; we both knew this offer was meaningless. As we approached the crowd, there was a quiet murmur that dissipated as we were let through. I hurried ahead of him, pushing my way to the center of the crime scene. We were too late; a red tableau unfolded before us. The distant electricity of raw violence remained suspended in the air. Some idiot offered us fresh foaming milk in a steel tumbler. Ranvir accepted it, downed his drink in a massive gulp, and wiped his mouth with his sleeve while

I held my mug and wandered among the blood and grist.

"Look around," said Ranvir softly. "Let's be on our way. There is no work for us here."

I am not a detective but something didn't add up.

"The sad bastard was an informer," he told me. "This is a show killing. It is a gruesome message that says, *Do not rat on us.* You understand?"

Was this one of Tiwari's informers on the ground? And why were all these people sticking around if they had done this?

"The gang is here because they did it," said my boss, as if reading my thoughts. "And they are telling us that they're in it together, so don't even bother. And they're telling each other that if anyone else rats he will meet the same fate."

"So why did they assign the case to us, sir? And why is the riot squad here?" I asked, gesturing to some new arrivals.

Ranvir whispered, "I believe the victim has a Maharashtrian name. And if *bhaiyas* killed him there will be riots all over the city very soon."

I broke through the circle of vengeful onlookers and meandered around the neighborhood. This place is a rural implant in a concrete city; acres of swaying, knee-high grass and herds of livestock have withstood the encroachment of builders. I soon found myself strolling into a wooded area on a gentle hill. This was a secluded spot popular with morning walkers and joggers. There was a parapet wall along the edge of the road upon which young couples whispered sweetly into one another's ears.

A family with two young children hurried past. "Look at the sunrise," said the mother, tilting her child's head up. The other boy hung back, gaping at the canoodling teenagers. I caught his eye and he stuck his tongue out at me.

It was indeed a magnificent sunrise. I wanted to shake these early-morning go-getters, tell them a man has died. But it was time to move on.

Back at the murder scene things were in flux. I stood behind Ranvir and looked for trouble among the restless. I watched my boss work the crowd. How can one describe him? He was short for his build. For the money they paid him, he delivered. His current tormentor was a colleague in the department: Tiwari.

My boss ran the Third Squad like an old-school thug. The department loved him and his results. They bestowed on him a deaf ear, a blind eye, and a license to do as he pleased. In the course of five long years he had cleaned up some of the worst vermin that Mumbai could throw his way. In the underworld his value soared. Announcements of the price on his head were noted on a blackboard near his chamber and they drew a soft response from him. He never dwelled on the fact that he was a target, and that one day this might all catch up with him.

Ranvir was soon wrapping up at the cattle ranch in Goregaon. He had assembled the rowdy crowd into a circle beside the sheds. Amid the urine and dung and buzzing flies, he asked them to drop their weapons—right now. It was a heroic scene. My fingers caressed my handgun and I had already picked my first target—the red-faced, stout bully with a bristling mustache. I could hear the birds and the bees and the sound of distant traffic in the distance.

"*Sahib*?" said Govardhan Bhai to Ranvir. "We were here to protect the poor guy. We couldn't." The rest of his gang looked on grimly and nodded.

Ranvir walked up to him and put a hand on his shoulder.

He spoke quietly: "Govardhan Bhai, I know you didn't do this. After all, he was one of your men."

"Yes, *sahib*." Bhai ceremoniously dropped his sickle to the ground and the rest followed suit. And then, seemingly out of nowhere, a shot rang out. It sounded distant but I felt the impact right next to me. The crowd hushed and I glanced around. The local constable who had accompanied us stood frozen and my boss looked horrified. Bhai was standing beside him but his eyes were bulging and his chest was bloody. Another shot rang out and this time we whirled in the direction of the sound. It had come from the hillock nearby. I knew this had to be a scope rifle.

"Down!" I screamed, summoning a voice I never knew I had. "Get down!"

"Everybody down!" my boss echoed. Most of the crowd obeyed and crouched on their knees, some right into the blood and gore. My gun was out and without much thought I shot three bullets into the hillside. Bhai looked puzzled; he reached out to us and stumbled. We grabbed his hands but couldn't hold him upright for long.

What followed was a tense half an hour in which a restive and increasingly vocal crowd of *bhaiyas* were barely in our control. We held our ground till two trucks arrived with more reinforcements. I glanced at the dismembered body of the informer one last time. It looked hopeless and forgotten. Death has no dignity sometimes.

Ranvir placed a hand on my shoulder. "The guy's name was Vithaldas Panduranga. You wanted a name, didn't you?"

I nodded. I needed to put a name to that body; it made him a person. We were given cover as we were whisked away. My boss was livid over the next hour while we drove into town, speaking on the phone with someone named

Mishra. When we reached our building Ranvir looked like he wanted to get his hands around Tiwari's neck. According to Mishra, the long-range shots had been fired by Atmaram Bhosle, a known cop-killer and gun-for-hire. It was rumored that the *khabari* gang that shared our building had asked for Govardhan's head in retaliation for Vithal. It was the second show killing that day.

In the media spin that followed, the episode was made out to be an encounter, one that Ranvir's team had staged. A well-known politician with a large migrant constituency raised a stink. My boss was forced to go on leave for a month while a departmental investigation took place. The ignominy of it all left a deep scar on Ranvir, and he was hurting even after he was cleared of any wrongdoing. The case file on Govardhan Bhai stayed in our records. We didn't want it, but it remained a recorded encounter, the only one where I had taken a shot and missed.

Nandini cannot rest. She leaves home furtively. She gets the address from Karan, heads to the Goregaon-Jogeshwari belt, and finds Panduranga's dwelling. The neighbors are of no help. She ransacks his abode for a trace of family and finds none. The building watchman comes up to her and they chat. He leads her to the *ghat* where Panduranga lies unattended. The *ghat* is a strange one and at this hour an old hag and a fat man ask for money to conduct the rituals. Nandini pays for ritual and a little extra for dignity. It is almost morning by the time the preparations are done.

"Who was this young calf?" asks the old hag. Nobody answers. "Did he have a good life?"

"*Mahamayi*," replies the fat man. "In Mumbai the good life is a seasonal thing, like mangoes."

"Light him up," the hag says. Flames leap into the sky. A good fire loves cow fat. But the flames burn out quickly and the act seems inadequate. The city lights blink as dawn breaks. Below the hill there are signs of life. They wait till the flames wilt. Another conch-shell note pierces the air, starting low and ending with a blast. The fat man wipes his conch with the folds of his *dhoti*.

"Gather his ashes," says the hag. "He wore no valuables—no necklace, no rings, and no gold fillings. What a waste, I shouldn't have waited."

The cab ride back is long and Nandini's mind roams.

It is a sultry dawn in the city, she thinks. Sleep at your own risk in this place because great men plot while you dream. The night is when webs are spun and bells are rung. So much happens. In the night the city yields to the will of those who hold remorse for ransom. This city of noir sleeps at dawn. The night's debris waits for the tide.

Karan is asleep when she returns. She wakes him up.

"Tell me you didn't do this!" she shouts.

Karan rubs his eyes and meets her gaze. He shakes his head.

"Say it loud, Karan, I need to hear this."

He tries to respond but no sound emanates. Outside the pigeons fly away in the breeze. The neighbors lie in their crumpled beds and try to drown the noise from the streets below.

"I hope somebody pays for this," she says.

After going back to sleep for a few hours, Nandini reads the full story in the newspaper and apologizes to Karan. For the next couple of days she will try to make it up to him.

Getaway

Driving lessons. She drives and you sit in the passenger seat with a seat belt around your middle, your mustache is slightly awry and one end tickles, your sides are hurting after your workout at the gym, and you are blowing air into your palms as you had been before taking a shot. You are being looked at, not for the first time, but this look is special. She keeps throwing glances but you stare straight ahead, refusing diversions. She overtakes a few cars and is honked at for doing so. You reach Chembur and she slips into the left lane and slows down. The road is broad and the surroundings have opened up somewhat. In the distance you can actually see a horizon that is slightly blurred by the smog. There is smoke in the air from tall chimneys that are the lifeblood of the Rashtriya chemical factory, a known consumer of oxygen. "Chembur blood samples are usually negative." That is what she has told you.

"What do you see?" she asks, parking on a side street. It's an easy description and, while you are no T.S. Eliot, you are succinct. You call it an industrial wasteland.

"Roll down your window," she says. You do so. "What do you see?" she asks again.

Lesson one, from this curator of cities, was learning to

see with all your senses. With the windows down you can experience what this factory is doing. It is ruining the air by smelling like sour eggs and burned toast. There must be some honest sludge somewhere too amid the deceptive green swamp that stretches up to the factory from the highway. Nandini has told you that you have a sixth sense but that one of the other five is usually missing. Which one? You've never asked.

You resume your journey. She takes the highway by the neck and drives through the wind. The sound of tires and the air rushing past the windscreen grows louder and louder, and she finally slows down below 100. She is testing you. You hold your breath, barely.

Lesson two, from this woman who holds your life together, was learning trust. Not in her driving but in her (and your) innate instinct to stay alive. She slams the brakes and swerves to the right as a bus ahead of you with no brake lights stops suddenly. Passengers disembark from it and you glimpse them in your sideview mirror as you speed past. The world is unaware an accident did not happen.

This could be called *distance learning*. A fair distance from the city you see trees and open farmland and a few people tilling it, some watering it, a scarecrow, a school with barefoot children, a train making slow progress, the wheels of a cart—and you feel the absence of punctuation and a mind on the mend. You feel rested. "Default settings," Nandini calls it. "They are very special. A normal person needs to reclaim them."

You make love in a motel. "Say fuck," she says. You cannot. "Say it out loud," she says. She does when you don't, she says it aloud with eyes closed, and it isn't an order but her body speaking. "Fuck," she exhales. In that room for the anonymous, the two of you find an hour to do your thing. For you it seems just physical but her intensity gets in the way and you begin to feel something that you have not before, and you realize that getting away from the everyday provides these moments. The ride back is silent, half drowsy but expressive.

"Are you in love?" she asks you.

You take your time to respond and then nod your head.

"How do you know?"

Love is metabolism; you know that. The heart beats a little faster from the anxiety and the anticipation that you feel around her. Love is insecurity; you can feel that because occasionally you truly let go. Love is a habit; you have a habit of staring at her when she isn't aware and when she catches you looking, she asks, "Why are you smiling?" You had no idea you were smiling. "Love makes you whole?" she ventures, holding you.

Does it?

"You want to see what love looks like?" she says, grinning into your face, turning the rearview mirror so you can see yourself. You look thrashed. There is graffiti on your cheek; a long scratch from her fingernail and two pinch marks.

When you get home she kicks off her shoes, throws down her bag and keys, pirouettes, hugs you, laughs, wheels around, whoops, spins, and stumbles, holds her head till it steadies, and then enters your den. You follow her in a happy daze and your eyes adjust to the dark and you see that she has used a fluorescent marker on your wall. She has written: *BRAHMAN, WOULD YOU KILL FOR ME?*

Encounter Thirty

When Nandini got pregnant her home became silent at night. The chawl members welcomed the silence but were unaware of the reason. Soon Nandini was visibly pregnant and then the neighbors congregated, played some games, and suggested names. The child would be a girl, they decided. She would have her parents around her little finger.

Karan stood tall when all this happened and tried to imagine what life would be like. He was anxious. All he wanted was a normal child, a healthy baby who would dribble, spit, wail, and still be cute. When there wasn't much time to go—perhaps a month—he was relieved by a lull at work. Every assignment was now a cause for argument in which Nandini played prosecution. But she was glowing, became a happy grumbler, and her appetite was hearty. Karan learned how vegetables were cut, sliced, and diced. Most mornings he made Spanish omelets and some nights he tossed a Chinese noodle.

And then, out of the blue, as it always happened, a call came and an encounter took place. That day Nandini was yearning for a Gujarati meal and he was to meet her for lunch near Bombay Hospital. He managed both, barely making it to the restaurant. They had lunch together, enjoying the meal, but that night she discovered Number Twenty-Nine because Karan had been careless—he'd left his gun and a spent cartridge on display.

She sat on a lounge chair with her legs up on a stool, the light from a lamp casting shadows on a wall. He could tell from her stare that she knew. "Why now?" she asked him, her hands on her belly, tapping, responding to the movement inside. Was there ever a good time? He had no answer.

The next morning there were complications. There had been complications before with autoimmune rejection, and she was taking medication for it, and for a while they had prayed and things had settled down. This time seemed more urgent and, as he rushed her to hospital, they looked at each other for reassurance but ended up fearful. His car did not let him down and it drove smoothly and quickly. They held hands till she went into surgery. The doctors did their best but could not save the baby.

For days after this Nandini went into a shell. She sat at home in that same dark place, looking at Karan expectantly when he walked by. He wasn't very good at discerning feelings and it was easy for him to be oblivious. But the sheer physicality of her stare raised a singular question: was he guilty? In their nuclear household this mishap was Number Thirty.

When she emerged from her depression she was still a little distant and there needed to be a confrontation to clear the air. He abhorred confrontation but now he wished he could instigate it. He said sorry many times in his head and finally out loud.

Was he sorry? Yes, now and then, and he felt sorry for her sometimes. He was also sorry for the perversion of what was good and the deification of what was considered bad, and he had stood in the land in between, where his job made him feel guilty and his boss told him that his misgivings were groundless.

Nandini listened to a TED Talk that evening. Again. She was an evangelist for such material. She found them uplifting, these stories of the valorous who could stalk a stage with a mic pinned to their collar, who used their hands cleverly to articulate stories, and before them the acolytes gathered, a junta hooked to phoenix-like narratives attempting to prove that life rewards those who believe in redemption.

She wanted an encounter specialist on a TED Talk. If only Pradeep Sharma would stand up in the dark under a spotlight, keeping his hands in view, and speak about gunning down baddies. What would this achieve? She felt people should know how cold and clinical it all was, and how desperate.

Karan himself would not be able to deliver a TED Talk, according to her. He disagreed, privately. Something told him that his halting manner, his pauses, his uncertainty, and his doubt would be less polished but more riveting. He would tell those gathered there about the unreal feeling that came his way before he pulled the trigger. He wasn't thinking, just like the manual said. There was no doubt, only unease.

"What are you, Karan? What kind of person are you?" she asked him. "You go to a barbershop and shoot someone who is seated and helpless. You go to a grieving son on his mother's death anniversary and shoot him dead as he kneels at her grave."

She was holding her scrapbook in which she recorded

his actions, culled from newspaper reports. Some days she wanted to destroy it, as if it was a part of him that could hence be excised and diminished. He could sense that.

"Do you know these people?" he asked her. "Have you read their stories?"

She wouldn't listen.

"These people have done nothing to you. They haven't threatened or even heard of you, and yet you walk up to them and kill them in cold blood."

She needed help. Maybe he did too. The next day the two of them were in the midst of a Sunday breakfast and it was obvious she hadn't slept well. She had her head in her hands and her hair obscured her face as she flipped the newspaper pages. She was still in her faded cotton nightgown that she had bought at an art exhibition and refused to let go of. He waited for her next salvo and it came.

"Who can do the things you do and then walk away to a restaurant to eat a leisurely lunch?"

He had done that, admittedly. What could he tell her in his defense? They had gone to that Gujarati restaurant because she wanted to go. Of course he was hungry, and he had done justice to the unlimited *thali*. The restaurant staff had gathered around him and beamed because they hadn't seen his kind of relish in a while. And now, after realizing he had come straight there after a bloody assignment, Number Twenty-Nine, she was playing that scene over and over in her mind. He hadn't even gone to his office to file his customary report. Assignments made him hungry. It was a physical thing that he thought needed no explanation.

"Nobody is a shell," he finally said. He was done with her staring.

"What did you say?" she replied, leaning in closer.

"Everything is questionable." This wasn't his best. He could express it better in local parlance in front of men but he couldn't tell her that he was a dumb *madarchod* or a grade-A *bhosadi* because he stuck to a job that wasn't plain and simple and whose reward was just a damn statistic.

He felt alone now. He always felt alone when people came at him saying he was heartless. But there was a way out. All he had to do was to show signs that he was affected. Perhaps by skipping a meal, getting migraines, developing an ulcer, shouting *Gaand maraa bhosadeke aulad*, suffering sleepless nights tossing and turning and mumbling incoherently, visiting temples after something untoward like a hit, or by confessing to her now and then that inside he was eroding and he was gutted—this would have made him part of the human sea.

"You told me your department is scared, and that you will become like the Class of '83. True?"

He nodded. But unlike the Class of '83 he had committed no crime, and looking around at his modest possessions anyone could tell he had made very little extra money.

"They are idiots," said Nandini. "I am scared that you will remain who you are."

"Who I am?"

"What are you, Karan?"

He had to think through this question. "I am a person."

"Are you trying to be funny?" She was shouting now.

He wasn't being funny. He meant every word. "I am a person, not a puzzle."

Later she went to the wall in his den. Below *Aham Brahmasmi*, she wrote: *A MAN WHO OBEYS.*

You walk to the nearest station and catch a train. You follow yourself, observing from a distance. You are a man with a hood holding a camera behind you, panning the compartment from your six-foot height. The most useless way of spending an hour in Mumbai is taking the train from Borivali to Churchgate. The slow train takes prisoners. You are jammed amid *paan* chewers, people with bleeding gums whose breath smells of halitosis and plaque. There are lice nesting around you, quiet lice that are hard at work making colonies in unwashed hair. You cannot prevent people feeling you up. You stopped being sensitive a long time ago. At Andheri Station there is commotion and at Dadar Terminus where people switch lines it will turn to mayhem. People will crush past in both directions. The mindless train moves on. At Bandra Station there is a Hail Mary—at least you thought you heard one. Phones ring, some vibrate against your knee, and one man's headphones shudder as the bass kicks in.

You exit at the Marine Lines Station seemingly on a whim. That was Desai telling you to go off and do the unexpected. Walk to Metro Cinema, he said, step inside, and watch a film. Doesn't matter what is running, stay with it. Leave the theater and it will be dark outside. Adjust quickly to the city's rhythm that has changed to red. Scan your surroundings. One of our men will be in some nook observing you. We wish to determine if you are being tailed. We have been told you are under watch. Be yourself, whatever that is. Desai snickered here despite himself, proving for once he was human.

Pick up your trail at Charni Road Station. As you stand on the platform, facing the Taraporewala Aquarium outside, do not look behind you. If someone comes up to you he will do so quietly. Ignore the buzz in your ear, the hair that stands on the nape of your neck, and your instinct to reach for your metal, because it will be too late. Someone does come up but nothing happens. A train comes and goes. Then another one. You think hard and now you want to do something slowly. You want to turn around and see who is beside you. The rest will be up to him. "Do what you feel you need to," you say.

It happens just the way Desai said it would. You control your unruly mind that is screaming at your silent hands. Your eyes blur with effort as you wheel around. You are hurting but you remain steady as everything leaks out of the picture frame, and only one face comes into focus: Evam Bhaskar. He belongs to your childhood. You belong to a place he created.

"Where have you been hiding?" he asks you.

You spend a couple of hours with him, unburdening, and nothing gets resolved. "There are no answers to the question, *Why me?*" he says.

So you ask him differently: "Do things happen for a reason?"

Book II

Department Records: Counterintelligence

Ranvir Pratap returned from his enforced leave of absence and it was obvious he hadn't forgotten or forgiven. It was hard enough handling him when he was his normal self. Right now he was exerting a threatening influence on his boss, Parthasarathy. Partha, forced out of his customary diffidence, had asked to meet Mishra.

"The problem with you, Parthasarathy, is that you were busy covering your ass instead of keeping your eyes and ears open," said Mishra. "What do you know of what went on between Ranvir and Evam?"

"Very little, sir," said Partha.

Mishra, the chief of counterintelligence, was an imposing and burly man who ate nails for breakfast. He had a sharp tongue—rare was the sentence that did not contain abuse—and he was proficient in many languages when it came to unparliamentary words. Mishra sat back and took a deep breath. There was no point in venting about this man who was a misfit in his current post and a passenger at best.

"Can I see the classified files?" asked Partha. "I believe they have all the details."

"They do because I handled it, Mr. Parthasarathy. They will come to you like a prepared meal. You think this will help you have a balanced view?"

"Yes sir," replied Partha. What he did not say was that he knew Mishra favored Ranvir and hated Tiwari.

"Fine. But you will have to read it here and make no copies. Is that understood? And one more thing: officially these files do not exist."

Parthasarathy was taken to an airless, musty room. There were three monitors and a pair of headphones on a table, with a lone lamp that shined its circular light upon various transcripts and two documents. It seemed counterintelligence had bugged Ranvir's office, Evam's facility, and their phones. He sat in the relative darkness and listened to the scratchy audio files. He was enthralled. This was living history. What unfolded was a complete picture on the origins of the Third Squad. Once the tapes ran out he had trouble breathing.

"Understand this," said Ranvir Pratap. "This is an informal meeting, you are merely my sounding board, I still question your credentials in the field of psycho-whatever-you-call-it, and whatever we discuss will stay within this room at the risk of my having to put you away permanently."

Evam Bhaskar trusted himself to nod. He felt privileged that his advice was being sought in the first place. Perhaps handling Ranvir's son the way he did gave Ranvir some confidence in his abilities. They moved toward Evam's small office. Ranvir entered and stood near the door for a moment, absorbing the contents of the room. He headed to the cushioned seat which had been left for him. Evam was eyeing him closely as well. Ranvir was not the tall, elegant officer people imagined him to be. As a physical specimen he belied his image. His defining features were his eyes and his fingers. Neither kept still unless they were wrapped around an object of attention. The man scared his superiors, thought Evam. He probably hated formal reporting, begrudged public shows of respect, and his standard expression would surely qualify for rank insubordination.

Most of all, Ranvir was an enigma (like Krishna in the epics, someone said), and Evam liked enigmas. Ranvir was a strict vegetarian, not that it really mattered. It seems he went to the Vaishno Devi temple every year and made pilgrimages at night to the holy shrine. This was fine as well; you can choose your gods even if you send people up to meet them.

Ranvir patiently recounted the history of the now infamous Class of '83. The members of this group were the most successful encounter specialists that the city had seen. He explained what had happened later with each of them. "This is what I have been asked to steer clear of," he said, "and I don't know how."

He then handed Evam a draft job description for the Third Squad. Evam read through the materials.

CRITERIA FOR SELECTION FOR THE THIRD SQUAD PREPARED BY RANVIR PRATAP

1. Ability to focus is crucial. While this is difficult to test, its absence can be spotted. Look for hyperfocus, and not for those who are hyperactive.

2. Ability to work at night. We cannot have people who sleep on the job, especially during long, boring watch duty or stalking assignments at night.

3. Loners work better than others. Lack of social skills and etiquette is not a deal-breaker here.

4. The nature of the job is such that emotional or friendly individuals will not last. There will be assignments with casualties. Team members will go down and this has to be overcome. I am not suggesting heartless, ruthless thugs, but I will still look at them.

5. Team members should be honest. We cannot have the team exposed because of the lack of honesty of any member. Failures will happen in this line of work. Each member of the team has to own up and tell it as it is.

6. Confidentiality is at a premium. The less the candidate babbles the better. Small talk in our case is overrated.

7. Lack of attention to detail can derail everything. If possible we should look for perfectionists, people obsessed with quality in execution.

8. Operatives should follow rules and instructions without exception. We do not need people who question everything, however intelligent they may be; even if their way is sound, the one that everyone follows is the best. It is a hierarchical setup and orders need to be executed instantly, without fail.

"The idea of this job description," explained Ranvir, "is to help narrow down a bunch of hopefuls into a smaller group who can then be short-listed after an interview. The chosen few can then be put on an intensive training regimen to further narrow the field."

This document seemed to be a general description, but

the behavioral approach it took was interesting. It was the kind of approach that Evam would have been proud of initiating. There was more that Ranvir had written.

DOES A MEMBER HAVE TO BE

1. AN ATHLETE? Historically, we've identified a group of physically fit men and women as potential recruits. But how does it actually help to have a strong athlete as a member? Do we still chase people down by running after them like in the movies? Do they have to climb mountains, cross rivers, or engage in hand-to-hand combat? Increasingly, we have to do focused legwork. We have to be dogged in pursuit, boring in execution, and intelligent in response. If things come down to hand-to-hand combat, we have failed.

2. A GUNSLINGER? Shootouts seem to be the norm in our perception of an encounter. It would seem that every operation has to end in a physical altercation including possibly an exchange of fire. The fastest with the gun and the one with the better eye wins. That is history. Encounters should be one-sided. Our pursuit has to be anonymous, our information good, and our closure ruthless. It doesn't have to be physical. If a bullet needs to be fired, we should do so through a scope which affords good aim, produces no return fire, and preferably has a stationary target.

3. AN EINSTEIN? We do need creative members on the team but they are not the ones we want in the field. In the field we need people who can execute. If we have to think too much on our feet, change the game plan as things emerge, and act upon instinct at that moment, then we are doomed to fail in the long run. Think of making a movie without a script, where the actor improvises the lines, the accidents on the set determine the plot, and the camera decides the focus. You will get a flop.

4. A WOMANIZER? Sorry, I couldn't resist this one. I was merely going by the popular perception of this department consisting of 007s—suave, cool, handsome, indestructible, and irresistible to women. Times have changed. History, thy name is Bond.

Evam liked this approach. It was a fresh, different, and maverick methodology. This team would comprise a unique vintage, very different from the Class of '83. What excited him was the fact that Providence had smiled. He was sure that in the list of his life's coincidences this was up there. How often does it happen that you have an agenda of finding jobs for four young men and someone walks into your world and describes them to a T?

"Ranvir, sir, I have explained this to you before but hear me out again. Imagine people who are different from us but the difference is slight. They are born that way and they are a parallel group of humans who coexist. They have some known limitations which curiously help in your context. And they have some peculiar qualities which you could stand to benefit from. There is only one problem."

"And that is?"

"They come from a spectrum disorder that includes your son." Ranvir looked shocked and Evam clarified hastily: "It is a wide spectrum and your son was at one extreme. The A-word frightens people, I know." Evam paused here for a moment. "What you need, Mr. Ranvir Pratap, are people we call Aspies. They fit your description. But it would be a bold man who would make that call."

"Aspies? I recall reading about them."

Evam explained as best he could, taking care not to make too strong a case. "Autism is called a spectrum disorder because each person is affected differently. On one end of this spectrum is a mild form that is called Asperger's syndrome, so mild that sometimes we meet such people without knowing it. While there is a greater awareness of this today, there are many in our country who are still unaware that they are Aspies."

"Refresh my memory—what causes all of this?"

"It's genetic. It's not because of upbringing or social circumstance; it's not anyone's fault."

"So it's an abnormality?"

Evam looked like he was searching for words, something that modern doctors and analysts do a lot these days. They are more careful with words than writers. "I would describe it as being outside of the norm; we who are the norm are called 'typicals.'"

"And unlike my child, these people survive, grow up, and live by themselves? They have a normal lifespan?"

"Yes. Contrary to popular perceptions and beliefs, their lifespan is typical and they are independent. With some exceptions, of course."

Ranvir scratched his head, for once. Nothing was resolved at this meeting but at least a seed was sown. And as long as Ranvir Pratap had a puzzle on his plate he couldn't rest.

A few weeks passed before Evam received a call asking for another meeting.

"Go through it again," said Ranvir once they were seated. "Just take me through this, slowly."

Evam tried to explain. He guessed that Ranvir would have done his homework. "Imagine people who are diagnosed late, perhaps even as adults, because what they have is not considered an illness. It has no cure or treatment and is a lifelong condition. You could be living with such a person, initially not knowing and then at some point feeling that something is 'wrong' without being able to put your finger on it. Often parents take such children or young adults to doctors. They suspect something is either wrong or something is missing. It is a small niggling matter that won't go away. It is not easy for them to describe what makes them uneasy."

"And they come to you after all the other tests have proven fruitless?"

Evam nodded, then flipped through four case files. He pulled one out and showed the cover to Ranvir. "Munna. That's his name. His mother thought he had eye trouble because he kept bumping into things, often toppling them over, and rather than appear guilty he seemed if anything a little surprised. *What the hell?* he would blurt, every time. He looked awkward somehow. His mother felt he was making faces at her even if he did not move a muscle. I brought him to a dart board in my office, made him stand eight feet away and throw darts. He was clumsy and the score was awful but the result wasn't important. The fact is, he would lose his balance throwing that tiny object—he actually fell once."

He showed Ranvir a photograph of the young lad. He had a man's face and a child's expression. Munna was looking away from the camera even while facing it. Evam took the next file and wiped some dust off it. "Tapas, a boy from Orissa. Thought to have some impediment because he didn't participate in much conversation, was extremely shy, took a lot of time to reply when spoken to, and when he did, he would drift off into unconnected subjects. On a hunch I asked him if he could recite poetry and he did so for the next five minutes, without a break. He reeled off three pages of Shakespeare, verbatim, without stopping. He was perfect to the letter, but I had a bad feeling. I noticed his diction was unvaried and there was no feeling. Halfway through, his parents looked toward me with an expression that said, *We told you so.*"

He lingered on the third file, turning it over and taking his time before opening it. "Kumaran," he finally said. "A bright child who is very good at math. He would go for treks in the city and return hours later, having forgotten why he left in the first place. He could not tie his shoelaces. They suspected dyslexia but it was never diagnosed. Kumaran is an obsessive sort and has unreal knowledge of unimportant and unconnected things. He is quite happy to be by himself in his world. I asked Kumaran to take a shirt off my rack and fold it. I watched him do it. He would measure every angle of every fold, computing, calculating, and when he was done he had a slight smile as if he had solved a puzzle in his head, an efficient puzzle that was resolved with a precise fold." The photograph showed the kid wearing a hood, under which his recessed eyes gave him a mysterious presence.

Evam took a long pause, the fourth file resting unopened between them, then said, "The fourth fellow remains a puzzle. I took him to the dart board. He stood, all six feet of him, erect, perfectly proportioned, fair, good-looking like an actor, and he did badly. He was a little surprised, I think, to be scoring low. And almost in disgust he turned away from the board as he flung his last dart. Bingo. It was a bull's-eye. I asked him to do that again, five times. He looked away from the dart board and threw. Five hits in a row, each was dead center; it was unreal. This was a rare gift. It wasn't chance."

"What's his name?" asked Ranvir.

"Karan," said Evam. "An orphan," he added, "like in the epics."

It was time for Ranvir to voice his doubts. "Nobody will question me if I recruit left-handers," he said. "Why are some people left-handed? I've researched it but I could never find an answer. Some people will question me if I knowingly recruit gays. For some reason the armed forces and the police approach it differently than, say, the fashion industry. But a gay person can still be a good cop, and I think we can all agree on that. Why are some people gay? I'm not sure we have that answer, do we?"

Evam had suspected that Ranvir would come at him from left field.

"Now, about these Aspies. Is Asperger's as simple as being left-handed? You said it's a spectrum, so is it possible that at the low end that's all there is, just a few traits related to communication, language, and emotive response?"

Evam interjected here: "Why these things occur may not be as important as whether these people can be effective in their job. And if their traits suit your needs, why not use them to your advantage?"

"Why not indeed?" replied Ranvir. "If we can wire robots to do a job, then why not use those who are differently wired?"

Evam winced at the comparison with robots, but attributed it to the free-flowing discussion.

"Are these people stable, these Aspies?" Ranvir continued. He was pacing around the office now, examining the shelves.

"You mean the condition? That's a great question. Yes, they do not 'improve,' nor do they 'deteriorate' with any of the factors. But the statistics are inadequate too."

Ranvir returned to his chair and sighed before Evam made one last heartfelt pitch.

"These are four self-aware kids who are comfortable with who they are. Today you can see them and hear them without preconceived notions and prejudice, and even speak to them online in a world without walls, where they have created a sophisticated underground culture of their own. They are precious to me, but few organizations find them employable."

It was an education and it was also the kind of development that excited Partha. Yet even before he could decide on a course of action that would calm Ranvir down, he found Tiwari at his doorstep. "Panduranga was compromised," he said. Tiwari carried evidence that pointed to Ranvir and his team blithely assuming that there was no obvious link between Atmaram Bhosle and him, but counterintelligence had alerted Partha. To Partha, it was obvious that the animosity between Ranvir Pratap and Tiwari was getting ugly and growing untenable. He had to intervene. He again called the chief of counterintelligence, who unsurprisingly began with a curse.

"The problem with you *myrandi* rice-eaters is that you come running to me holding your backsides the moment there's trouble. Of course I won't meet you."

Partha explained the situation patiently: "Sir, I hope you know that I'm just filling in temporarily. I've extended my contract just to calm things down between these two."

"I'm not so sure they should have given you an extension," replied Mishra. "You are an academic *banchod*, Parthasarathy; we all know that. You studied dirty toilet paper to unearth clues about civilization. What do you call it again?"

"Evolutionary psychology," Partha replied.

Eventually Mishra relented and they mutually agreed to plant someone in each team's office as an impartial observer. There was already one such person on Tiwari's team, an intelligent, multilingual Trojan deputized by Mishra himself. But Mishra refused to spare anyone else. "Let Tiwari hire one of his own and send him to Ranvir's office. I just hope he manages to stay alive."

Tiwari summoned his tag team of Kamte and Pandey to call for one of his new recruits, Vishwa.

"Sir?" queried a surprised Kamte. "Vishwa? The guy is too green behind his ears. He'll wet his pants at the first sign of trouble."

Tiwari was in no mood for advice.

Vishwa was a short man who wore a red *tilak* on his forehead. His hair was well oiled and perfectly parted. One side of his mouth was perpetually occupied by *gutka*, a potent combination of tobacco and *catechu*. That was the source of his bravado. The fellow was shape-shifting; in the office he looked like a peon, in a railway station he could resemble a coolie. Tiwari called him a universal socket, one who would fit in anywhere.

His briefing was brief.

"Remember: you do not know me, you never came here, and nobody will come to your rescue."

Vishwa gulped, swallowed his *gutka*, choking at its bitterness. He hit the back of his head with his palm to stop coughing.

"Tomorrow you report to the front," Tiwari instructed. "There are four wolves out there and one lion. Please keep a close eye on the wolf called Karan, especially after office hours."

"What should I do if he sees me following him, sir-*ji*?" asked Vishwa.

"Say your prayers."

More *gutka* went into his mouth before he found his voice again. "Sir-*ji*, is this an important job?"

"*Jaanbaaz*," replied Tiwari with a smile. "You could bet your life on it."

The next day Vishwa reported to Crime Branch under the guise of a *chai-wallah*. He was assigned to the pantry. He did three rounds on the first day and broke two tumblers. He was so on edge that the first time he saw Ranvir he spilled tea all over the aluminum tray he was carrying. Goose bumps were sprouting along his arms. Gods were queuing up in his head and he named them all under his breath. This *kuphiya* was going to miss the honor roll.

The first week was uneventful. Yet his digestion was shot, his face had lost color, and he grew suddenly fearful of shadows. He arrived at Tiwari's *adda* on the weekend looking like a ghost.

"Anything to report?" barked Tiwari.

"One suicide case, sir-*ji*, nothing else."

"Is something the matter with you? Why are you shaking—have you given up *gutka* or something?"

Vishwa's struggled to get any words out.

"Somebody bring him some water," ordered Tiwari. Pandey arrived with a full glass from the cooler and Vishwa drained it.

"So what exactly were you doing for a full week out there?" asked Tiwari.

"Sir, I drove the jeep. Karan-sir does not like driving. He found out that I could drive and from the second day I became the driver."

"Good. So you went around with them?"

"Yes sir. Ranvir-sir and Karan-sir both go together, and I drive."

"What did they discuss, *bhosadeke*? Do I have to keep prompting you?"

"Sir-*ji*, they kept complaining that there were no assignments. They said they would soon have to look for employment in a laundry or a car wash."

Tiwari was delighted. "Excellent. That's good news. What else?"

"They were asked to go check out a suicide case. Mr. Ranvir said it was an insult that he had to cover such silly cases."

Tiwari laughed and examined the lines on his hands as if what was written there was finally coming true. "Anything else?"

"That's it, sir," mumbled Vishwa. He wiped his brow with a cloth that he had wrapped around his hand. It had red stains.

Tiwari sat back and glared at him. "Then go back tomorrow."

Vishwa wanted to die, he wanted to curl up in a corner and bid the world goodbye. "Sir-*ji*," he said, stuttering, "I do not w-want to go back."

"Why?"

"I think they know who I am. Mr. Ranvir keeps looking at me."

"*Gandu*, I am looking at you too!" shouted Tiwari. "You are supposed to be a *bahurupi*."

"I think we are wasting our breath," Pandey whispered into Tiwari's ear.

"Look at this hopeless fellow. What's bothering you?" Tiwari pressed.

"Sir-*ji*, they asked me if I was from Bihar. I said yes. Then Karan-sir took me to the pantry. He held my hand tightly and brought me there. The place is dirty and the walls are full of soot from the stove. Karan-sir asked me, *Do you know what our team is called?* I shook my head. He held my head with one hand and pointed it toward the wall above the stove. With the other hand he scraped the soot." Vishwa let out a sob before continuing. "Some lettering appeared on the wall in capitals. Somebody had carved into the wall with a knife. Two words that every Bihari dreads. Sir, he then took a penknife, asked me to close my eyes, and he carved it on my hand." He held out his hand and looked away.

Pandey unwrapped the cloth that covered the bloody hand. He turned Vishwa's palm upward and stretched it under Tiwari's nose. On it, etched in red, were the words *RANVIR SENA*.

Kamte let out a low whistle. The Ranvir Sena was one of the most feared militant outfits in Bihar, famed for ruthless executions. It was banned by the Indian government.

Tiwari cocked his head and clucked his tongue. "I get the message. They know who you are and where you come from."

"You did what? You carved the guy's hand with a knife?"

Karan examined the signs that had given him away. On his shirtsleeve was the blood of a man, and outside the window warm winds had been blowing hard all morning. It was a dry, bad wind. The koels in the trees called out for rain and the wind chimes on balconies were rattling and whistling off-key. He knew this was the season when arguments quickly grew hot, a time when people fought for no reason. He should have kept his mouth shut.

"Yes," he said.

She bit her tongue. "What did you carve? Your name? I believe your name serves as enough of a warning these days."

"Actually, our team has been given a name by Mr. Tiwari, one that belonged to a murderous gang in Bihar. He calls us the Ranvir Sena."

"How nice," she replied. "And do you have a coat of arms? Perhaps a motto too? Tell me, what is your motto, Karan?" she said incredulously.

"For by wise counsel thou shalt make thy war." Karan recited it without hesitation or irony.

They fought that day; they fought like hell. And that night Karan roamed the chawl and the street outside trying to tire himself to sleep.

Encounter Thirty-One

Nobody knew where Kumaran resided. He came and went like a commuter with a day pass. You acknowledged his presence only when something went wrong in the Special Branch building. Since the building was old it required constant repair. Kumaran was the handyman and people often went to him for whatever needed fixing.

The fixer learned from dismantling. Kumaran's fundamental life principle was "dismantle." Anything that came his way was broken down to its most essential level. His office desk had four drawers which were full of mechanical and electronic parts. Occasionally some of them would come to life and emit beeps. He would raise an eyebrow, rummage through the drawers, locate the objects, and dismantle them further till they finally died.

Kumaran had a satchel bag that held his possessions. It had become part of his anatomy. In the course of basic training and the years thereafter the team tried to wean him away from it. They couldn't. The camouflage on the canvas fabric had gradually faded. Kumaran would hang it over his right shoulder, draping the strap across his chest so the bag rode his left hip.

Naturally, Ranvir was compelled to know what was

inside. At one briefing session he suddenly decided to conduct a public inventory. Kumaran stood stone-faced as Rana sorted through the bag and recited its contents loudly.

"One Ponds talcum powder that smells of flowers," he said, turning up his nose. "One green banana." He held up the slightly crushed fruit. "One cell phone that has been dismantled." He couldn't pull out all the pieces. "What is this?"

Kumaran peered inside. "A radio-controlled detonator," he replied. "One that I defused."

The inventory continued: "A long single pencil shaving in a plastic box." It almost looked artistic, if out of place. "One notepad." Ranvir flipped through the pages. "Drawings of arches, doorways, and windowsills. Where from?"

"VT Station," replied Kumaran.

The rest was spread out on a table. There was a black-and-white photograph of Ramana Maharshi, a book by Richard Feynman, a Polaroid self-portrait with blurry edges, and a slip of paper that said, *Mum's the word*.

The last item puzzled Ranvir the most. Yet despite this public revelation of his most personal possessions, Kumaran remained an enigma. He wasn't the usual vending machine of death that people expected. (Neither was the rest of the squad.) He certainly didn't look the part; he was lanky rather than lithe, had poor motor function, and, to add to that, he was clumsy with a weapon. His aim was poor and his hunting skills were not predatory. But Ranvir still felt he had potential.

We slinked among some parked vehicles on the approach to the chawl. The targets were holed up above us in one of the tenements. Behind us was a concrete wall, a dead end—a term we did not care for. Kumaran looked at it, as if for the first time realizing we were trapped in there. He should have thought this through better.

"Sir, should we not spread out?" I whispered.

Ranvir said nothing.

"Sir, we're bunched up like goats at an abattoir." This was Munna trying to be funny.

Ranvir ignored him. We were unhappy that Kumaran was in charge because we didn't think he was ready to lead an operation. "Are you sure they are there?"

"Yes." Munna's Adam's apple bobbed as he spoke. "Nobody has stopped us thus far. We cleaned up the whole building and nobody fired, nobody shouted."

Ranvir remained confident. "You have studied the methods of these guys so you should have anticipated this outcome. This is a gentle gang, almost a helpful one."

Munna, Tapas, and I lurked in the shadows, on our toes, each with a lethal weapon. Our adrenaline was pumping and we wanted to storm that tenement and remove the targets. We were held back by Ranvir's stern gaze. What's the point of training so much if someone who can't handle a weapon has his way in the end?

It had taken us six months to reach this end game, half a year of painstaking detective work that no one likes to hear or read about. For some reason we were losing a number of old folks in a particular locality to seemingly random accidents. Old men and women were falling off staircases, tripping over balconies, and suffering electric shocks from household appliances. Five such incidents happened in the locality in a single week and the Special Branch was called in to investigate. Use your brains for a change, we were told.

Other crime branches were busy with more obvious cases.

We started by examining the circumstances in meticulous detail. We questioned all the family members, thought up all possible motives, and harassed the neighbors with enough questions that by the first weekend we had ruffled just enough feathers to stir suspicion in that quiet corner. Suspicion breeds enmity, which in turn breeds informers. Yet there was no breakthrough. The last call we made was to the nearby hospital to check their records. There were no revelations there, and no postmortems had been carried out either.

Ranvir called us in for a meeting.

"I would like to study those who are still alive," he said. He had to explain that further.

"Study how these old folks live, what they eat, what they drink, what they keep, and what they throw away."

He saw us looking puzzled. "Just do it," he ordered.

We marshaled some youngsters from a college to use as "researchers." We chose five random elderly folk who lived alone. After a few visits that often became extended hand-holding sessions, we developed an inventory of all objects in their houses with descriptions—condition and look and feel. We then compared the lists and drew up a common inventory of items. *Godrej almirahs*, radios, medicine cabinets, razor blades, discolored mirrors, and old magazines. All of them had stashes of cash, and bundles of notes were stowed in unlikely places. Their jewelry was often kept in packets within jars in the kitchen below the rice and *daal*.

Three days later I dropped by the station at night to do some catch-up on other cases. I found Ranvir hunched over his desk, poring over our reports.

"What have we found, Karan—isn't this a treasure trove?"

"Looks to me like trivia, sir."

"It's amazing the kind of stuff one learns. What do you think was the most versatile household utility device of the earlier generation?"

I listed a few that I had seen: "A walking stick . . . or reading glasses and pieces of string?"

Ranvir shook his head. "It's the pin. Every house is full of them, in many shapes and sizes. Pins for cleaning ears, pins in place of fallen buttons, pins to dig into your teeth, and pins to file papers. Have you realized what we have replaced them with?"

"Sir?"

"The earbud, dental floss, and, of course, the new-found Velcro." Ranvir went back to studying the list. "I think we are ready."

"Ready to file the cases, sir?"

"No, we are done with the living. Now we're ready to study the dead."

We rustled up the case officers from each of the five most recent accidents and ran these lists past them. Remember what you saw when you went in and tell us what's missing, we said. They went through the lists and ticked most of the items.

"It's basically the same. Most of these items were there."

"Any money?"

"Money? You mean cash? No, there was no money around."

"No bundles anywhere?"

"No."

"Loose notes, change?"

"None."

"Are you sure? There must have been some loose change."

"No sir, there was none."

"I see. What about the *almirahs*? Were they rummaged through, untidy?"

"No, they were clean enough. I guess old people have good habits."

"You're telling me that in all these instances you only encountered orderly *almirahs*, and that no cash was lying around in any of these apartments?"

Ranvir let out a long sigh, one that celebrated discovery and promised retribution. "We have a case, gentlemen," he announced. "Five, in fact—of murder, followed by petty robbery."

Kumaran had now blocked all the exits, encircling the chawl completely. But he then sat back and refused to advance. The rest of us were getting bored and restless.

"We are not going in, not now," he said.

"Then when, when it's dark?" asked Munna.

"No, let's just wait this one out."

"We've come here to wait? Why are we even here? You could have called us later," Tapas piped up.

I was not interested in this debate. It seemed to me that the best we could do was to throw some smoke bombs and shoot our way in.

"Trust me," said Kumaran. And so the matter ended there.

~

We had established the crime and the motive. The mode

of killing was painstakingly simple: a nudge or a poke, or a simple but effective domestic accident. We didn't know where to begin looking for the perpetrator. Ranvir went around humming tunelessly and asking the same question again and again: "Who let them in, who let them out?'"

It was getting on our nerves.

Phase two of our research began: we sat as temporary watchmen in an apartment block in a typical suburb, watching the goings-on for three whole days.

"Getting the vibrations yet?" asked Ranvir.

I was beginning to sympathize with watchmen and their drudgery. Back at the office Ranvir emerged from a hibernation of deep thought and asked for the dates of the incidents. It turned out that all took place in the first week of the month. "Payback time," said Ranvir, seeing the light. We went after the bill collectors.

We found them quickly. There were three of them, in their late teens, bad eggs given to minor offenses. One was with the gas company, one was with the electricity board, and the third was a newspaper delivery boy. They had teamed up some six months ago—we were looking at a nascent gang, one that might have gone on to bigger things had we not caught up with them.

Ranvir Pratap invited Parthasarathy for a chai and *bun maska*. They met in an Irani café over breakfast. Parthasarathy was convinced by the findings. He also agreed with Ranvir when he said that there wasn't sufficient evidence to convict these killers through the courts. It was well known in police circles that the burden of proof was a mantle that Ranvir flung with impunity, and he took no chances unless a quick verdict was certain. Parthasarathy did not fight the decision but he made it clear that this should not be a typical encounter, the kind that involved Karan. There should be no shooting.

There were a couple of new members on the team who had arrived quietly. We watched them suspiciously because they did not fit in. One was a thickset civilian who was fiddling with the electrical panels of the apartment where the gang was holed up. The other was a middle-aged man who was poring over some blueprints. I could glimpse outlines of gas cylinders and pressure pumps.

The chawl was still deserted and its inmates were milling around outside, a murmur gradually rising. We did not have too much time. What was really going on? Kumaran remained stoic and continued fiddling with some kind of detonator. I was growing curious watching him. Ranvir seemed satisfied with the progress.

"Why don't we smoke them out, sir? We could get them out alive."

"Cannot," said Kumaran.

"Cannot or will not?" asked Munna.

Kumaran paused. "The last incident they engineered involved an old woman," he said.

"So?"

"She lived on the sixth floor of an apartment block."

"Okay. So what happened?"

"She was blind. They walked her by the hand to the elevator shaft. They had managed to open the sliding doors even though the elevator was on the ground floor below. She fell down into the blackness."

Ranvir watched us closely. "Feel anything?" he asked. "Sympathy, anger, the urge to do something?"

I felt nothing and looked away. The gun in my holster grew heavy but it remained in place. These boys were multiple murderers and perhaps deserved whatever came their way. But I needed orders to get going.

"At ease, my little sharpshooter," said Ranvir. "This one is not for you. There's a better way. We have to do to them what they have done to these old folk. And we have to ensure the public doesn't find out." He gave Kumaran a quiet nod.

Kumaran asked us to fall out and scatter. He didn't want us in the vicinity when he executed his plan.

We were astonished but we followed his orders. Tapas, Munna, and I packed our equipment, turned our backs on the chawl, and started to walk away. At that very moment there was a massive explosion. The two civilians in Kumaran's team had engineered something—they had used gas cylinders to pump inflammable gas into the chawl, then shorted the power supply. Glass shattered and blew out from the apartment, followed by flames and a blast of black smoke billowing out from the windows. The three of us turned around and gaped. Our guns were instinctively in our hands.

The ensuing scene was unforgettable. Kumaran was crouched behind a car watching the results of his effort. He rose to his feet slowly, then turned to face us. His expression was one of deep satisfaction and vindication. He smiled and his teeth gleamed. I had never seen him smile before; I would never see it again. The first hail of bullets started from left to right. They zinged past us, hit the wall behind, and zipped past again. The line of fire caught Kumaran and drew spurts from below his knees. He buckled, looking surprised. The second hail came from the opposite direction at the same height. By now Kumaran was down on his knees and flailing. He caught that hail with open arms and he never came to again. The spurt of firing died. It was the death rattle of a cornered gang member who was mindlessly letting loose with his weapon. Kumaran lay grotesquely in a crumpled heap. The three of us stood with the best weapons that the force had, cocked and ready, but feeling quite useless. We looked up at the destroyed apartment and then in unison toward our boss. Some part of Ranvir Pratap died that night. We could see it on his face, just a fleeting glimpse.

The incident made the papers the next day. A chawl had suffered an electrical surge. A fire started and some gas cylinders had exploded. Three youngsters were caught in the blaze and were charred to death. A police team was in the vicinity but could not help them in time.

"A domestic accident," said Ranvir to the press, as he handed out a list of domestic do's and don'ts. "We have been experiencing many of them in the past few months, as you must have noticed. We should all be careful."

Tiwari read the official report and smirked. There was no mention of any gunfire. Kumaran's fate was recorded as an accident; he was known to be clumsy with a weapon.

Inside or Out?

Nandini was away and I had roamed the streets trying to distance myself from thoughts of Kumaran and the time we spent together. Sometimes the crowded streets of Mumbai can get your mind full of things you do not want to remember. Linking Road, Bandra, is full of honking cars, its sidewalks are crowded with hawkers and teenage shoppers, mostly girls wearing three-quarter leggings and large hoop earrings. Their feet peek out of brightly colored sandals with toenails that are aflame. I catch myself staring sometimes. I walk again. A fellow lies on the sidewalk, legs spread wide, his head lolling to one side; his clothing is threadbare and his hair needs a wash. I look for needle marks as I step over him. I find plenty of them in a tattoo parlor with a line out the door. I join the queue of youngsters just to see what happens, then give my place away to a boy with torn jeans and studs. He shrugs.

I keep moving till it darkens. The streetlights come on and the sodium vapor takes hold. The streets are yellow when I leave. I walk briskly to my door, happy the day has gone by. The chawl is eerily quiet; there is no footwear in front of our door. I enter and reach for the switch; the phosphorescent tube flickers on. There is a Post-it on the fridge that says, *Eat*, one on the sink that says, *Wash*, and another on the liquor cabinet that says, *No*. I fix a drink and down it in one gulp. I fix another in a hurry and head for my den.

And then I pause. It hits me. The question comes like it has before and I cannot move . . . Am I inside or out? I place the drink on the floor and feel the door. My hand finds the doorknob. I turn it slowly, enter cautiously, and shut it behind me. It is pitch dark. My ears buzz. I reach inside my pocket and fish out my lighter. I place my left hand against my face and flick the cap open. A flame leaps and gray smoke spirals.

I turn slowly to face the table and lower my hand. I blink. It's true, I am there as I had feared, seated at the table. I have been there all day. I walk slowly and drag some dust to this man who lacks courage, who sits alone in the dark the day after, frozen.

The man raises his eyes, slowly removing his gaze from the blank sheet of paper in front of him. Helpless are his eyes and the hand that writes. He places a palm on my shoulder as he rises and he walks into me.

The bell rings and we freeze. We hear: keys on the key ring, shoes sliding across the floor, Post-its getting torn up. Breathing.

"Karan?"

One of us should speak.

"Karan, are you going to sit there all day?"

Things have changed. Nandini has changed. And I have not. I get asked the same questions all the time—why doesn't she come in more often? I peek out and she is seated on the floor facing away from me. She must be biting her lip, since I expect she would have said something really harsh by now.

"I liked Kumaran," she says finally. "And I'm worried you will be next."

I leave my den and sit beside her. She doesn't speak for a while and she doesn't look toward me either but she places her hand in mine. We watch TV till our eyes glaze.

"Fix me a drink, will you?"

She drinks it quickly and proffers the empty glass for a refill.

"Happy hour?" I fix her another.

"I'll be a lush in my old age."

I try to imagine what I'll be.

"Will you wear your uniform? Please?"

There is no getting away. I drag myself to my wardrobe where everything has its place. I kit myself in my very best. It isn't mechanical, not in the least. Crisp khakis with a greenish tinge, shiny belt, cap, medals, epaulets, shoes. She gives me a hug from behind, buries her nose in my uniform. She loves the feel, the smell, and the "look."

"Stand down, officer." I step back and she keeps looking at me.

"You thought it wouldn't fit?" I ask her.

"No," she says. She looks into her glass, at the amber fluid, before it goes down her throat. "It fits, of course it fits. God knows it belongs."

Evam Bhaskar

Around the time Ranvir Pratap and Evam met and discussed the recruitment of Aspies, someone in counterintelligence ran a check on Evam. They kept him under surveillance, opening a file titled "Evam Enterprise." He was an astute businessman in what Mumbai called "the unorganized sector." The crèche that he ran for autistic children and their parents was just that: a crèche. It was very profitable. There was another side to Evam Enterprise that was profitable and quite bizarre.

The CI department expected their chief, Mishra, to expose Evam. "Now is not the time," he said. Evam was linked to both Ranvir and Tiwari. Mishra was a chess player who saw many moves ahead. To him this whole affair seemed headed in the right direction. He made a notation on the file that said, *One day someone will clean up this Special Branch.* That would be him, of course: Mishra, the modern Hercules.

"What's the purpose of living?" asked Evam of himself.

He had no appropriate response for the question. He had no audience either. It was a humid night and he had a few mosquitoes for company. He was staring at a computer screen which showed a sensuous girl. She gestured and she made a sound every time he clicked.

"Touch me," she said.

"For what purpose?" he asked. A mosquito vied for his attention; it landed on the vein of his right wrist, which rested on the mouse. He watched it settle.

"Do you know my name?" he asked.

"Touch me, Evam," she pleaded.

Evam Bhaskar was a social misfit. In his dreams he was a miscast hero but in life he was just another abject Mumbaikar. He peddled sex for a living and ran a crèche for idiot savants on the side. As a qualified psychologist he was hard-pressed to explain this.

Each thing Evam did clashed with everything else. This did not tear him apart but it made him contemplative.

"Why, Evam?" asked the girl, questioning his silence.

Evam clicked. She smiled, pirouetted, and shed her garb.

"Is this living?" he asked. The mosquito hovered and landed again. This time it drew blood.

He poked her with the cursor.

"Big boy," she teased.

Evam slapped hard, his left hand missing; he swiped again and the mouse clattered off the table and hung by a wire. There was a buzzing sound around his ears.

The girl moaned.

And Evam cried.

"I am so sorry," he said. For what? "So many things," he whispered.

After a while he recovered. He walked to a window and peered out at the night. A breeze ruffled the curtain and he took a deep breath. His dead father spoke to him. *Find a way, my son,* he said.

Though his father departed early he left behind a settled household and two words of advice that he repeated to himself as much as to his only son: "*Raastha dhoondo.*" It was a decree that had a sense of urgency: "Find a way, don't dawdle or hesitate because the likes of us have started on the wrong foot." That summed up Evam's life. From the grape boughs and grain fields of his village, to Mumbai and a doctoral degree in child psychology, and his two strange businesses, life was one long attempt to "find a way."

"You want to study child psychology?" His mother wanted to know why.

"I don't know."

Dr. Evam. He had it carved on a polished teak plank with gold-painted lettering. He had to make a living. The thought of a government job crossed his mind. He applied to a general hospital in Mumbai and stated his specialization.

"Child psychology?" asked the registrar. "We only have openings for gynecology."

When he tried to explain further he was waved away. "*Raastha dhoondo,*" he was told. In this case it meant, *Go, get lost.*

Finally he set up his own practice. He decided he would consult for special children. Nobody came at first. His operation flirted every now and then with financial ruin but he kept getting money from unlikely places at the most opportune moments. He kept faith and he put up a sign that said *Rahath* and waited.

They eventually came. Desperate mothers showed up to Rahath with their children, not for a cure but to cope, and he helped them. Their children were fine by themselves. At his place they could make faces, make mistakes, they could be themselves and nobody would notice.

This practice was numbing: mind numbing. Initially he marveled at the sheer variety, the inexplicable range of issues that cropped up when the wiring in the brain was even a little off. And then he began to yearn for a simple solution that would calm minds responsible for children with such issues.

There was no solution. If you had a child like this you had to learn to lead a different life, and it wasn't easy. What was easy was to say that these kids were just a little different, and that we should learn to accept the difference rather than try to make them normal or beat ourselves up when that did not happen. Autism was hard to live with, and it was getting to those who came to Rahath. He realized that he was just a caregiver, effectively running a crèche for the parents as well.

Over the years his practice began to focus on milder forms of autism and its variants. His primary goal was to find gainful employment for this group, and he began to make presentations to corporations and government departments. It was hard work trying to change mind-sets.

Evam glanced at his watch and groaned. He had woken up in the middle of the night again. He was still seated in front of a screen that had also fallen asleep. His hands were covered with bumps and he scratched a few bite marks. He sat for a while and then got up to drink some water. The city was quiet, the street sounds having tapered. The bed didn't look inviting. He sank into his chair again and shook the mouse; the screen came alive.

"Big boy," she said, smiling. She breathed deeply.

He was captivated by the sound of her breath. He could almost feel it on his shoulders. He smiled back.

She waited. "Evam? Is that you?" She was blind. That took some effort; that took so much programming. "Do you know my name? Could you say it?"

"Giselle," he said without thinking. "What am I doing?" he asked himself aloud, not for the first time. He was moved to write a confession. Some part of him wanted to confess and another part wanted a record in case something happened to him. Dealing with horny, reckless cops was a risky business.

The Minds of Men

It's time for a summation. I live in a lonely planet. I write a page every fortnight for a girlie magazine. It's sandwiched between scantily clad pinup girls and some unclad ones. It's a good place to be because I dispense advice for maladies that arise from reading girlie magazines. The column is titled "Tiger Balm." Like any good balm my column hurts while it heals.

I've never met the editor of the publication. As an introduction, I sent her samples quoting fictional letters and advice. She liked my style and said my feedback was "sharp" and very "original." She gave me three months as a trial period. I think their pictures were very good and so many letters came. Life went on.

Q: Will masturbation weaken me?
A: Yes. For about sixty seconds.

Q: I have a hard-on that won't go away.
A: Sharpen a knife. Then shave a pencil till you break the lead.

Q: We like the photographs. That's why we buy the magazine.

We don't need you and your advice.
A: You need a girlfriend.

Q: My girlfriend left me. She complained, saying I have bad breath, that I smell like sweat all the time and never shave. What should I do?
A: Reach out to National Geographic; better still, Animal Planet.

And then came the question that changed my life. The first U-turn in my life came up when some idiot who was in the throes of penis love wrote in:

Q: What care does my penis need?
A: Treat it like a temple treats a lingam.

I meant to say . . . Forget what I meant to say. My column was done, over, finished. There was outcry and outrage and I was out. I realized that my column would not have lasted long anyway. Some part of me wanted to just let it all out; I did so. I let go in an online blog. There I told people what I really felt, no-holds-barred. It was irreverent, insolent, and sometimes abusive. People loved it and commented in kind and it became a joyous slugfest. Was this some kind of escape for me?

A continuous stream of mothers and their children traipse into my clinic seven days a week. The children make faces, they break all the toys, and they break my heart. The mothers come for succor and I have to bear their burden for a few hours. For much-needed relief, I hide in a room with a computer and play games and watch porn for hours. The girlie magazine experience gave me an idea.

I got hold of a young visual artist who was also a whiz with computers. His name is Giri. Giri is supremely gifted and equally lazy, and I suspected his hormones were raging too. I described my assignment and watched his eyes widen. I gave him a challenge and in just seven days he delivered a program.

"Sir, you have no idea what I had to do to get the right sounds."

I was the test market for this site. Male, single, never married, with a poor social life. This thing had to excite me, it had to hook me and keep me occupied. It did all of that. I am a strong believer in sound. The right sound can do wonders, as much as touch or feel. Giri had captured the sounds I wanted.

We worked hard on the image. We developed a screen called MORPH. Based on your data and your preferences an image gradually takes shape. After refining it further for another month, we went live with "Giselle." Giri and I stood in front of my PC and he ceremoniously pressed a button. I logged in and fed in my details. MORPH went to work and my Giselle appeared. You have to see her; she is a marvel and she is mine alone.

Giselle is easy to use. If you are honest in creating your personal sketch, your Giselle will then appear. In India she is a little rounded. You can rest your eyes on her for she is sexy and you can touch her through your mouse or, better still, your touch screen. She moans in six different ways depending on where you touch her.

The sound is incredible. Each note has been carefully chosen and the pitch and the timbre are perfect. Keep hitting those buttons and you could have a symphony, an aria, or a blockbuster harem session. Giselle started as a free site, but when it began to take off, I did the sensible thing and after making a few improvements I added a paywall. I have money in the bank now and the best part is nobody knows who owns Giselle.

And this thing keeps me busy too. My young friend has engineered the site such that I get to know who logs in, when, how often, and what they click on. I get a whole lot of data that I use to analyze profiles and usage patterns. I have realized that most people are weird in their private moments.

I told you I am a trained psychologist. I took eight long years to qualify. My college, which was in interior Maharashtra, was forever on strike. I spent the first three years improving my English, which is now bloody good, thank you very much. What was missing and finally developed in Mumbai was a sense of dress and social skills.

I came to Mumbai to make a living. It seemed like the kind of place where I might become successful. When I first arrived here, I felt out of place and lacked confidence. I called everybody "Sir."

Dealing with difficult children is a hard practice. It's very challenging to see nature's mistakes. It's even more challenging having to live with them. Let me define *mistake*: nature's biggest mistake and evolution's all-time screw-up is making the majority of us very much like one other. We are a dominating majority. We live in a uniform think tank, we swim rhythmically in an empathy pool, and we have lost the ability to deal with those of us who are different. And when someone different comes along we cannot handle it.

Right now I am observing the habits of the heaviest

user of Giselle. Giri, my young wizard, has sent me the data on this fellow who seems hooked on my invention.

IP Address: Mumbai, India
Declared Age: Midthirties
Marital Status: Single
Usage Style: Chaotic

"Sir," says my computer friend, "this guy must have busted some of the keys on his keyboard by now. He keeps hitting them so rapidly that I've had to reengineer our response timings."

This prime customer of ours, who I had been tracking closely, seemed to have a serious problem. I wanted to help him out if I could. My professional calling egged me on and I felt compelled to answer the call. But how?

I sat at my computer and ran a few searches. I fished around in the profiles of those who have posted on my blog, I followed some dead ends, and I finally found a match. His blog postings were a mix of Hindi and English. His thoughts were staccato and his questions were naive. He kept referring to women as *Aurat jaat*.

And now I was in a quandary. I wanted to get through to this user—for his sake. How do you go about doing it? Giri traced the IP address and he spoke to a friend and they got hold of the location. It was a police station in South Mumbai. The person was a cop.

Giri's asking around stirred some feathers. I received an anonymous note saying that all information and records pertaining to Tiwari should be deleted forthwith, or else I would be in trouble. Of course I did no such thing.

After a week the user was back online. And then I was paid a visit by a man named Pandey who questioned me about who I was and what I did.

"Psycho what?" he asked me. "Are you qualified for such a thing?"

He wasn't satisfied when I said yes. A few days later he called saying he had a puzzle that only I could help solve. He set up a meeting with his colleagues at the police station. While I could hardly wait to see the biggest user of Giselle—I had visualized him a million times in my head—I was also apprehensive.

The Bahurupi Sena

Informers were called *khabaris* and they were compensated either in cash for the *khabar* or they were offered amnesty by the police for past infractions. The other term used for *khabaris* was "zero." Zeroes had no official standing with the police and certainly none with the gangs. They were invisible men operating in a no-man's-land. A legion of such zeroes visited the rear portion of Special Branch. This two-faced army was colloquially called the Bahurupi Sena.

There were no niceties in the rear office. The place had a concrete floor, stone walls, exposed wiring, and it was poorly lit. The approach to the building was crowded and outside was a bazaar that extended right up to the doorstep. Cheap junk was sold on the sidewalks, on the roads, and in temporary shelters. People shopped here en route to the nearby railway station. The shops had no names and nothing could be tried on or returned. Things were sold in twos, threes, and more. There was an energy, a must-sell-today kind of energy. Buyers looked around furtively and for good reason. The material was a steal; was it stolen? There were many wallets on sale and countless pens. Were these people shopkeepers or were they pickpockets?

All efforts at clearing this mess were thwarted by Tiwari.

He found this bazaar a good camouflage for his operation. His men and their extended network could sneak in and out without notice. Nobody knew the size of this subterranean network and very few were aware that its tentacles spread over the map of Mumbai. Mumbai informers lived hand-to-mouth and the cops exploited them. Tiwari was given a stack of cash every month which helped keep his network on a short financial leash.

"There is no love lost in my department," said Tiwari. "The world hates an informer."

Ranvir watched Tiwari's progress and famously said, "This will not last."

He was wrong. The Bahurupi Sena flourished. Things were going well for the Bahurupis, and thanks to their information preemptive arrests were on the rise and many crimes were getting solved faster. The focus shifted from hunting for clues at the crime scene to letting informers loose. They came back with names. The hit squad had less and less to do.

The clashes between Ranvir and Tiwari began with minor issues, the first salvo coming from Ranvir. He issued a three-point memo that said, *No paan chewing, no spitting, and no loitering.*

Tiwari responded, *Please define loitering.*

The reply: *Leaning on anything when on duty, sitting on anything other than your chair, scratching any body part in public view, speaking to anyone for more than a minute.*

Everybody knew that Tiwari chewed *paan* leaves. Each morning, a *dhoti*-clad denizen from the Hindi heartland would arrive with twenty-four neatly packed bundles. The first packing layer was a rough leaf that was covered by newspaper with a top plastic cover. The process of unpacking was gradual, with each layer thrown into (and sometimes outside) a dustbin. By the evening the *paan* would have marinated into the newspaper and the plastic turned a bloody color. With so much mastication it was inevitable that spitting would follow.

The clash of cultures spilled into the work zone. Parthasarathy held a meeting to try to defuse the tension.

"Gentlemen, this is a rapprochement meeting. Now please air whatever is on your mind, but no mud-slinging and no personal insults. Clear your misunderstandings and let us try to be positive."

"You have done well, Tiwari," said Ranvir, to begin proceedings. "For someone who has come up the ranks, you have done very well indeed."

Tiwari looked a little surprised. Was this a loaded compliment? Perhaps Ranvir was trying to emphasize the fact that he was an IPS officer. These Indian Police Service types liked to distance themselves from the rankers.

Ranvir turned to Partha. "Mumbai has no patience for subtlety, so the city gets what it deserves. Tiwari's method seems to be working. He bugs the bad-asses of Mumbai. He plants bugs in their bedrooms and boudoirs and records what happens. He tracks the pimps, the whores, and their clients—and he bugs them as well. He threatens the underlings and the weak links in the gangs. And you, sir, give him a bundle of cash to dispense with impunity. There is enough dirt in Mumbai for our friend to thrive."

Tiwari reddened and had difficulty composing his thoughts. He lacked finesse and so his reply was emotional and incoherent. "Ranvir *sahib*, unlike you IPS types, we've had no time to learn language. We grew up middle class. There is no poetry in our houses. You want to know why?"

Ranvir shook his head. "No," he said.

"Well, I'll tell you anyway. It cannot pay our bills. *Sahib*, to police Mumbai you have to grow up in Mumbai, like I did." Tiwari switched tracks; he went off on a personal journey: "My father was a devout family man. We all worshipped him. I was a small boy when he suddenly passed away. After he died my uncle took me aside and showed me what my father did on those evenings he came home late and those weekends when he was on the road."

Ranvir wanted to interrupt but Partha held him back.

Tiwari rambled on: "My uncle took me to the infamous neighborhood of Grant Road where there was a dancer, a *mujrewaali* called Tabassum. I hid behind torn curtains while Tabassum danced. Later she placed a hand on my head and I shuddered. I could only see the grime, the dirt, the peeling walls, the cheap makeup, and the fake laughter. I had to find my own way home that night."

"Why?" asked Partha, amid his doodling.

"Because my uncle stayed behind."

"I see."

"That night I saw the world through my father's eyes. I walked the lanes of that notorious district. And I saw men wander those streets. I stood in front of one *jaali* room whose curtain was pink. Many men came. They were unsteady from drink and they spoke loudly. They arrived like heroes and left like thieves. There was a dark corner in that alleyway. As they left they sprayed the wall of that alley with piss till the smell made me gag. Mr. Parthasarathy, I learned about sex that night."

"What did you learn? I hope you didn't—"

Tiwari shook his head. "I learned that sex is like going to the toilet."

"Is that where you go for sex?" asked Ranvir with mock politeness.

Partha intervened. "Rana, let him have his say."

"Is there a point to this story?" asked Ranvir.

"My father led a double life that nobody knew about," said Tiwari. "That destroyed him; that information finished him in my eyes. I couldn't sleep. I realized the power of information that night. Information can make a man and it can finish him too." He stood up with some difficulty, walked over to Ranvir, and faced him head on. "Ranvir *sahib*, in my language, my station as a cop is a *thana*, and I am a *thanedaar*. This is the real Mumbai, my Mumbai. You are welcome but you do not belong here."

Tiwari's World

You have no official identity in this city, just like the million or so others who reside in Mumbai's slums. There are no land records in your name though you have laid claim to a small hole in a dirty chawl where you shit into a plastic bag and throw it into a bin. You do not get any bills for electricity or water because you have tapped them both illegally. You buy things in the gray markets where no one makes out receipts. Your SIM card has a phony address and you have neither a passport nor a ration card. Your name does not appear in any database, nor does your photograph. You have never been inside a bank. There are thousands like you in the slums among the poor, the criminals, and those who are both. You are untraceable and a nightmare for the police.

You are in your early thirties and you make a living selling cell phones from a small shop in a slum. Your suppliers are crooked and your material is fake but the phones work and you offer free repairs. Your cousin sits at the rear of the shop behind a partition and hacks the codes of every phone brand and model and installs every update as well.

You are such a fake that even your name, Pappu, sounds

phony. That's what everyone calls you. Your part-time job as a *khabari* exists because of who you are. The cops cannot trace the likes of you without an informant network. You took up this precarious job because one day a minor don bought a phone from you and he got traced. When he was released he came after you, took you away, and cut off one of your balls. You nearly bled to death. Then you had recurrent nightmares, and they had robbed you of your prowess in bed. The ignominy dragged you to Tiwari, who took care of the hoodlum. You became a *khabari* in return. You have grown weary of ratting and your wife wants you to come out into the open, buy a small apartment, open a bank account, and adopt a child.

You have gathered your courage and asked for a meeting. You are taken through a low door from the street outside and the two men who accompany you do not touch you but they own you, the way they shepherd you through a narrow corridor without windows to a small room without windows that has one yellow light, one table, and one metal chair upon which you seat yourself without being asked. You face a wall, the light comes on, and you see your hunched shadow. Opposite you is a stuffed seat and Tiwari enters without a sound and sinks into it, and before you know it his hand is on your shoulder; he has turned your face to the light and memorized your every pore.

"Speak," he says. "Say something."

You blurt your name and where you are from and he holds up his hand and stops you.

"I know who you are. Do you want to live?" he asks.

"Yes," you say without thinking.

"The answer is always yes," he replies matter-of-factly, then leans forward. "Why?"

"*Why?* What do you mean *why?*" You laugh nervously.

"What happens if you die?" he says softly. "Have you ever thought about it?"

You shake your head and lean back as much as you can because he's bearing down on you and he reeks of sweat.

"Let's say you die here in this room. It has happened to people—they have come here and they have had strange seizures. What will really happen if you die? You think you are worth something, worth preserving for someone like me?" His tone remains soft through all of this. Tiwari shifts his seat closer and the grating sound echoes in the small chamber. He is right next to you and you have to look into his eyes and you find yourself disoriented by his relentlessly questioning but dulcet tone. "What can you do for me now? What you have told me in the past is history. You are telling me you want to just walk away . . . and then? I can give you some money and send you away. What will you do with your pathetic existence—go back to your booze?"

"I don't drink, Tiwari-*ji*, I don't touch it."

"To your needles and hash then."

"Only *gutka*, I take only *gutka*, I swear."

"Fine . . . You can leave but don't ever call me again."

"That's it? I have to go back to that serpent's den wearing an informer's badge? You told me you would protect me."

"Why should I? There's no pension in this business."

"Okay, just give me my money."

Tiwari pushes a small packet across the table toward you, which you pocket quickly without checking the contents. "Your wife spoke to me," he says. "Actually, I called her today. You can't keep her happy, can you? Fucking eunuch. I hear even Viagra failed."

The son of a bitch; the fat, shameless slob. Will he stop at nothing?

There is a fine line between information and intelligence, and Tiwari had the instincts of an assayer in these matters. It's hard to distinguish between the two when most of your material is hearsay and half-truths. Before Tiwari took charge it was assumed that what was forced out of somebody was true and what came to the door as barter needed to be vetted.

No one had actually seen Tiwari get physical in an interrogation. He considered it a failure if someone on his team had to lay even a finger on an informant. And yet he was very effective. His mind was one with those who showed up. Wastrels, petty thieves, convicted criminals, and devious rats would surface at headquarters and within minutes of meeting him they felt exposed. Such was his understanding of their minds. It was quite extraordinary. Tiwari believed he could cajole a man to give up his life. Seriously. Those who ratted to him often died violent deaths. None held him to account.

He is a fat man, shaped like a dome, bald with a shiny patc, with small cycs that look at you without malicc and a soft voice that makes you feel like he's telling the truth and that you should trust him. Trust is dear to Tiwari and he conveys this repeatedly to each and every one of his *khabaris*, dwelling as well on the catastrophic consequences of any breach. In his own office, whether in front of colleagues or in the interrogation room, he is a changed person, a man playing a video game, the arena a fantasy world where he hunts quarry and on a good day information appears like a vision would. His diffidence disappears and he seems confident, daring, manipulative, and masterly—a throwback to Machiavelli and Marquis de Sade.

Outside his office Tiwari reverted to who he once was, a different person, one who he wasn't in love with. His favorite food was sweet, and his constant nightmare was having to converse in English. He was much more comfortable with the broken Hindi that Mumbai had invented, a form of expression that was efficient rather than poetic. In his run-ins with Ranvir, Tiwari suffered. In Ranvir's presence he was slow with his thoughts and those that formed took time to find expression. Ranvir had a quick tongue with acidic lace. It was no contest.

"You are a metaphor for what is wrong with this new Mumbai," Ranvir said to him.

"Metaphor?" What could that be? It sounded like a pill he had taken some days ago. He was getting riled but he didn't know how to retaliate.

"You are a tradesman in the wrong profession," Ranvir continued. "A common shopkeeper in the police force."

It was no secret that Tiwari had a bazaar mentality, a faith in barter, and a conviction that what could not be purchased actually had no value.

"Mr. Ranvir, everything has a conversion rate," replied Tiwari finally. Perhaps a decent Tiwari quote but not his best. "Everybody has secrets, even you. One day my information might find you."

Tiwari suffered from domestic depression. In his household the language was culinary and the principal medium was clarified butter. Milk rose in the morning and curds set in the evening. The cow, Gomaatha Gai, was the family deity. She occupied the kitchen and presided over Peth Puja.

Tiwari grew up visibly unfit, fat in his briefs, an object of self-loathing, with bulges and folds that tested his school uniform every year. In school he was prime material for ragging. The bullies sated their hormones with his puppy fat and squeezed his tits. He grew to dislike the full-length mirror at home and his self-worth reached a nadir in his teenage years. In private he exacted revenge on small animals. He was quick to catch the noisy pigeons that made *gutur-gutur* sounds, shed feathers, and dirtied his small balcony. He would twist them by the neck and toss them as far as he could. Many street dogs in the neighborhood bore marks where he threw stones or had used a stick on their legs. Their helpless sounds and cries did not disturb him.

The neighbors complained at this sadism. "I am a vegetarian," he replied. "You people slit the throats of animals, let them bleed to death, and then eat them, so don't talk."

There were some worries in the department about his emotional stability, but there were never any untoward incidents. At work he trusted no one and he operated without a formal structure, a practice that made him indispensable. He had a flunky named Kamte who ran around and did odd jobs for him. Recently and against his wishes he had been asked to accommodate a lateral hire, a man in his thirties who was proficient in many Indian languages, a skill which would be useful in interrogations. He was fluent in English, which earned him respect from Tiwari. The recruit was named Pandey. Pandey deigned to do whatever he was told; clearly he was capable of more.

This was in essence Tiwari's immediate team. Most of what had to be remembered and retained was in Tiwari's head, and to be fair he had a phenomenal memory for facts and faces. He was also a good judge of a certain kind of person, one who had something of value and could be bought. But he had no understanding of people like Ranvir who spouted values that were not monetary.

Tiwari adjusts the rearview mirror and picks his teeth. He spots a young girl in the mirror as she waits to cross the road. Her hips catch his eye and she tosses her hair and smiles at someone. He is startled. Blood courses to his unmentionables and he squirms.

"*Aurat jaat* . . ." he says helplessly. "Women are such a mystery."

He sits awkwardly in his jeep, his feet apart, barely squeezing into his tight pants. He drives erratically. He has a meeting today that could change his life. He touches the plastic feet of the Kanhaiya on the dashboard and then spits out the window. He glares at every car that pulls alongside him.

The temple provides sanctuary for his thoughts. There is a crowd and for a while he loses himself amid the din of the believers. He should hurry. Back in his office his boss Parthasarathy will be waiting for him to return. (He is in fact already sitting in Tiwari's smelly chair and holding his nose.)

When Tiwari returns, his underlings Kamte and Pandey are standing outside his office. "He has come," says Kamte breathlessly. Tiwari nods, lifts his belt above his belly, and barges in. As he walks in he considers this life form called Parthasarathy. Such a dry chap. His face has no color, his eyes are like water, he has no taste, wears pale shirts, and his handshake is limp.

Parthasarathy had never seen field duty. In the eyes of his subordinates he lacked credentials. His file was so thin and his job experience was woefully short. When questioned about this his laugh was hollow. He was a placeholder for the position of head of Special Branch, brought in because of the untimely death of his predecessor. He had been in charge of the succession committee which had just one member because the others had begged off. Nobody wanted to get between two vindictive types like Ranvir Pratap and Dharamdas Tiwari. Partha had grumbled that neither of them seemed fit for the role and then bought himself a six-month extension.

"Tiwari-*ji*, come, take a seat."

He falls into the visitor's chair in his own office, which protests immediately by expelling air. It is hot and sultry and the room feels like a sauna. He opens a shirt button hoping for a sliver of relief.

"The name of my successor will be announced in several months, giving us room for a smooth handover."

"Why the delay, sir?" blurts Tiwari. "What do we do in the meanwhile?"

"More of the same," replies Partha.

The room falls silent until Partha finally dismisses them, letting himself out even before Tiwari has struggled to his feet. In his journal Partha notes, *Will Ranvir and Tiwari be on their best behavior these next six months? I suspect they will be at their worst.*

At his desk, Tiwari rings a bell and Kamte and Pandey fall over each other as they enter. He pulls out his pistol and they recoil. The instrument of war tangles with Tiwari's pocket and belt buckle. He pulls the trigger and a dull click emanates.

"Chai, sir?" asks Kamte. "Can I get you some *vada pao* to eat?"

Tiwari fondles the pistol and looks into the snout with each eye. "Oshiwara," he says finally. He needs an outdoor interrogation to get his mind off these office battles.

They walk deliberately to the jeep. No directions are given yet they reach the same suburb in Oshiwara where foliage is thick along a deserted road. They pull over onto a grassy knoll. Nobody speaks.

"Off-duty hour," Tiwari eventually says.

"Happy hour," says Kamte.

Tiwari pulls out a bottle of liquor from the glove compartment. Kamte has brought glasses and the three of them drink for a while. In a few minutes a police jeep will arrive with a scheming informer, one who thought he was clever.

Tiwari turns to Kamte's young colleague. "Pandey, how's your English these days?"

Pandey nods. "Good, sir." It's in fact his strong suit, and he narrowly missed becoming a teacher in a Hindi Prachar Sabha.

"Good. Today's interrogation will be in English."

A man from Goa had information on a iron ore mining case. His name was Sequiera and he had been beaten up, seemingly in the last couple of days from the way the blood had dried. Tiwari frowned, visibly unhappy.

Good *khabar* can make you smile. You can see the effect it has on Tiwari's face. The moment sometimes arrives after days, and other times it arrives suddenly when you least expect it. Information has an expiration date, so the sooner it is gleaned the better. Pandey asks his first question that night in English and Sequiera replies. Tiwari and his team look at one other and they can barely contain themselves.

That night Tiwari has a recurring dream about a woman. He is naive and he is awkward and fulfillment eludes him. As the night drifts away he sleeps fitfully. While Tiwari sleeps a night bus passes by his window. The night tour was growing popular because Mumbai by night is a different beast.

Nandini looks tired as she sits next to the driver with a mic in her hand. She usually makes a few closing remarks. Tonight she has an enthusiastic group and she will let them talk.

"Nandini, tell us more about Mumbai."

She cocks her head as if deep in thought. "In this Mumbai anything can happen." She pauses. "Your turn," she says. And they set off at each other with rapid-fire dialogue.

"Mumbai, my perfumed garden."

"Creeks that reek."

"A vast pond that feeds big fish."

"Where minions labor."

"And time travels by train."

"Snatches of song, whiffs of a better life."

"Shop windows."

"*Nullahs*, *galas*, gullies, rickety cabs, and drab buildings."

"Dug-up streets that drop you home."

"Poseurs on street corners and roadsides."

"Wake up, makeup."

"Carry your cubicle to your cubbyhole."

"I want, I need."

"The next best thing."

"It's happening, man."

"The giddy blur."

The bus has passed and Tiwari tosses and turns like a whale caught in low tide. A nerve flutters in his arm and his mind flits between the crass and the nude. Fuck it, the mattress is too firm. As dawn breaks he struggles to his feet, downs a coffee, and heads for the mirror.

"I can see you, Tiwari," he tells his reflection.

He opens his pantry and reaches for his stash of biscuits. He has bottles filled with sweet rusks, cream biscuits, and the local *naan khatais*. He crunches a handful.

Down below are the tiled rooftops of Mumbai. An unused chimney stands over a small schoolyard. Noises filter upward: scattered horns of the impatient, children shouting while playing, a municipal truck gathering garbage, and a querulous *namaazi* clearing his throat into a mosque's megaphone.

Thoughts swirl in the recesses of his mind. He touches the burning bulb to feel the heat and looks in wonder at the burn mark. He is restless and scratches himself near his Adam's apple, drawing blood. He washes the nick and it smarts. He has a shower and changes into a white *kurta* and pajamas. It is a Sunday, a day that heightens his innate fragility.

Tiwari's home makes him despondent. His family life is like a physical ruin. He is a bachelor and a virgin and even now the proximity of a woman gives him goose bumps. Surprising, given that he has three sisters, but then they are much older and still treat him like a child. In his teens he had to take turns and wash clothes and share a bathroom with them, and the place was a mess with their clothes and underwear drying inside at all times. His mother was big-boned (and so were his sisters) and she had hairy forearms and a deep voice and she smothered him. She was inordinately fond of him. At school his shorts were starched and flared, his shirt was tucked in tight, his hair was oiled and parted down the middle. His mother would comb his hair to heighten the parting; one wave of hair went left and another went right. His head resembled the pages of an open book.

"You should have been a priest," his mother says every now and then. She pictures her son standing like his forefathers once did in the Dashashwamedh *ghats* in Banaras. They stood bare-chested with water climbing to their midriffs as they stepped into the river of sacred ablution called the Ganga. It was a long line that was broken by Tiwari's father, a line of priesthood. Tiwaris were men who were proficient in Sanskrit, a language that was never a mother tongue; it was a sacred and elaborate script that spoke only to gods.

He sits up in bed and rubs his distended stomach. "I have only pawns on my team," he grumbles to himself. "But at least I have real work, I am busier than ever. And Ranvir? He has a small team. Munna, Karan, and Tapas; but they are idle. They sit around their office doing crossword puzzles in English."

He needs ammunition against this trick squad. He has something but he isn't yet sure what it means. In typical Tiwari fashion he had sent Pandey with a key to snoop inside Ranvir's lair. This was Pandey's first test. Kamte had to cover for him, standing the whole night outside the Special Branch front porch on one leg and then the other, losing his balance. Pandey ran down the batteries of his flashlight rummaging through the place, taking pains to set it back exactly the way it was. He let himself out in the morning through the small window when the security detail changed over.

He found very little because there was hardly any paperwork in that office. In desperation he riffled through what was lying around and made some notes. He shared these notes with Kamte before meeting Tiwari. Kamte examined the disjointed sentences which made no sense to him.

"Your promotion is doomed," he informed Pandey. Secretly he was pleased the young challenger had failed.

They trooped into Tiwari's office unshaven and unkempt and found him looking restless. He clearly needed good *khabar*.

"*Kya*?" Tiwari asked. "Found something?"

"This is what Pandey found," said Kamte as he tossed the notes carelessly on the man's table.

"Pandey?" said Tiwari. His voice carried hope, his tone feared failure.

Pandey did not want to be laughed at, or worse.

"Actually, I didn't understand these scribbles so I consulted somebody. He told me these are their call signs."

"Call signs?" Tiwari looked toward Kamte, who shrugged and turned to Pandey.

"Call signs are pilot nicknames," read Pandey from a sheet of paper. "Pilots in the air force give themselves nicknames. They engrave them on their headgear, use them in their radio communication, and even call each other by those names. Usually the names are aggressive, reflecting high levels of testosterone." He looked up and saw confusion.

"Continue," said Tiwari. He liked this boy Pandey. He spoke English like Ranvir. Initially he had been suspicious of him because he had been thrust upon the team by Parthasarathy.

"Pilots have a different alphabet," said Pandey. "For them, A is for albatross, not apple; B stands for braveheart; C for Cherokee; D for daredevil; and I for Icarus, the chap who flew too close to the sun and fell."

"These are local boys, sir," said Kamte. "B must be for *behan* and C for *chod*."

Tiwari laughed. "*Behanchods*," he muttered.

"Yes, sometimes they use cuss words for their targets as part of the game," said Pandey.

Tiwari rubbed his face with his hands, picked up a random sheet, smoothed it out, and peered at the words. Each sheet contained four lines:

TAPAS
Agent Code: 16
Call sign: DIFFERENT
Favorite line: I am the best kind of different.

He paused and looked toward Pandey for explanation. They moved on to the next one.

MUNNA
Agent Code: 11
Call sign: LOOKOUT
Favorite line: R-U-ALL-THERE.

Pandey moved quickly to the third, the file for the now-deceased Kumaran.

KUMARAN
Agent Code: 10
Call sign: PRENATAL
Favorite line: I got Mother's blood.

"Mother's blood?" asked Tiwari. "Kamte, do you have Mother's blood?" He picked up a pencil and scribbled.

"Kumaran was an orphan, so . . ." suggested Pandey.

"So?" Tiwari sucked the end of his pencil. He was growing irritated. "Give me Karan's sheet. I know you've intentionally been keeping it for last."

Pandey read it aloud.

KARAN
Agent Code: 26
Call sign: PUZZLE
Favorite line: I am a person, not a puzzle.

"This is the only one that makes sense," said Tiwari, glancing expectantly at his two underlings. "Though what he says is wrong. He is a puzzle, not a person."

"The whole thing makes them look vulnerable," said Pandey.

"I agree," said Tiwari. "These hit men are big, strong guys. Each is six feet tall, sturdy—quiet, yes, a little aloof, and perhaps a little awkward too. But think about the things they do. It's frightening. These sheets of paper are childish. I think we need to show this to a psychologist. Let's give all this to that Evam fellow. Pandey, can you get ahold of him?"

The next day Evam received a sealed envelope from Tiwari containing copies of the four sheets.

Tiwari's Office

The space Tiwari inhabits describes him better than any résumé. There is no color scheme to speak of, unless dirty gray is considered a shade. The flooring consists of ceramic tiles that have cracked in many places from moving around heavy furniture. This is nondescript, government-issue furniture with each item bearing an inventory code painted in white. Some misshapen cushions have been added by Tiwari and they have made many misshapen bodies a little less at ease. They are encrusted with sweat patches and the embroidery has grown threadbare. There is a rectangular table in the center of the room with a Formica top. On it is a jug of water, three glasses, and geometric tea stains. Tiwari sits on a big, roomy thronc of a chair. Thc placc has a smell, an ingrained fragrance that is part cheap barbershop and part third-class railway compartment.

In sum, people of a certain background could come here and feel comfortable.

Tiwari's assistant Kamte fixes his *paan*, positions his spittoon, arranges his *gaddis*, and listens to his every word. Tiwari shifts around constantly, revealing an agility and alacrity that are at odds with his size. Any transactions that are discussed stay mostly in his head. He communicates through handwritten notes in a mix of English and Hindi. Over time he has developed his own peculiar shorthand.

Evam arrives at ten thirty in the morning and Tiwari is on to his second *paan*. Kamte watches the juice build up in that elastic mouth. He can smell the *katha* and the *choona* as they mix inside it. Tiwari's plump lips pucker and his cheeks swell. It's time for the spittoon. Kamte!

He wipes his mouth with a small hand towel. And he gets back to chewing.

Pandey watches Evam enter Crime Branch and he is not enthused. Evam Bhaskar doesn't look like a psychologist. He seems harried and he's wearing a variety of charms. Around his neck is a black thread with a silver trinket; he wears two strings on his left wrist and three rings with large colored stones on his fingers, all presumably for good luck.

Pandey looks from Evam to Tiwari, then wonders what he is doing spending his time with these two. He is reminded this is a police station by the uniform that has begun to chafe him. Closer up, Evam looks reassuring. He has a pleasant face and sharp eyes that don't miss a thing. At least he's not a fool.

Evam spots Tiwari and halts in his tracks. His mind is spinning. He is thinking to himself, *This is the sex-starved policeman who batters his keyboard to vent his frustrations. He looks like a village* panchayat *leader. I wonder what his Giselle looks like. Comely? Yes, certainly comely. Rounded hips and upwardly stacked. Homely? Yes, certainly homely. Clad in a low-cut blouse and a see-through chiffon sari.*

They shake hands all around. Tiwari has a plump and sweaty palm. Evam sinks into one of the roomy chairs and wipes his hands on the sides. His deliberate gaze travels the length and breadth of the room. Tiwari is asked to give some background on Ranvir's team. He relates a tilted version. Little do the others realize that Evam helped Ranvir pull together his team and that he knows each member quite well.

Evam summarizes: "You are telling me that a fellow officer has assembled a private militia: a modern Ranvir Sena. And that he has done this in the police force. He has been given carte blanche by his superiors; for good reason, evidently, because the Third Squad has the most successful record that the Special Branch has ever seen. What I cannot see is a problem."

"Look deeper," says Tiwari.

"Let me get this straight," says Evam. "You are insinuating that there is something wrong with the team that Ranvir heads, and you want me to prove it?"

Tiwari nods. "You are the expert. All I can tell you is I have questioned more people in my career than anyone else in the police force. You have to respect that. My problem is, I am not able to say what I want to say."

"Try speaking in Hindi," says Evam with a straight face.

"Okay. In Hindi, the word for crazy is *pagal*, but the word I use for these four is *ajeeb*."

"Meaning strange?"

"Yes. The Third Squad is a ragged outfit with many obvious flaws. You are a psychologist and I am sure if you spent time with them you would discover something. There is something very, very wrong. Have you seen them?"

Tiwari has a scrapbook containing four photographs, passport-size portraits that he has pasted on white sheets. No smiles and no expressions; nothing remotely passes through their eyes as each stares at a point a whisker away from the camera lens.

"Don't they look like specimens, Mr. Bhaskar?"

When Evam glimpses these photographs he sees the familiar history of Evam's Ward. He sees social blindness, visual-motor issues, visual-perception issues, and poor prosody. But right now he pretends he sees nothing.

Tiwari scratches himself and examines his fingernail. "I have interrogated hundreds of people, Mr. Bhaskar, but all I can get out of these four are long, strange replies, and those only after an irritating pause. They have no volume control; one moment they speak loudly, the next moment I can barely hear them. Yet they speak in monotone. And they will never look you in the eye. I have tried staring directly at them." He bites some dead skin from his finger and spits it out. "In interrogation terms these four are guilty. They are hiding something. If I didn't know they were cops I would have arrested them."

"The Third Squad is called a crack team, Mr. Tiwari," says Evam. "They are heroes."

Tiwari is discomfited. He trusts his instincts in matters like these and he has to get to the bottom of this puzzle, but he can't clearly enunciate his worries. "Among them I worry most about Karan. Once he cornered me in the bathroom and said, *Come with me to the shadow lands.*"

Evam tries to reason: "The team probably doesn't often to speak to outsiders, which is why they might seem false and unconvincing."

"Sorry, this simply doesn't add up: these awkward, clumsy men have an unbelievable five-year record against skilled gangsters. Either they are crazy, or you and I are."

Evam sits up. "That last statement is quite true, Mr. Tiwari. Let's look at ourselves. I, Evam Bhaskar, am supposed to be a trained psychologist but actually I make a living peddling porn. I run a site called *Giselle*; she is a girl who moans if you touch her. And you pay me money every time she moans. Am I not mad, truly mad? And you? You look like you just touched a live wire. You might be a police bigwig but you are so horny that the only way you can stay sane is by hammering your keyboard. Where do you fall on the madness charts?"

Tiwari bites his nail again and draws some blood. All pretense is off now and this is a moment when anything can happen. He laughs. "Yes," he says. "We are a little mad, you and me. Just like this crazy city."

Evam shudders. He examines his own fingernails. The urge to bite is catching. "I cannot make heads or tails of what I am doing these days." He walks up to the window and looks out for a while. Policemen were meant to be well-trained, upright officers with the personal habits of gentlemen. Psychologists were not supposed to be quirky businessmen who preyed on a sex-starved nation.

Tiwari watches Evam, whose nervous energy is now visible. "Mr. Bhaskar," he says, "did you have a chance to review their papers?"

Evam places the papers in front of him and quotes, "*I am the best kind of different.*" And Evam thinks in his head, *It is such a poignant statement. Each of them has realized he is different. Each knows the others on his team are as well. And that is what binds them. They are different from the rest of us—not in any dramatic way, but in the kind of things they are unable to do, their quirks, the things they do not respond to, the things that give them trouble; simple everyday things.*

"*I am a person, not a puzzle,*" says Tiwari, now repeating Karan's line.

Evam half nods. "That really says it all, Mr. Tiwari. To

most people these four remain strangers. But they are not really all that strange."

Tiwari is still unconvinced. Evam leaves quietly without shaking hands.

That night Evam notes in his diary:

> *Four grown men on a hit squad; they cannot communicate very well. They have few friends and fewer acquaintances. How can they tell anyone what they are all about? They invent call signs, like pilots do. But these are a different kind of call sign. These are calls for help, the kind that float online looking for buoys in the ether.*

"Karan, what are you doing?"

I am sitting on the edge of the sidewalk. I have removed my right shoe and sock. The swelling has started. "Split ends," I reply.

A girl was crossing the road. She had a hand cupping a ear and she was talking. An auto rickshaw caught her ankle as it swerved. The phone came loose from her hand and tumbled into the street.

"Split ends?"

Nandini looks toward the street. It divides into two up ahead. There is a temple in the middle of the road that will not budge. The morning *aarti* has started and we hear the bells ring.

"Yes," I reply. I nurse my ankle with one hand and rub it vigorously with the other. Two boys stand next to me. They have handed me the bag of groceries that I was carrying.

"I see what you mean."

She folds her hands as the bell reaches a crescendo and flames appear in three circles beyond. The boys take an apple each and run. I straighten. The girl with the phone is trying to reassemble it. The auto rickshaw has gone and the driver hasn't heard her rant. She is young and her hair is loose.

"She needs to brush her hair," I say. I test my foot and I feel I'm ready.

Nandini looks quizzical and follows my gaze. "Karan," she says a little loudly, "she is too young for you."

"Her hair; it has split ends," I say.

We walk for a while.

"How do you notice these things?" she asks me.

I just look at where I'm looking.

An old man is crossing the road carefully. He has peered left and right, and he clutches his walking stick tight and steps off the sidewalk. There's a gap in the fast-moving traffic. He has just enough time to make it before the red BEST bus that has stopped gets going again. Nandini follows my gaze, hurries to the gent, and helps him cross. The bus rumbles by and she is back.

"Karan, I asked you something."

"The old chap was so careful but his fly was down," I tell her.

She grabs the bag of groceries from my hand. "You are impossible. Why would you notice such a thing?"

I cannot explain what the eye follows. Nobody can. "You are looking nice today, Nandini."

The wife steps off the sidewalk in a huff.

Nandini worried about a scene that's been lodged in her head. She had a 180-degree view of her surroundings, revealing glass-and-concrete towers that sat indiscriminately among slums. The roads that tied them together were battered and the sidewalks were apologies for the lost art of walking.

This vista of urban bondage and posh ruin outside the chawl was truly the age of Kalki. Kalki's age was not a number, she felt, but a state of being, and Mumbai was concrete evidence that the Indian apocalypse was around the corner.

"Take your pick from these Mumbai ghettos," she told her audience at a seminar. "These are cheap places, locations for auteurs from Hollywood who wish to shoot an Armageddon or script an apocalypse. Is it too late to conjure up an unlikely hero?"

At home she worried about her husband and his career. Where was Karan headed, and what would happen to his department? It did not take her long to figure out that Karan had one very specific skill set that was useful to the police. But that way of policing that Ranvir and his team represented was increasingly out of sync with the times. Ranvir would soon be isolated in the digital age where information was paramount and social media could protest effectively against the methods he used.

It seemed the era of encounter squads was coming to a close. *Times have changed* was the easy explanation, but it surely had something to do with the successful record of the encounter teams who, despite the glare of public disapproval, a glare which was harsh and unsparing, managed to eliminate hundreds of gang members. Extortion calls had ceased, kidnapping and murder had declined, and the Bollywood and construction syndicates were breathing easy. The higher-ups in the police force now said they would heed the call of their collective conscience. *Do not take the law into your own hands* was the new dictum.

Soon an item appeared in the newspapers that clearly pointed to a downsizing of two of the hit squads.

Everybody concerned read this report. Tiwari muttered a sentence aloud: "*No decisions have been passed on the other two squads.*" He looked at his two underlings. "Why not?"

Evam read the report seated in his ward with mixed feelings. Nandini reviewed it and had mixed feelings too, but for different reasons. Ranvir wasted no time and requested a meeting with Parthasarathy.

"Should we even take this seriously?" he asked Partha.

"Yes, I'm afraid so, Rana."

"If I have no work then that is good for my city," said Ranvir, ever the diplomat.

"It's good for Tiwari too," said Partha. "But you must also realize that he will pull ahead in the succession stakes."

Ranvir was prepared for this discussion. They both knew there was a mole in Tiwari's team, a boy who Ranvir thought was a younger version of himself in many ways. It was time to let Partha know what Tiwari was capable of.

"Do you know where Tiwari is right now?" Ranvir asked.

"Should I?"

"He is brothel-hunting, Mr. Parthasarathy. Your potential successor is out to discover his true self. Trust me, it will be ugly."

How does male chauvinism happen? wondered Pandey. *In what pigsty does it breed?* Every time he saw his boss Tiwari in the vicinity of women or heard him speak about them, he understood something more about chauvinism.

"Women are a breed," said Tiwari for the millionth time. "A breed apart."

Many of the *khabaris* who landed up at the station

were pimps and Tiwari was friendly with one of them. His name was Ustad. Ustad was summoned to handle Tiwari's libido. He arrived around three in the morning, a time when watchmen fell asleep. They left in a taxi to a nearby station.

"Where are we going?" asked Ustad. A jovial Tiwari made him nervous. His phone was buzzing because these were the busiest business hours.

"Today you have to blood me," said Tiwari.

Looks like he wants a freebie, thought Ustad. "There are many ways to do this, *janaab*," he told Tiwari. "But none are good."

"Doesn't matter." Tiwari was feeling light-headed.

They boarded a train that headed into the western suburbs, alighting at Goregaon. From there they took an auto rickshaw and Ustad provided directions lane by lane till Tiwari lost his bearings.

"*Patli galli*," murmured Ustad as they arrived at a dead end.

Tiwari was brimming with anxiety and the thought of a guaranteed fuck made him restless. He had applied cologne and carefully combed his hair. He sat at the edge of the rickshaw like an eager groom on his wedding night.

The last stretch was a walk through grime. They stepped carefully around a squatting child. Old Hindi music emanated from a small structure with dim lighting. The illuminated sign said, *Zabardast Massage Parlor*. They climbed broken stairs and a man with stale breath and downcast eyes brushed past them on his descent. Curtains parted and there was a room with a bench; they sat and waited. From the darkness came Giselle. She had shape—just about. She looked like she was wearing props from old films and greasepaint decked her features. And when she spoke Tiwari felt at home. She had a gruff voice, a voice whose timbre was perhaps wrecked by sordid phlegm.

She took Tiwari by the hand and led him to her cave.

This can't go wrong, thought Ustad as he popped a *paan* leaf into his mouth. He had chosen someone mature and experienced.

Inside a room that smelled of cheap disinfectant was a bed that had sunk in the middle. The bed groaned deeply as Tiwari sat on it. Giselle had dark eyes; she stood before him with a winsome smile. Tiwari froze. She walked to a corner and undressed, then returned in her underwear and stood before him.

"Come and get it," she said in Hindi.

Tears formed in Tiwari's eyes.

She placed his hand on her ample breast. "Squeeze," she commanded.

He squeezed. "Giselle," he mumbled, now fully aroused. He grimaced as he removed his belt and pants. A tear dropped onto his bare thigh.

"Where is your pain?" asked his Giselle, a little puzzled.

Tiwari pointed at his head, then smiled through his tears as she went down on her knees.

Her ministrations eased his pain. But he kept crying. All through her kindness he wept.

As they walked down the stairs Ustad looked at Tiwari nervously and waited for him to say something. He didn't speak till they reached the station.

"Take me back there tomorrow," he said.

The spooked Ustad finally let out his breath. "I will take you once more, *janaab*," he said. "But next time you will have to pay."

The next visit would see Tiwari completely let go. He would not be kind.

Back in his flat Tiwari asked, *Who am I?* as he let hot water steam his skin. Deep into the night in a place called home, in the room he had been brought up in, he finally found a side of himself that he liked. Things seemed different after the suburban tryst. He stood under the hot shower for a long while till the room steamed up and the mirror disappeared. He worked up some suds and a couple of soap bubbles floated into his face.

"This is what I need," he said aloud. "I have found what I was missing. She will be my regular. Once a week she will be mine."

He wore crisp whites and settled into his bed and examined his phones. He usually carried four of them at all times because these were the tools of his trade. The phones had a color code and there was a hierarchy. An official number that was widely available was usually picked up by Kamte. The next couple of numbers were answered by Pandey, and the fourth was his personal line which was divulged only to the best among the rat pack. None of these phones had rung in the last eight hours. He kept checking the signal strength: four bars, full battery. The personal phone was forever in Tiwari's pants pocket. It nestled in his V front and was on vibrate. He loved that feeling.

Another day and another train ride and this time Tiwari is humming a tune and drumming his hands on his knees. Ustad watches him and sees the pent-up energy. This man has clearly imagined the next visit and he has a list of things he wants to do. They catch an auto rickshaw at the station and the driver tries to be funny when they tell him the address. All the streetlights are working and the place seems more grimy than usual.

As they walk the dark alleyway Tiwari falters. They stand briefly below the sign. Ustad knows better than to press on.

Tiwari is down to a whisper. "I don't trust myself today," he says.

Please don't whimper, thinks Ustad.

"Will I regret this?" wonders Tiwari aloud.

"Perhaps," replies Ustad. "But you might regret turning away too."

They stumble up the stairs.

Giselle wears a floral gown. Her makeup is layered and the edges show. There is no drama. She leads Tiwari away. It will be a night of pain for her but she doesn't yet know it.

Tiwari finds a side of himself that wears her down. She goads him on initially in a practiced manner but then Tiwari takes over. He learns the meaning of the words *zabardasti* and *manmaani* as he forces himself on her again and again till her cries are genuine. He cannot stop. He has her in his control and he revels in that feeling of power, her audible pain heightening his pleasure.

When Ustad leads him away Tiwari is very quiet. They walk down the stairs in silence.

"What happened?" he finally asks him.

Tiwari grins. "She refused to tell me her name. I kept asking her and she refused."

"I see."

"I asked her to say my name," says Tiwari. "And she did, again and again. *Tiwari, Tiwari, Tiwari.*" He imitates her and it sounds awful. His grin gives way to a look of wonder as he examines his fingers, his hands, and the rest of his expanse. "She kept saying my name, *miyan*," he repeats, hearing it in his head. He flexes his fingers and hands, then does a full stretch with his arms. "*Randibaazi, miyan! Randibaazi!*" he shouts.

Ustad worries at his tone. "Why do you need to know her name?"

Tiwari shrugs. He wants to remember her by her name. His first conquest.

Later, when they are in a cab, Ustad's phone rings. His face darkens as he speaks. He suggests a good doctor. He then turns to look at his fat customer. Why, why did he have to hurt her so badly that she needed medical attention? Who is this man sitting beside him?

"Why are you in this business, my friend?" asks Tiwari, noticing his expression. "Just for the money, or for the kicks?"

Tiwari is blissfully unaware of the dark thoughts churning in Ustad's head. Ustad is no psychologist but he has seen enough men and the things they are capable of. Very rarely is he surprised anymore. He knows one thing for sure: there is no end to violence, just as there are no limits to pain and pleasure. His customers are capable of inflicting madness on others and themselves. This Tiwari looks harmless on the surface, but he needs violence because it gives him a voice.

Department of Counterintelligence

Parthasarathy had a visitor, an underling who was thought to be deaf and dumb. He stood before him and said nothing. It was common knowledge that counterintelligence sent such emissaries who were mannered in the tradition of yore, a sinister tradition where the invite was delivered as a wordless missive. *Please come. You know where.*

He walked with him to a jeep outside with an *888* license plate. They traversed a short distance, and next to a famous *bhelpuri* joint they climbed a staircase that led to a single unmarked door. The door opened to a small square room, lit like a cave and whose walls bore the mark of its occupant, Mishra. It was a personal office. In the *sarkari* world this was an aberration.

On the wall were photographs of Mishra's family, some clippings from newspapers bearing his likeness, and some quotations from people whom he presumably respected. There were portraits of leaders like Gandhi and Nehru that seemed left behind from the previous occupant. Mishra's taste had rubbed off on every inch of that office. The furniture seemed to have come from his residence and there was good-quality leather and polished teak wood.

A faint smell of tobacco lingered in the room despite the daily scrubbing.

Yet the place was a mess. Papers and files fought with books and magazines for floor space. Staff had learned not to touch a thing. There would be hell to pay if even one piece of paper was out of place.

Mishra removed his reading glasses and placed them on the table. Once Partha sat down he swept the papers away, and they fluttered to the ground. Partha watched the show in silence.

Mishra was to the point; he had dragged himself out of another meeting for this. "I need to get back quickly so I'll be succinct. Your ass is on the line. One of your sharpshooter teams has a maverick at its helm, about whom I am hearing strange rumors. The other team is headed by an unscrupulous businessman who has been spotted visiting whorehouses and has seriously injured a woman. We are beginning to look like a bunch of squabbling *chutiyas*. Ranvir Pratap and Tiwari are fighting with each other like your post is somebody's goddamn inheritance. Mr. Parthasarathy, you're getting paid a salary for this?"

It was a loaded opening. True to form Partha shook his head with ambivalence.

"You did nothing," added Mishra. "You should have intervened. Why didn't you?"

"I had my reasons," replied Partha.

"You mean allowing all this to happen—"

"Was perhaps the best course of action," completed Partha.

Mishra sat back and cupped his mouth while he lit a cigarette. He wore a slight frown because from the corner of his eye he could glimpse a folder containing his chest X-rays. A small shadow had shown up. *If we let this grow,* the doctor had said, *it will eat up your lung.* Mishra had learned a lesson at the clinic, that doing nothing could be life-threatening.

"Sir, shall we go through the material on the Third Squad together?" asked Partha. "I'd like to talk you through it."

"Be brief."

"Some years ago, when Ranvir was put in command of the Third Squad, he was tasked with assembling a team. He went about it in his own way. The normal course was to contact HR and admin and put in a recruitment request. They would assemble candidates from various internal resources, since there was no shortage of officers who wished to get into the encounter squads. But Ranvir started with a document that laid out a different set of qualities he was seeking in his personnel. It was a selection manual that he prepared himself."

"I remember it well enough," said Mishra.

"Talk about going against the grain. Ranvir Pratap turned conventional hit-squad recruiting on its head. He waltzed to the other extreme. Look at his team: two of them had weak legs, most were sensitive to bright lights, one was clumsy beyond belief and couldn't shoot, they were all poor communicators, and none of them knew the slightest thing about teamwork."

"All very fascinating, but it's history," said the chief. "Do you have anything concrete for me?"

"I had three of them tested by a psychologist," Partha replied quickly. "Munna, Kumaran, and Tapas took the test."

"Test for what?"

"Autism. Asperger's, actually."

"I see. And?" He eyed the other papers that Partha was carrying.

Partha nodded and handed over a note from Evam.

The chief read quietly. His face remained expressionless, but the fact that his cigarette died in the ashtray was a clear sign of his attention. "Interesting," he finally said. "What do you make of it?"

"Sir, what medicine does not need is literature. Unfortunately, that is what Asperger's has in spades. And it's easy to understand why."

"Why?"

"Firstly, they say it is not a disease. They describe it as a condition, a predisposition. Then they tell you there is no cure. The diagnosis comes from administering tests that are basically long lists of behavioral questions. Failing this test places you in a category. Imagine being told, *We are happy to inform you that you finally belong—but to a group of outcasts who make us very uncomfortable.*"

"Quite a story, Parthasarathy," Mishra said with amusement. "You know, this reminds me of an experience with my daughter. She had what we thought was a bad squint. Turned out to be a lazy eye. One eye was lazier than the other. The doctor had no cure. I called it a case of idiopathy."

"Meaning?"

"Meaning the doctor was an idiot and the patient was pathetic."

Partha did not know how to react; he looked down at his shoes.

"Where is this written test that you administered?" Mishra inquired.

Partha pulled out a bunch of other papers and handed them to Mishra.

The chief flipped through a yes-or-no exam. The questions seemed innocuous, which disappointed him a little. He read the first question aloud: "*Do you expect other people to know your thoughts, experiences, and opinions without you having to tell them?*" He continued to read on silently until he reached question 48. "*Do you tend to procrastinate?* Procrastinate—is that what we're doing?" This seemed to cause the chief a measure of grief. "Mr. Parthasarathy, are you telling me that based on this behavioral test, these simple observations, we can declare someone mentally fit or unfit? These questions make me nervous—even I could fail this test."

"All the best tests look simple when you take them," said Partha. "If the tests make you self-conscious, they won't work."

"Why can't they construct a test for normal people to take? After all, how do people know if they are normal in the first place? Let us say such a test existed—do you think Ranvir, Evam, or Tiwari would pass it?"

Partha chuckled, pleased that his name wasn't included with the other three.

"If a person is intelligent enough to finish this test, I wouldn't worry too much," said the chief. "But it's hard to take all this seriously."

"We have to, sir," said Partha. "On record, I mean."

The men fell silent until Mishra changed the subject: "Could you tell me more about Rana? I respect him, and so do many of my colleagues, but I haven't been able to get a clear sense of him."

Partha felt the need to unburden about this man who

worked for him, who was so good in so many ways and yet refused to ever toe a line. "Where do I begin?" he mused.

Some tea and biscuits arrived and the chief poured the tea himself. He was glad he didn't have to add milk or sugar—milk clouded good taste and sugar drowned it. Partha took this first sip tentatively, anticipating the hot brew. It was a light blend that had been steeped to perfection. He let out a deep sigh and the chief acknowledged the approval by looking less severe.

Partha broke the reverie and spoke in a confiding tone. "Rana has his own way of doing things. Right from the beginning of his career he followed a different method. He gets things done. He has an acute sense of right and wrong, and he is impatient with the slowness of the justice system. Ranvir always says: *I wear many hats and all of them fit.* He is the policeman, the prosecution, the judge, the executioner, and the priest."

"Parthasarathy, are you worried?"

"Worried? About what?"

"About Rana and Tiwari."

"Why do you ask that?"

"I'm guessing here."

"I suspect something bigger is brewing between them," confessed Partha. "I wanted to back Rana, but honestly, Karan and his colleagues scare me. They are so ruthless and their boss is headstrong and righteous. They are like vigilantes. And times have changed because the media will come down hard if they feel the police force is administering summary justice. So I am trapped between two troublesome options."

"Parthasarathy, place these tests on record. Make it look like we suspected something about the Third Squad and commissioned these tests—and that now, sure enough, our suspicions have been confirmed. And please protect Rana from this. I don't want anything on record that says he knew this from the beginning. I will in the meanwhile destroy the other material." The chief suggested administering the test on Karan as well.

Partha agreed to do so immediately. Ranvir had taken a month's medical leave but was still in Mumbai and accessible. Then Partha realized he should be going. They shook hands a little awkwardly.

"Thanks for your time," said Partha, not knowing his own fate at the end of the meeting.

"My pleasure." Mishra sounded less cold. "May I take the liberty of quoting something personal?" He didn't wait for Partha to respond. "It goes like this: *Maybe some men aren't meant to be tamed. Maybe they just need to run free till they find someone just as wild to run with them.*"

Partha understood that the chief was backing Ranvir to the hilt, which wasn't surprising since both were IPS officers. He wondered where Mishra got this quote from. Could it be a book like *The Art of War*? "May I ask your source?" he asked.

"I do not read profound books," said Mishra, smiling for the first time. "But I do watch *Sex and the City*."

The Test

After the test, which took me more than an hour, I emerged into the sunshine. I was wearing dark glasses, feeling like an aviator from a squadron that flew birds through clouds. I shielded my eyes. The test was not agreeable and it had left me feeling queasy. I felt as if a probe had been lodged inside me somewhere.

It seemed that the Ranvir Sena was in the crosshairs, and Ranvir and the three of us had been lined against a wall. And since Ranvir was on leave and I was reporting to Parthasarathy for a month, I felt exposed.

I headed home, taking the long route by foot. The hair on my neck stood against my collar, my insides were churning, and the queasy feeling would not go away even after I arrived home and set my eyes on my Nandini.

"I have a headache," I told her. "They hired a psychologist to give me a test."

I had a coffee but it wouldn't stop my yawning. Nandini gave me my prescription pills, which some idiot doctor said I needed to keep me calm. I popped them into my mouth in front of Nandini's watchful eye, then went to the washroom and spat them out.

"Don't you go into your room this early," scolded the wife. "Talk to me first. I've been waiting for you."

I needed my room right then. I needed to sit at my desk. I needed to read something that could distract me.

"What's the psychologist's name? Do you have his address?" asked Nandini.

Should I let her into my childhood, that one last place that was mine? It didn't matter; she searched my shirt pockets and found his card. Evam Bhaskar. In my presence she called him, pretending to be a mother with a special child. "Can I come now?" she asked. When he said yes, she got up abruptly and left me alone there.

Evam arrives just as Nandini does and escorts her into his ward. They enter the facility in silence. There are the usual number of children and some mothers there. They greet Evam with warmth and for a few minutes he is occupied with them. Nandini watches, fascinated. She discerns a difference in the kids; it's not too hard to make out. They smile readily and some of the mothers look at her and smile too. When she smiles back they are by her side. They need to touch her . . . and they do. They need to talk . . . and they do. The questions begin.

"Where is your child? Bring your child next time."

"First visit? You should come here. This isn't like the other places."

Nandini takes a wrench to places locked up inside her. There are moments she will remember, moments she will never forget. A couple of hours go by. As evening shadows form Evam takes her aside. And he talks to her because he needs to, and then he cannot stop. Not all that he says adds up but it fits in with that day and that moment.

"Empty your mind of the words that people gave you, the clichés and the pretense. Spend time in places like these and you will never go to a place of worship again. What gods will you seek after these children have knocked on your doors? You go home and find questions that ransack your mind. There are everyday dreams you have seen that have been left behind."

She lets him continue on and says nothing.

"We do not have the grace to deal with difference. People go mad because the differences are minor, and yet they are unforgiving. That is all that occupies them. I can hear them yearn. *Be like me, child. You are mine. Talk like me.* And when they don't, they shout at me. *Show me the fault line, doctor*, they tell me. *And set it right.*"

Fittingly, Karan had foggy dreams that night as a blanket of smog hung over the city like a slow-building cloud seeking form.

Evam sat in his office and wondered what would happen to Karan now that the tests had been handed over to Parthasarathy. Life had come full circle. The young boys that he had nurtured had grown into fine young men, they had found tough jobs, and they had done well. But things were turning against them. This need to continue to test them and perhaps brand them as "different" was disturbing. What could he do to help them?

Mumbai transforms people into characters, thought Evam, reflecting upon the colorful crew who had surrounded him the past few years. Tiwari the mind setter, Ranvir the vigilante, and the slew of associates both living and dead. Each of them was custom-made; they had no creed written against their name. Among them was Karan with one foot in each camp: a neurotypical on the one hand or an Aspie if you wished to brand him as such.

Evam decided to write a letter to Parthasarathy defending Karan against those who would seek to label him. As an academic, Partha needed some convincing that among all these people who comprised his force, Ranvir's team wasn't the one that was really strange.

Karan's chart resembled a rock amid a circle, as if it were a meteorite heading to earth. The scoring was marked below:

Your Aspie score: 123 of 200
Your neurotypical (nonautistic) score: 94 of 200
You seem to have both Aspie and neurotypical traits.

"Can anyone take this test?" asked Mishra, the CI chief, lighting a cigarette and then looking at it distastefully.

Parthasarathy nodded. "It's readily available online. This is intentional because many Aspies don't even know they have the condition."

"Then I suppose even I could be one," said the chief, stubbing out the cigarette and coughing. "The questions are deceptively easy."

Partha consulted some papers he had brought and then continued: "The world is divided into the neurotypicals and Aspies. While Karan seems to be on the cusp between the two groups, the other men on the team clearly showed up as Aspies."

"What should we do with them?" asked the chief softly.

"Sir, if you met these guys you would know that they are not very different, and without orders they are not dangerous."

After a while the chief shook his head. “It seems like more than that to me. It seems like Ranvir is rearing his own private species.”

“Sir, with all due respect, that sounds a little extreme,” replied Partha.

The chief shrugged. He wasn’t here to discuss anthropology. “What about the Fourth Squad? Soon you will tell me they are all engineered mutants and that’s what an encounter team needs.”

Partha smiled weakly. “So what do we do now? I only have a month left to run this operation.”

Mishra fiddled with another cigarette for a moment. “Let’s say we put Karan to a test. Is there someone who can give him instructions?”

Partha nodded. “The mole Desai normally deals with Karan.”

“So let’s given him a series of assignments and see how it goes. Leave the usual instructions for him. Observe him closely and report to me. I know there is some risk but we need this capability till we can build it up all over again.”

Partha was reluctant. “It’s unpredictable without Ranvir supervising.”

The chief drummed his fingers on the table and then pulled out his pipe and a packet of fragrant tobacco. He spent a few moments cleaning his pipe, tapping it, eyeing it closely, and then filling it.

“Shall we go ahead then?” asked Partha.

The chief was busy lighting his pipe but he seemed to nod almost imperceptibly.

“Women are always right about these things,” said Nandini. She pressed the iron down on his uniform, the steam hissing out. "What are these white patches below the arms, and here in the collar? They never go away."

"Sweat," said Karan.

She splashed some water on them and ran the iron again. "I told you the gas cylinder was leaking and I knew it the moment I entered the kitchen in the morning. I was right, wasn't I?"

"Yes, you were."

"If I hadn't insisted you would never have replaced that cylinder—and what did the gas company tell you?"

"It would have burst in your face, they said."

She picked up the shirt and bit a loose thread with her teeth. "I didn't tell you but I had a feeling about that boy Sudhir next door. I told him to wear a helmet and I even spoke to his mother. Finally he bought one, and guess what?"

"I know, I know."

"Of course you know—he had an accident a few days later." She looked up at him to see if he was still listening. He had almost nodded off to sleep. It was eleven p.m. and he'd had a long day. "I haven't been sleeping well lately," she added.

"I know," he said again.

"Karan, I have a premonition, a bad one." He was alert now. "I keep waking up in a cold sweat. I shouldn't be saying this but I think you should take a leave—a long one. We could take time off and travel."

"I can't. You know I couldn't just leave work like that."

She slammed the iron down. "You don't get it, Karan. I am not being frivolous. I know this may sound foolish, but I'm really worried about you. It just feels like something's going to happen, and everyone else realizes it too, but they're all standing around like spectators."

"Nandini, why do you have to—"

"Fine, forget it. At least take care of the rat."

"Where is it?"

"In the kitchen, inside the trap. Just dump it in a bucket of water and be done with it. And please shut the door when you come back."

"Sorry," he said, after returning from the kitchen a few minutes later. "I can't do it."

"You can't kill a rat?"

"It's just so small," he said. "I tried, I lifted the trap and there were squeaky sounds, I dipped it into the bucket but it started splashing around and I could see really small bubbles come up. I couldn't leave the trap inside."

"Aaaargh."

They didn't speak for a while and the ironing continued.

"Can I just set it free outside the chawl?" he asked.

Encounter Thirty-Two

A smog-ridden city gets a hazy dawn. Sunrise arrives an hour late on the western seaboard of Mumbai. The orange orb rises slowly, reluctantly, as if the municipality has to winch it up from the Arabian Sea. The city develops a weak and watery gaze.

I hold my breath and let it go and it floats away like the thought I slept with, a thought that I do not wish to remember. I stray to my window. Potted plants struggle in windowsills while a seedling which has taken root inside a water pipe thrives. A woman spots me from a balcony as she hangs up clothes. She drops her arms and adjusts her sari, covering her breasts. I turn away slowly, pretending I haven't seen her generous curves.

The household is asleep and I have to leave early. On the refrigerator is a scribbled message that says, *Movie this evening?* I want to reply, but how can you say no?

"There are many ways of saying no, Karan," Nandini once told me. "One way is to just say it."

I had returned to the office building the night before. Police buildings have poor security because we are smug and we do not expect thieves. So it was all very easy. I wanted to find out what these people thought of me. As I walked the corridors I snuck into the records room and to my surprise I quickly found what I was looking for: notes from Parthasarathy and even Evam.

Partha writes in longhand with a fountain pen using lots of loops and flourishes. He has a theory for me and people like me, and a category too: the category is called Asperger's syndrome. Evam uses a typewriter. That machine is worn out and some letters look faded. This is what he said:

> *Your question is: is he capable of violence outside of instruction? I am not sure that can be predicted. There was a case of an encounter specialist who turned rogue and was conveniently called a deviant. That fellow was violent, genetically violent. On the surface there was nothing wrong. He was clean. But this cold, ruthless man began to act without instruction. They tried telling him to stop and he couldn't. Bloody mystery. It seems he was trying to clean up all of Mumbai. Finally he killed himself. And he left a suicide note that had one word. "Atonement."*

Atonement. I like the sound of that word. I can relate to it. I like Christian themes like redemption and resurrection. I also like the thought of reincarnation. What I don't like are descriptions like "slow-witted," "socially awkward," and "unable to sympathize or empathize": that, according to them, was me.

Partha has made a notation in Evam's file:

> *But what explains Karan's ability to shoot? Even in the glare of lights he can pick off targets. It is unreal. Find out how. If you feel we do not have time, tell me so.*

There was also a memo from counterintelligence that contained my name. I was a mystery and they don't like those. But I could explain myself to them if they bothered asking because I have spent many months doggedly reading about how the eye sees, how the brain senses and analyzes, and then how the muscles act. I am a "neurotic reader," after all.

Mind-reading, empathy, imitation learning, and the evolution of language come from neurons in the brain that we call "mirror neurons." Autistic people have very few. People like me with so-called minor forms have a few more mirror neurons than the truly autistic, but not quite enough. We cannot look at you and feel for you. Your feelings and gestures do not fire mirror neurons in our brains. So we do not empathize, and hence our communication and interaction seems off-key.

But I have one mirror neuron that fires beautifully every time I have a gun in my hand. That's because I have seen Ranvir with a gun and he is the best. We practiced day and night. I watched and I have learned. People dare not blink in our presence.

The morning sounds of the chawl: the *bhaiya* on his Enfield with the milk cans, the newspaper vendors dropping and sorting bundles on the pavement, and the cleaning *chokras* chattering in different tongues. A few bikes start up and one car refuses to. I sip my morning cup and slip out of the door sideways and shut it quietly. Outside is clear, or so I thought. I bump into my comely neighbor, inappropriately, and ruffle the front of her nightgown. She frowns and untangles her hair from my shirt button, seeming irritated. I should say something but I can't find the right words.

I tiptoe past a door where an old woman lives. She has this habit of calling out to me.

"Manu? Is it you?" she says, every time.

I don't get it. Her hearing is so good yet her eyesight is so awful. Should I tell her she's making a mistake?

"Manu *beta*, could you raise me up?"

That makes me stop. I enter her room for the first time and help her sit up, get her glasses, and pour her some water. And I leave before she can say anything else. When I reach my jeep, the sun hits my eyes and suddenly all my unspoken thoughts and words come out in a rush as if someone pressed a button in my head.

I was thinking last night that I should stop sleeping in the den. It's not a place of rest.

I wanted to reply to that note on the fridge, saying, in a nice way, that I might not make it to the film. And I wanted to tell my comely neighbor, who thought I was a pig, that people who do not speak are not as rude as those who do.

As I start my jeep I check my pockets, my holster, and my briefcase. I drive slowly, take three right turns, and arrive right back where I began. Nobody has followed me today, and the chawl is as I left it. I fiddle with my phone. Should I make a call? Who should I call?

I call Ranvir Pratap. He likely will not answer since he's on medical leave, but going through the motions is still comforting. I hope it's nothing serious. I cut the engine of the idling jeep and wait, then hang up. My thoughts drift to whether I should have left home the way I did: like a thief.

Nandini told me, "Sometimes you should wake me up before you go, even if I don't like it."

"Wouldn't that inconvenience you? Wouldn't that cause another—"

"Argument? Karan, without conflict things will die."

The phone rings. On assignment day it always sounds different.

"You are in play," says Desai. "Are you set?"

"Yes, I'm already on the road."

"Good. Fill up your tank and head for Flora Fountain."

There's a line of cars at the gas station because of an imminent price hike. I am stuck between cars and have to wait. I try to remember what today is all about. I have already visualized how it will happen.

My eye is a fitted lens that pans the scene inside the office building. I slow time and movement breaks down into frames. The target, a gifted assassin, will emerge from an elevator, in one motion, to take in the tableau and pull his weapon. That is the moment I will shoot, even as he progresses into my vision. It will be close, heart-thuddingly close. It is heady to imagine this happening. The rush comes; it comes to me in one smooth wave and that is the only recoil I allow.

The man I have pursued for two days is a lowlife. The more I get to know of him the less I like what I'm doing. This one's not worth my time. He looks like a regular guy, of medium height, light-brown complexion, dark hair, normal features, and a forgettable profile. But he's a gifted assassin and I've been chosen to kill him.

There are a few things that are different about this assignment.

"Don't look like yourself when you go," Desai had told me, his voice cracking.

"How do I do that?" I asked.

He said nothing.

"Why?" I tried.

"It's nothing personal," he said. That meant it was. This was Desai at his obtuse best.

At home Nandini walked up to me, put her mouth to my shirt, and bit off yet another loose thread. She always had something to say on days like this.

"You're on assignment, aren't you? I know it, I can feel it."

As I let myself out I bumped into the child from next door. He looked startled. "Sugar," he said, pulling a cup out from his pocket. He smiled. I carried that smile with me. I needed it.

I'm standing at the head of the stairs facing the elevator shaft. It's an old Mumbai building in a district whose best days were captured in glossy coffee-table books. The staircase is wooden and the lift is an old open-door Schindler that clicks and rattles. The lift doors are made of metal grating in a criss-cross pattern and they have to be manually operated. There are two doors on this sliding lift, on opposite sides, and my information is that this weasel will emerge in front of where I stand.

The elevator arrives and the attendant pulls the sliding iron mesh aside. And he emerges foot-first. In my frame I see one hand holding an attaché. The other moves like Napoleon. He is half out when he meets my gaze and his other foot has dragged by the time he meets my bullet. The frame shifts. One hand is still under an armpit where his gun has begun to glint. The other has spilled the attaché. The frame moves. The attaché splits wide open as it falls. It slides to my feet.

The man keeps walking toward me with a look of frozen surprise. He was fractionally slow. My disguise had worked.

I think it was the way I stood. I wasn't facing him as he would have expected. I had half turned and I pulled off the shot with my back facing him.

He is close enough to whisper to me as he begins to fall. He comes to rest with his head on these photographs that have spilled from his attaché. He still looks surprised and, peering down, I am too. The photographs are of me. Me at home, me in the jeep, and me with Nandini eating at roadside stands. He had blown my cover and I was his target. He had tracked me and shot these photos and I did not know.

I lay my police badge down on the floor to keep people calm. A team arrives breathlessly from the nearby building. I collect the photographs and head home.

"What have you brought?" asks Nandini.

"Something personal," I reply.

"Wash your feet," she reminds me.

This is how you leave death at the door. That night I clean my gun in the chawl veranda under a moonlit sky and stay on my knees long after. I ignore the curious eyes of children with imagination. I am not a hero today. For the first time what I have done is personal. It feels different. All along I had practiced to be a hunter but today I am the hunted as well.

The next day Desai calls and I cannot speak. Something has changed inside me.

"I knew you would get him," he says. "He was very good. Were you wearing a disguise?"

Partha called the CI chief and he was kept on hold for five minutes. Finally he came on the line and his tone was impatient.

"What happened?"

"Karan got him. The target had been following him and had all his details it seems. God knows who tipped him off."

"What do you mean, God knows, *banchod?*" screamed Mishra. "Find out the fucking leak, take some bamboo, and plug it. We cannot have our sharpshooters getting compromised."

After a while Mishra calmed down.

"I have to say, Karan is as good as he ever was," said Partha. "I admire his skill level. He is the only one who could have pulled this off."

"You should admire his resolve more than his skill," replied Mishra. "Give him the difficult cases. He is your best man. And please keep an eye on Tiwari. I don't want any more leaks."

"Sir, in light of your vast experience, do you see any holes in Karan?'

Mishra took his time before replying. "Of course he has weaknesses. I have studied his cases and I can see them."

"Sir?"

"You're once again asking me to do your work for you."

"Sir, please," pleaded Partha. "Do you see an end game?"

Mishra finally relented. "Karan's file is interesting. There is no consistent genealogy in his thirty encounters. But there has been an impact on him. What has and will continue to diminish him are encounters that pose questions."

Book III

Encounter Thirty-Three

"Imight take a long walk," joked Nandini when her contract came up for renewal. "Frankly, I'm getting tired," she added.

The rest of the Heritage Walk team sat in silence till she couldn't handle it.

"We all do this for a reason, right?" she said. They nodded. It wasn't for the money, they all liked to say. "Fine, three more months," she finally relented.

Nandini was a popular guide and her tours were usually sold out. She had a different take on the familiar, so even locals would come by to visit places they already knew. A walk with Nandini became a reason to visit old haunts. People swapped stories from their previous visits and it was fun. The society that organized these walks could not afford to let her go. The money they raised was useful for their charities. Nandini knew she couldn't leave, so why not force them to let you go? She decided to get wacky. She thought she could put people off by announcing a Dharavi Walk, one that squeezed you through the heart of the big slum. They ended up with a waitlist. Her follow-up to this was the Grant Road by Night Walk that covered the red-light district. This had an even longer waitlist.

She bought new shoes, unique ones for each of the

walks. She dressed differently and she spoke in a local dialect in some of the places they went to. It bordered on the theatrical. Things happened on these walks because they involved living spaces and people, not monuments, relics, or history.

She bought a map of the city, an old one. She bought many old maps. And the walks became Tracing the Map, returning to a moment in time where the landscape and topography was revealed in its absence.

She wanted to buy peace with Karan. She wanted him to think about what he was doing. It was best not to push too hard, for men who dance on the edge of knives shouldn't be questioned about where they stand.

She knew Karan was still following her. She still tried to follow him sometimes too. Yes, she would admit to it. The Karan Walk she did alone. She saw him leave every day but sometimes his manner would give him away. There were days he would touch the head of the neighbor's child on the way out, a reminder of the glaring absence in their own home.

Today was the Other Dharavi Walk. They started by visiting Nariman Point, Cuffe Parade, and Breach Candy.

"These are the shore temples of Mumbai," she said.

There was no shock and awe. All they could see were bland straight-line structures, drawn to fill pockets. At least there was no pretension.

"Rich men have built their Dharavis," she explained.

There was a poverty of architecture, an absence of planning, and a complete lack of maintenance. Each building showed up the next.

"There is an aesthetic somewhere," promised Nandini.

She led them to the waterfront as the sun set and

the missing aesthetic arrived. The looming darkness hid the structures and the lights began to blink. The bays of Mumbai were beautiful by night.

Water lapped the concrete walls and some spray scaled them. Today was another day. Another man would meet Karan for remembrance.

Tiwari sits in his office and stares. He has spent the last hour goggle-eyed, watching a ray of sunlight traverse his desk. Dust particles busy themselves in the yellow diagonal.

"Collider," blurts Pandey. He has read about the new scientific experiment.

"What?" says Tiwari.

Pandey the linguist looks at his boss and his young, alert mind finds new words; moribund and desultory describe Tiwari today.

"Sir," he says, "this Dr. Evam has designs on you."

Tiwari shrugs.

"Our immediate concern should be the next twenty-four hours, sir," Pandey suggests. His confidence with his boss is increasing by the minute.

Sunlight disappears. A cloud bank moves in, ready to deposit. There is a strange light outside, a precursor to rain that seems to affect Tiwari. "I am unable to get off this chair and do anything," he despairs. "What weighs me down?"

It is the weight of suspicion's ax that rests upon his plump shoulders. He wonders what Ranvir must be up to and thinks he should be second-guessing him. Tiwari wants this over quickly. When you are helpless in battle you would rather see the end than watch your wounds take shape. It is a gray August evening; it is a time when rain follows rain. Cups of hot tea haven't helped. Tiwari wraps his arms around himself and reflects aloud.

"My *khabaris* are common folk. Their daily life occupies them. They have to defend themselves against hunger, despair, corruption, and disease. One of them will have to deal with Karan, this man who is like a lethal ghost."

Pandey has to say something. "Sir, you think Ranvir-sir will do something?"

Tiwari sighs. "Let me spell it out for you. One of my best *khabaris* has to catch a flight to the Gulf of Oily Wealth. I have to make sure he gets away. And the singular problem is that he is on a police hit list and his name was assigned to Ranvir's team. Imagine, I have to protect one of my men from the police force. I cannot do it officially so I can either hope that Ranvir's team does not find out, or I have to be devious."

"How will they know if you don't tell them?" asks Pandey.

"There are leaks everywhere, Pandey. One day you will understand. Anyway, if there's no movement from Ranvir's team, it means my *khabari* is safe."

The call soon comes.

Tiwari sits up with a jerk as he listens. He loosens his collar because he needs room to breathe. "Karan is on the move," he mutters. "They have cut him loose. He has that walk we all know by now, that slow, deliberate shuffle he adopts when he's hunting. It's a strange thing to look at; it's almost as if his feet do not belong to the earth."

"They are wasting no time, sir. Target?"

"There's only one," says Tiwari. "I can see a sure thing. Karan will try to kill him by the day's end."

The thought of a killer on the move captivates Pandey. "Sir, we will have him followed?"

"Easier said than done." Tiwari starts to pace the room. How do you follow a madman with a gun? How can you even find someone who could keep up with Karan's meanderings? Karan was a wanderer when he killed. You never knew where he would go next or the path he would take. "When the time comes he disappears," says Tiwari. "Give me my phones. I will assign my lookouts in every locality. My people are in every suburb."

"We still need to tail him, sir. Someone should try to get evidence."

That's a good idea. "Like who?"

"People who are familiar with the roads. The weather forecast is grim, so we need people who can find their way around in such conditions."

A light goes off in Pandey's head. He examines a list of their men and picks two names. He chooses two former classmates of his, Dilip "DJ" Jadhav and Kunal "KK" Kirkire. They have interesting backgrounds. Like him they were graduates in the humanities, which in India was a degree for wastrels. The two were also part-time musicians who played cover songs at social functions. In no time Jadhav and Kirkire were the new-age jobless: English-speaking, confident, some would say cocky, and proud of their state of hopeless enlightenment.

We filched toilet paper so we could write. We bought the girlie magazine Debonair *so we could read. We saw* Waiting for Godot *and stayed till the end. We would spend our daylight hours in a café. We would hang about, busy-looking and broke.*

Nothing matters. None of this matters if you believe you have potential. The best years are always ahead.

These thoughts ran through their heads while they were seated in a canteen.

DJ became a bus driver and KK a conductor. Together they handled Route No. 84 Ltd., a bus route that was an institution. It was a long and winding journey that traversed the length of Mumbai's western suburbs. Every morning the two would meet at the Mantralaya building near Nariman Point. KK would smoke a cigarette and DJ would empty a *gutka* packet into his mouth. They would then walk to Hutatma Chowk and board the first service of the day. They would end up in the distant suburb of Goregaon. From there it was back to the *chowk*; another smoke and another *gutka*. And they would do this loop till the day elapsed. They would stand at day's end on tired feet and spit into a gutter. For ten years this was their life.

One day DJ says to KK, "Kirkire, *you* drive this bus from now on."

"Why?"

"Look into my eyes," says DJ. "What do you see?"

KK doesn't need to look. "Retinal discharge. It comes from boredom and the fear of daydreaming and falling asleep at the wheel." KK peers down at his own legs instead. He has varicose veins to show for the years of standing all day long on the bus; they were ugly, these knotted threads that stitched his legs together. He could not bear the sight of them.

Tiwari's offer to join the police force came like manna to the duo, who had been classmates of Pandey's years earlier. It gave them a chance to put their feet up most of the time. When asked, Tiwari was blunt.

"Your job description? Rat on your neighbors and rat on your friends."

They were tasked with keeping track of three localities, places where they roamed and whose people they had known for many long years. And they had to divulge anything notable that happened; they had to follow people from time to time to unearth secrets or gather information. They buried their qualms and their misgivings. An honest job had been no friend of theirs.

The Karan assignment was their first serious mission, and they dropped everything when Pandey called. Tiwari gave them a Handycam. It was small and easy to use.

"Take this and shoot Karan," he told them, laughing at his own joke. The two stood and stared at Tiwari. He showed them a portfolio of Karan. Almost every photograph had him looking down at some point below the camera. "Memorize this face," he ordered.

The two stared some more.

Tiwari got up from his chair and paced the room in a slow shuffle. He looked like a drunk trying to walk straight. "Remember this walk," he told them. "This is how he moves."

Examining the two, Tiwari had doubts. DJ and KK were a little frantic and they sometimes held hands. Tiwari was terrified of the sight of men holding hands. These two were constantly touching, and even now a hand was over a shoulder. Tiwari looked at Pandey, who shrugged.

"Any questions?' Tiwari asked them.

DJ held up his hand. "Sir, is he a criminal?" he asked. "I mean, is he dangerous?"

These were two tough questions. "Yes and no," said Tiwari. Again the irony delighted him. It was best these two remained clueless.

The rains started early. The clouds had gathered through the night and a humid stillness had camped over the city till it felt swollen. The clouds broke at five a.m. just as the milk vans and newspaper vendors began making their rounds. The first showers pooled the debris on the streets and sidewalks. The drains swirled and the night rats scurried for cover. Street dogs sought shelter under awnings and morning walkers held umbrellas, scoured the skies, and marched onward.

It was a weekday. Office-goers took an additional five minutes in bed, did a couple of additional stretches, had a wistful moment in front of a mirror, and then got into the zone. White collars, blue collars, and day workers dressed up, wired themselves, and left hurriedly, half-expecting the heavens to open up. The drizzle intensified and by noon it looked like a monsoon.

DJ and KK were in limbo when Tiwari called. He asked them to get going. He said he would provide minute-by-minute instructions.

"Just keep rolling and keep shooting. You'll spot this guy Karan soon. Do not let him out of your sight."

They cursed in unison and stared at the cloudy skies.

"Father Sperm," said DJ.

They stared at the wet streets.

"Mother Egg," said KK.

They eyed each other with mock seriousness.

"We are bastards all."

They spent a full day in the field and the rain made it messy. They pulled out all their rain gear: plastic caps that covered their ears, plastic gum boots that bit their feet, and black plastic overcoats that made them sweat. They looked like a couple of miserable crows. Outside the water had started to flow along the sidewalks. Armies of umbrellas marched from station to station. Cars and buses honked ceaselessly and tempers flared. A few children from the slums laughed at the madness and walked on the road dividers, holding out their spindly arms and gathering water.

A bus rushed past, splashing them with murk from the gutter. KK kept a straight face. Water was collecting in his right shoe and tickling his toe. The damn boot wouldn't come off easily so he had to bear with it.

"Who is this Karan fellow?" asked DJ. "Is he important enough for this?"

KK was perceived to be the senior among the two and had been given some additional instructions. He had been asked to keep a fair distance.

"He's a VIP. He's also mental."

DJ shrugged his shoulders. He motioned to their Handycam. "Is this waterproof?"

"Yes and no," said KK, mimicking Tiwari. They laughed for a while. The two had long since found solace in misery. "Let's go."

It is a day for disembodied voices. The first is when a call comes from an unregistered number. There is no introduction, just a set of orders and a promise of more to follow. Where has Desai gone? Karan is given five minutes. Then the same voice calls again. "Ready to go," it says.

He walks to the cupboard and opens the drawer. The gun is dull and heavy. He holds it in his right hand, cups his left hand under his right wrist, and takes aim in the mirror. Outside the rain is pelting down. He pulls on a raincoat, yanks the hood over his head, and steps out into the streets.

This is a dream, he tells himself once again. He glances down and watches his feet move. His hands stay dry in the raincoat. He walks with no purpose because it isn't yet time. Karan crosses the road, walks awhile, then crosses back again. Voices follow in his wake. So do KK and DJ.

Nobody is supposed to know Karan's assignment today and, curiously, no one actually does. He is carrying a new phone with him and takes orders from a new controller. After half an hour of meandering he stands listlessly under a bus shelter. Life pauses as he watches rain thread its way down the metal roof. He feels uneasy. He likes a clear plan that is of his own making, but this assignment is different. The quarry is known but the staging is impromptu and this makes him nervous. In his line of work he needs to prepare, get under the target's skin, and understand how the person would react. He has to choose the place and time. This ensures there's no room for surprises.

But he has learned not to question Ranvir. If Ranvir Pratap wants to keep the staging unknown then he surely has his reasons for it. Ranvir is a stickler for detail and he makes his team go over every step again and again till he tells them to fuck off.

"No more thinking now. You hear me?"

"Yes sir."

"If you want to be successful, don't listen to inner voices."

"Yes sir."

"Don't worry. Just rely on yourself to execute. You have been trained well."

The traffic light at Worli Naka turns red. Karan crosses the road and then another. A boy is selling books wrapped in plastic sheets. He looks hungry. Karan hands him a bill and picks up a pirated best seller. He holds it above his head for meager protection and walks. He takes the road to the seaface. Angry brown surf is scaling the wall and the parapet is getting a drenching. Karan stands out of range. Young couples are sitting on the wall with knees bent and arms wrapped around each other, as if daring the sea.

He needs a distraction to occupy his mind but doesn't find any. Finally he turns, walks in the opposite direction, and hails a cab. "Dadar," he says, and the cabbie takes off. It is an old Fiat. It rattles and shakes, the roof is low, and he has to crouch. Outside it is pouring. He rolls up the window but a gap remains. The cab has wipers that swing uselessly and the cabbie leans out of his window with a cloth and wipes the windscreen as he drives. It is a dark afternoon. At Dadar he gets out near a bus stop and catches a bus to Horniman Circle. He sits at the back and pretends to read a newspaper. It takes over an hour to get there.

In the backseat of a taxi, DJ and KK strain their eyes to keep track of the red bus.

"This is like a treasure hunt," says DJ. "What's he doing?"

KK is listening to some music and doesn't respond.

The cabbie is humming a *bhajan*. He has white hair and vermilion on his forehead and he looks like a pandit.

At Horniman Circle they jump out in a hurry. It's four in the afternoon and the rain has subsided to a light mist. Karan walks to Flora Fountain. He keeps crossing the roads on the way. After a few minutes they realize he's doing this without thinking. There is no pattern. Karan stops at a *paan-wallah* and buys some *mawa* in a small plastic packet. He opens it, grinds some in his palm, tosses it into his mouth, and walks away.

"You think he knows we're following him?" asks DJ.

KK snorts. "You fucking moron, can't you see that he's also following someone? We're traveling like a convoy, all of us following each other."

Ahead of Karan is a man of medium build who is doing his best to move in an evasive manner, zigzagging ahead. Karan seems to be tracking him expertly by keeping some distance and many people between them. Every once in a while Karan gets a call. And then he waits and allows the quarry to disappear. Then he moves away in a different direction and magically catches up with the man.

"He's being guided by a team on the phone," whispers DJ.

"Why are you whispering, you moron?" asks KK.

They are taking turns running the camera. So far they have a street-side documentary of Mumbai on a rainy day.

KK calls Tiwari and describes the man who Karan is following.

"Keep following him," says Tiwari. "And be careful." He hopes Karan doesn't discover and then target this twosome. That would be a travesty.

But DJ and KK are careless and they run headfirst into the man they have all been following. He is wearing a white shirt and dark pants. His shirt is open to his navel and a heavy gold chain hangs around his neck. He's talking on the phone while holding an umbrella in his other hand. He walks right into KK and drops the umbrella and then the phone. He curses, glares at KK, and hails a cab. As the vehicle draws near he peeks into the window and says, "Airport?"

The cabbie nods and he gets in. And then Karan passes right by them and hails another cab. "Airport," he says. And they are off.

"Fuck." KK looks around for a cab but there are none to be found.

"Call Tiwari," says DJ. "Tell him we need wheels."

Karan's cab is old and slow and he's having a hard time keeping up with the other vehicle. During the long ride to the airport he gets three calls. His controller keeps urging him to hurry up.

"You are losing your quarry!" he screams. "What were you waiting for?"

"I didn't wait for anything," says Karan.

"You were standing around and getting *mawa* made for yourself. Do you think we cannot see you? Is this a time to indulge your vices?"

Karan takes a deep breath and counts to three. "Mister," he says with a degree of annoyance, "I thought I was being followed. There were two guys who were blundering about behind me trying to act smart."

"I see," says the surprised controller. Why would someone follow Karan? "Are you sure you were being followed?"

"Yes, I'm sure. I've never seen anyone as amateurish as these two. They were also filming my movements."

There's a long pause and a murmur of voices in the background.

"Don't worry about who is behind you. We will take care of them. Be alert when you reach the airport. And do not harm this guy."

"Could you repeat that?" says Karan. This did not make sense.

"Do not harm this fellow. He's a decoy. We know it but we are pretending we don't."

DJ is on the phone with Tiwari. They are on a local train and making good progress. Tiwari asks them to head to the departure area outside the international airport. They get off at Vile Parle Station and rush to a cab, but the driver refuses to move till he has four passengers. KK breaks into Marathi and tells him he will finish his family, his society, his ancestors, and his unborn progeny. KK is not an impressive physical specimen but his eyes are raving mad. They get moving. It is still raining. The skies have darkened again and it is 5:45 p.m. when they reach the airport. They keep some distance from the building and train their camera and wait. The phone rings after a while, jolting them alert.

Tiwari is down to a whisper. "Go to the parking lot," he says. "Karan is headed there behind that same fellow."

"This better be good," mutters DJ.

Tiwari hangs up. They hurry toward the parking lot. Cars are rushing by in every direction. The streetlights blink on around them, forming patterns on the water that has collected on the roads. They are completely soaked and equally miserable.

"This was your idea," says DJ. "Following a wordless, expressionless piece of wood all around town. Seriously, just tell me, man—who is this guy?"

KK considers the request and then relents: "He's an encounter cop. He kills people for a living. The bad news is that he is very good at it. His name is Karan."

DJ swallows. "An encounter cop? Of the shooting variety? *The* Karan?"

KK nods. DJ does not want to hear what he's hearing. "He doesn't look or behave like an encounter cop."

"DJ, for once you are right," says KK. "Just relax."

They are standing under a bus shelter near the parking lot. A cab draws up with tires screeching. They recognize the license plate and in an instant Karan gets out. He is wearing an overcoat and he walks toward them with his hands in his pockets. He stands at the other end of the bus stop and observes the arriving cars.

The camera is now running. Karan gets a call. He holds the phone to his ear and through the drizzle and the honking cars they hear him arguing with somebody. He stands in the rain and his shoulders slump.

"What should I do now!" he shouts.

He shuts his phone and shoves it into his inner pocket. Taxis are streaming in and people are spilling out and running toward the terminals with wheelie bags. The normal approach to the terminals is clogged and cars have lined up beyond so passengers have to trudge over from some distance.

DJ and KK are breathless. They can sense something is about to happen. KK's phone vibrates. He slides it to his ear and hears a strange noise. After a moment, he realizes it's the sound of Tiwari burping on the other end.

"Nothing has happened yet, sir," says KK. "But this man we are following, he seems tense."

Tiwari laughs nervously. This is a crucial operation for him and he isn't happy that he has to depend on DJ and KK for its success. "There will be two people who look the same," he says. "One is a decoy who will arrive first; the other man, one of my best informers, will come later. We should allow him to catch an international flight and escape."

In reality, they both arrive at the same moment. KK peers through the rain and spots two men stepping out of different cabs. They are both of medium build. Each wears a light shirt and dark pants, and both have phones glued to their ears. Now what? Karan glances from one to the other. He dials a number.

"There are two," Karan says to his controller. "The rain has picked up again and they look the same. What should I do? There's no time."

They watch Karan write something on his palm. He curses as his hands are wet. The two men have gathered their luggage and are heading toward the terminal.

"You want me to what?" he shouts again. "You said to follow this man, and I have done so. You said to lose him, I did that. Now you say he's a decoy and you want me to shoot him?"

The phone squawks.

"The other guy!" shouts Karan. "The other guy, the real guy is also here. I can get him." He listens intently, shaking his head, clearly unhappy. "You want me to shoot the decoy and not the man I'm supposed to? I don't know anything about the decoy." He listens again. "Fine, if those are the orders. Just say it again, say it aloud." He pauses and then nods. "Okay, I got it."

He's in a hurry. Karan glances at his palm, dials the smudged number, and looks up. "Hello," he says, then waits.

Both men are again on their phones.

"Abbas?" he says, then pauses for some kind of response. Both the men look around but Karan remains uncertain. They are approaching the entrance of the terminal.

Karan speaks again: "Abbas *bhai*, you are wearing a white shirt and black pants. I can see you. Don't ask me where I am."

One of the men halts in his tracks.

"Abbas *bhai*, turn around please," says Karan.

One of the two men moves first. His white shirt is wet and so are his dark slacks. He darts his head from side to side. And then the other man turns around as well. There are two flashes of light and two muffled thumps. Karan shoots the second man in the knees, two shots in rapid succession: left knee, right knee. DJ and KK watch in horror as blood spurts, the man drops his phone and crumples, his hands stretching outward for support. He falls slowly onto his shattered knees and he screams. His shirt falls open and the headlights of a car illuminate his bare chest; no gold chain. Karan notices that and shoots him in the head—a single shot in the middle of the forehead. The man falls backward, a pool of red spilling onto the road. DJ and KK realize they are running toward the fallen figure out of sheer instinct. Their camera is rolling and they focus on the man's face. He is far gone. DJ falls to his knees next to the guy's brains and gags. KK whirls around to find Karan right behind him. His eyes are dark and his manner is calm. He holds out his left-hand palm upward. The right still brandishes a gun. KK gives him the Handycam. Karan drops it onto the road and crushes it with his boot. A phone rings.

"Answer it," Karan orders.

"It's okay, Mr. Karan," says KK.

"I said answer it. I'm not going to ask you again."

KK drops the phone into a puddle where it fizzles and dies. He then looks up and Karan is gone. DJ has fled to the bus stop. He's leaning against a pillar with his mouth open.

There's a small packet of *mawa* lying where Karan had been standing, its red color bleeding into the other red puddle by KK's feet. In the distance they hear the rumble of the Western Express Highway, red buses trundling along on the overpass beside yellow-black taxis. One of them would be the 84 Ltd.

They walk the long road, bare-headed in the rain. They reach the bus stop and take the familiar ride to Goregaon.

DJ cannot stop babbling. Something in his brain has become dislodged. KK sits next to him and tries to ignore him.

"My mother told me not to deal with you," DJ tells KK. "She always said you were trouble. *Nothing good will ever come of that* chokra, she said. *He looks wild and he looks stupid.*"

"Thanks," says KK without moving an inch. "You want to know what your mother needs?"

"That guy fired three shots. He didn't spray bullets. Instead: one, two, three; left knee, right knee, forehead. Is this a movie, brother? Are we in some kind of movie?"

"You were filming it," deadpans KK.

DJ looks at his shoulder bag as if it contains a snake. "We are in danger," he announces. "People will think we still have all this on tape and now they will come after us. The whole underworld will be on our case. Abbas's *bhais* will be drooling over our pictures and sharpening their knives. And that shooter Karan will come first. He will need only one shot for me."

"He should aim for your mouth first. It's always open," says KK.

"No, first he will get you. You were the one making calls from there. But you were so calm, man. Didn't you see Abbas writhing on the ground?"

KK pats his damp hair with a handkerchief. At least the traffic is moving smoothly, the office crowds returning home on the other side of the road. "Do you have any battery left?"

DJ looks at him blankly.

"I'm asking about your phone, you dildo. Come on, snap out of it."

They eventually alight at Nana Nani Park, a haven for old souls. They sit there and wait for nightfall.

Dilip Jadhav and his best friend Kunal Kirkire are about to part ways after the most eventful day of their lives. A curious exhilaration has exercised pressure on their bladders. They relieve themselves in Brihanmumbai Public Sauchalya, a dark alley where the pavement slopes toward a gutter. These men have aged in a single evening. Somewhere they long for the days of their youth.

Day Two

The airport encounter made the newspapers the next day, and there was a color photograph depicting the body lying in the pouring rain with a plane taking off into the clouds overhead. It was a dramatic shot. Some footage made it on the nightly television news as well. Importantly, Karan was named as the alleged "rogue officer" who, it was claimed, had taken out the wrong person in a botched encounter. The long rap sheet of the "victim" wasn't mentioned. All of Mumbai instead saw a file photograph of Karan in uniform. He looked young and dashing, belying the picture that had been painted of him. To those in the force it was obvious who had instigated this.

Immediately after the incident, Tiwari started working the phones and raised hell. When nothing happened he called on Parthasarathy, asking for immediate action against Karan. He wanted a joint meeting ASAP. with Ranvir to demand an explanation and perhaps some blood. "We cannot set a precedent by doing nothing," he kept repeating. "This is not a mistake. It is rank insubordination." For once Ranvir was quiet when spoken to.

Parthasarathy knew this thing would not die down easily because the gangs would go after Tiwari. This was a breach of trust, and in the *khabari* business it was a serious offense. Anticipating trouble, Tiwari had tried to deflect blame and had gone ahead and released some details to the press. But he needed an official response from Partha.

Where was Karan?

That night you harbored guilt. (Evam told you that this was natural.) You walked the streets holding a collapsible umbrella, you wandered into flooded alleys, and you whiled away time sitting in small Udipi establishments run by the Shetty clan, drinking strong South Indian coffee. You were hungry. You went to the Madras Café in Dadar TT, taking your time to finish a plate of *idlis* and a huge family-size *dosa* that you had to fold into thirds. You were tired and wet and miserable but you could not rest. You rode trains aimlessly for a few hours till the services began to dwindle. You wished you could go home quietly, wash your feet, and creep into your bed. You kept your phone switched off.

You were scared. (Evam told you that this was natural too.) You had no idea why you were scared. You had done something wrong. But it wasn't that simple. If it was that simple you would have been fine after a while. You had done what you thought was right and you did it without thinking. Your second nature was not what you thought it was. You were human, not just a killing machine that followed orders blindly. You should feel relieved to know that. But you were scared.

You wished to know what Ranvir Pratap thought about what you had done. *He is your umbilical cord*, said Evam. Now you knew why you were scared.

You wanted to call him but you waited. For once in your life you thought, *He should call me*. But he didn't.

Why? Why, Ranvir Pratap, mentor of good men, why this silence? What would you have done in my place, sir? You have trained me and trained me well, so well that people do not believe someone like me can be normal so they dig into my past, into my every gesture, wanting to make me out to be some kind of aberration.

Will Nandini understand if you say, *Yes, I did shoot, I killed a man but I let another one go. There is a man alive because of me.* Will she see this the way you do?

This morning you awoke in an empty compartment of a train parked in the depot. You switched on your phone but kept it on silent. You watched it flash every now and then. Desai was calling relentlessly. He, this man you have never met, would likely end up at your house very soon.

Finally you answered his call and he sputtered for a while. You could hear some noises in the background, the hum of a familiar air conditioner. He wasn't alone—he was probably with Ranvir, the mole with the master.

"You got the wrong guy!" shouted Desai.

You looked at your hands while you lied. You were mechanical in your pretense. It was easy as long as you did not think.

"You want me to believe you made a mistake?" shouted Desai. "You were supposed to shoot the decoy, damnit, not the real Abbas."

You asked him something and he shouted some more. "How does it matter who the decoy was? What do you mean was he also a killer?"

But it mattered to you who you shot. You had realized that yesterday. You could not pull the trigger on a man who you had not studied, whose résumé you had not assimilated. You had to know that your quarry deserved your attention.

"You were given an order, Karan."

You nodded, but they couldn't see how you were torn like never before. Then you did another thing that your training taught you not to do: you spoke.

"*Dans ce pays-ci, il est bon de tuer de temps en temps un amiral pour encourager les autres.*"

"Karan, are you hallucinating? What are you saying? It sounds like garbage."

You translated for him: "Desai, it's strange how it's good that from time to time someone dies so others don't."

Parthasarathy and Ranvir met in the morning and argued for a while. They had to handle Tiwari and calm him down. And they had to make an assessment of Karan. This could have been an error—after all, there was little time, it was raining, and he had to take a shot in a narrow window. But this was Karan. Both were disturbed. Should they have informed Karan in advance? Were they wrong in presuming that a police officer would follow orders and knowingly kill someone he didn't know anything about, who would be simply collateral damage, and at the same time allow a known offender to escape? If he felt such a thing as a conscience Karan could have shot at the decoy and missed. But why did he have to kill Abbas? It was hard for Partha to comprehend.

"Karan never misses," said Ranvir. "It's the only part of his résumé that's still intact."

"I believe he is now AWOL?"

Ranvir nodded, looking disappointed. In his books, Away Without Official Leave was desertion. This was the second cardinal error that Karan was making. He should have reported back after the assignment.

Ranvir had called Evam at the crack of dawn, seeking an explanation.

"He probably expects you to call him, Mr. Ranvir. He wants you to speak to him," Evam said, trying to figure out why Karan was on the run.

"And what about his actions yesterday?" Ranvir's tone was accusatory.

Evam tried to provide some sort of explanation: "Aspies have a very strong sense of what is right and what is wrong. For them it is black-and-white, with no shades of gray. They cannot compromise in these matters and they don't respond well to half-measures. So I am not surprised that Karan chose not to shoot the decoy. Personally, I think that was . . . Actually, let's leave aside what I think."

"But what's shocking is that he then chose to shoot Abbas," replied Ranvir. "How do you explain that?"

Even Evam didn't have a satisfactory answer for this. A man who was trained to hunt spends stressful hours building the justification to track a target, chase the target successfully around the city, and in the final flush of the dance, at the very moment when he is to pull the trigger, he is told to "let him go" when he knows the rotten bastard will get away for no good reason. But could that man be excused for . . . It *was* hard to explain.

"In such situations of extreme stress, Aspies are affected more than others," said Evam lamely.

"That's great," replied Ranvir. "So what will our Aspie do next?"

This was beginning to look like a true "rogue officer" situation, a nightmare scenario that the police dreaded.

Despite the strained circumstances, Nandini decides to go

ahead with a group visit that she had committed to months earlier. A large Volvo bus arrives at the chawl, eats up a lot of space, and causes a traffic jam. The chawl has dressed up for the occasion, lights strung on trees and balconies in place of the usual clotheslines.

"We eat whatever we can pronounce," says the superintendent of the chawl to the group of tourists that Nandini has brought with her. "It's that simple. If we can't pronounce it then we don't serve it. In the posh neighborhood of nearby Breach Candy they love Italian cuisine, and in the upmarket Warden Road they adore French dishes. I cannot order those things. I only know how to order simple things like *kozhi* or *kombdi wade* or *kalya watanyachi ussal*."

"The chawl is the beating heart of the city," says Nandini. "Which is why my husband and I decided to live here and not in the police quarters."

The group listens intently and smiles. Others from the chawl in the reception party are eager to have their say, and they speak to the visitors in turn:

"We listen to music that we can sing: three easy notes set to a repetitive beat, a nice chorus that we can shout out loud, and songs that everybody in the vicinity can recognize and join in. People say it's boring but for us it's a community thing. We do not attend concerts in Rang Bhavan, we cannot afford the Zubin Mehta performance, for example, and nobody here has mourned the decline of jazz in Mumbai."

"We decorate our houses with what we can make ourselves. Anything handmade, preferably by a family member; like cushion covers that are embroidered with brightly colored flowers, or curtains that are patchwork from older clothes, and watercolors painted by wives that show women from Rajasthan with pots on their heads."

"The city will never admit that the chawl has more character and local flavor than the skyscrapers." This statement gets a small cheer.

"The Parel chawl is in a mill area, a place that saw real industry that made real products. Now all these fancy buildings have white-collar workers who do not know how to do an honest day's work. They come in fancy cars, these young kids, and they cannot even change a lightbulb."

"Some of us took to drink and others snorted things. Why? No idea. Why not? Maybe because that allowed us to sleep well. No, we are not cynical, but we become a little defeated after we hit forty. At fifty we are looking at our children and counting the ways in which they are different from us. That gives us hope."

Nandini walks back with the group as they board their bus. "I'd even be happy to raise a child in this atmosphere," she tells them. "There is glitz, there is charade, there is glitter, and there is sham—it all coexists, and it's messy, like life. Did you see the kitsch inside each home? Have you witnessed anything like it before?"

The leader of the group speaks to her quietly. "Actually, one of the highlights of this visit was supposed to be meeting your husband. I promised them they would meet an encounter specialist. So sad he was away. I hope he wasn't on another macabre assignment."

Nandini laughs. That is all she can do. She has no idea where Karan is. Her calls went straight to voice mail. She visited all their haunts last night, hiring a taxi and spending hours searching places she thought he might be. She was initially calm, very calm. She was sure she would find him.

But when she didn't, it began to hit her hard. She called Ranvir and he sounded worried. That wasn't a good sign.

"He'll get in touch with Munna and Tapas," he told her. "I am sure he will."

"What exactly happened yesterday?" she asked him. "Could you please tell me the truth?"

He told her exactly what happened and she listened quietly.

"Mr. Pratap," she replied when he was finished, "I have never supported what my husband does and he knows it. But after last evening, whatever he did, I am proud."

Ranvir didn't reply. He himself was conflicted for once. He needed time to sort out this messy affair in his mind. If only this bloody Tiwari would cool off for a bit.

The second day passes by slowly. You have found a hideout and you drop off to sleep for a while in the afternoon. Nandini comes to you in your dreams.

"Karan."

She is standing behind the door. You have shut your eyes. You can do this. In your right hand you hold a gun. Your left hand reaches for the door latch.

"Karan!"

Squeeze the latch, slowly but surely. Take aim two inches above that perfect mouth. Say her name as you do it. She will widen her eyes.

"Karan!!"

The door squeaks as it opens slowly. You open your eyes. She stands framed, beautiful as ever. You squeeze the trigger and hear a dull click.

"Very funny," she says as she peeps into the dark room. "You have a call from a man called Evam."

She shoves a phone into your left hand and leaves. The door shuts and an unknown number glows in the dark.

"Hello?" you say.

"Where were you yesterday, Karan?" asks Evam.

You trace your face with your fingers. "Dr. Madness," you whisper.

He laughs. "Man with a gun. Can we meet?"

The simple question vexes you and you hesitate. "Can't we just talk on the phone?" You suspect everyone right now.

"No, it is better we meet."

"Fine," you reply.

"Good," he says, and he hangs up. Why did he even call? Perhaps they were tracing your location. You don't care because your movements were quick and obscure. You could lead sniffing dogs to their death.

You dream of lunch at home as your mind wanders. You have lost your sense of taste. You laugh a lot at the table. Your wife stares at you, wondering, wanting to join in.

"Karan!"

Your hand holds a fork and your plate is empty. You drop it and take a deep breath and the smell of agarbattis makes you sneeze. You turn to look at the shrine in the corner. There are fresh flowers. She has prayed.

"Karan, about yesterday." She looks at you and you brace yourself. "Was he a bad man?" This unfailing question is the arbiter of reason in your marriage. Your answer is the glue.

You don't have to force yourself to nod. She sighs. For once you had made a decision she would have been proud of. Shouldn't you tell her who this dead fellow was? You will yourself to stop justifying what you have done. Your boss Ranvir Pratap must have gotten the message—you still need a good reason to kill.

The third day is difficult because you are tired and yet you have to be constantly on the move. Your movement has been random thus far but you realize there is a pattern setting in. Someone will inevitably pick up your scent in the next day or two. *Every mind is trained*, Ranvir would tell the team. *Thought has a pattern, a signature, and a trace*, he would say.

Your phone is giving you trouble. You keep it switched off but you are so restless, wanting to get in touch with Nandini, Tapas, Munna, Ranvir, Evam, your stillborn daughter. You start convincing yourself they cannot get to you and that you are finally anonymous, a true Mumbaikar at last. And so you go back to sleep.

You join a group that is out on a nighttime Heritage Walk led by Nandini. Walking after dark with a professional like Nandini is a different experience.

"My friend asked me if I was the type that is constantly outraged. She said she meets people who are always expressing their dismay about the city."

"Does it come with age?" someone asks.

"I guess so." She stops suddenly and laughs at something. "Stand still. Look."

There are two street dogs and they are both interested in each other. The places they sniff make you want to gag.

"Drag your eyes away from Animal Planet. Look back here. Tell me, what do you see?" She points to a shadowless spot. Is that a trick? You look to the source of light, a single street lamp above.

"It is quite late," someone says. "And this street has people milling about."

"What people? I don't see anybody."

The hair on the nape of your neck stirs for some reason. Damn, the road is deserted, the sidewalk bare, and the sky? No clouds, no breeze, and no personality. This could be a film set.

"You are making faces, did you know that?" she says, placing her hand upon yours, acknowledging you for the first time.

You rub your hands on your thighs. A car is coming around the bend, preceded by its lights.

"We should get out of the middle of the road. Now. Why don't you step aside?"

She jumps up onto the sidewalk. The lights swerve and travel across the wall, straightening into your face. Blinding beams, white light that dances and makes colored circles in your retina. Then it's gone. You catch the tail end of the light. The car has a police license plate.

She rubs her eyes. "Are you there? I can't see."

"Still standing."

"You didn't even try to come to me. What's wrong with you?"

You had been dreaming of mountains, grasslands, flowing water, and a weak sun; it feels like the onset of winter. You are rubbing your hands again.

"Karan, walk with me."

"Do we have to hold hands?"

"Just for a while."

"Nandini?"

"Yes."

"How did I end up like this?"

You wake up now, rubbing your eyes. It's still Day Three. You switch your phone on briefly and you receive a message in code. It's from Lookout. *We must meet in person*. He mentions a place in Gorai Beach, an unmarked shack that you know. You set off in a roundabout way. It will take you two hours to get there.

On the train you have an out-of-body experience. One part of you exits the crowded compartment and clambers onto the roof, catches the overpass railing below the Dadar bridge, vaults onto the road, and goes home. Someone stamps your foot with a heel for dreaming and not moving. You look him in the eye till he turns to stone.

At the shack you lose it, you completely fucking lose it when you see Lookout and Different. The two of them are there having taken a dare, having flouted every written rule to meet you. There is no holding back. All the months you have spent together with these two you hardly spoke, never had a drink, a chat, or a night out. And yet it didn't matter. You could feel what you never felt before and perhaps they did too because you actually hugged each other. It was awkward. They wouldn't let go for a while. Who was to say that you were Aspies? You were happy to stand there looking—not at each other, but just looking around. Occasionally you smiled, laughed, or shared a cigarette. It was a strange constellation in the dark on the beach with wind and sand, salt and sea, and perhaps some ghosts you had set free. Nobody was there to take anything away from you at this moment. Tapas had brought what you liked—red meat, tenderized, cooked medium. Munna had a bottle of spirits that had no label, fittingly. You sat down, the three of you, threw your heads back, and drank from the bottle till the last drop. Someone shouted later that night, someone sang, and a dog or two came by to check your litter and settle in the wet sand.

Day Four: Encounter Thirty-Four

The next morning you woke before sunrise, as you were trained to, and Tapas and Munna convinced you that the right thing to do was to go meet Nandini. *Nobody can stop us*, they said. You observed their faces in the half-light and you saw them for the first time. You felt a kinship and the feeling was warm, fuzzy, and comforting. This was foolhardy but it was the right thing to do and so much in keeping with what you had done at the airport.

"How long will you run?" asked Munna.

"Who are you running from?" asked Tapas.

"It's risky," you replied. The decision was taken, and as you sat in the jeep with the two of them and headed south, you had no more questions.

Cool air rushed past as you ate up the miles. You peered out at the empty streets. You occasionally looked behind as well to see if you were being followed. And you imagined what Nandini would be wearing today besides a slight frown.

Between the suburbs of Khar and Bandra the highway department had created one-way streets and roundabouts to tackle the traffic jams. The three of them were in a jeep and the morning sun had broken through as they entered Khar, heading south. Munna in dark glasses was driving and Tapas was next to him in the front passenger seat. Karan was in the middle of the backseat and his gun was with him as always.

They turned onto a one-way bylane. Ahead, on the left side of the road, they spotted a colleague. He was bare-headed and was waving at them. But how did he know they were in the jeep? That question came just as Munna dimmed the jeep's lights and slowed down. The man was carrying a folded newspaper with him.

"Move it!" shouted Tapas. "Something's not right, damnit!"

Munna gunned the gas, but the jeep struggled to gather speed. Out of nowhere a large SUV threw on its high beams and tore directly at them from the opposite side. It had obviously been lying in wait. Two staccato bursts of gunfire suddenly erupted. Glass flew from the jeep as the windscreen shattered. Behind it Munna lost his dark glasses, his eyes, and some part of his head. Tapas lost his teeth but gained a strange smile. There was a splatter of fluid onto Karan's clothes. He was sitting erect and miraculously he was unscathed, not even a scratch. And so he survived the gunfire. It seems he did not realize what he did thereafter: without thinking, he took his gun in hand, looked into that den of the SUV's lights, and let off two shots—one where the driver would be, and the second one next to him where the shooter might be.

Munna must have fallen like a rag doll onto the steering column, as the jeep swung sharply left. The vehicle smashed into a handcart that was reserving a spot between two parked cars, then climbed onto the sidewalk. The SUV continued to scream ahead and slammed head-on into a passing car. The car's driver had no safety equipment—no air bag or seat belt. He took the steering column in his stomach, the windscreen in his face, and part of the engine block in one knee, momentarily losing consciousness. Meanwhile, one of the assailants flew out of the SUV and landed on top of the car's hood. He lay there and leered. He had a hole in his head. Stuck inside the SUV was the driver. A neat cavity was drilled through his nose bridge; the back of his head was missing.

Karan claims he does not remember what happened next. At the hospital, a bystander would later emerge from sedation to tell the story. He said what Karan did would give him nightmares for the rest of his life. Karan had jumped out of the car and fallen awkwardly. He had scrambled like a primate, pounced on a third occupant from the SUV, and pulled him apart with his hands. And then Karan sat down on the edge of the pavement and did not move.

"Catatonic state," said a doctor who quickly arrived at the scene from his nearby apartment. Karan emerged from this state within minutes, asking for biscuits and tea. He only had a few bruises and scratches. But he was drenched in other people's blood, and had skin under his fingernails.

They used brute force to bend metal and towel-covered hands to pluck away glass before lifting the injured driver from the unfortunate car. He was mumbling incoherently, but someone caught a sentence: "They were coming down a one-way."

An ambulance arrived and a paramedic dealt with him and then turned to treat Karan. He was gone. It seems he waited for the injured man to be placed in the ambulance and then disappeared from the scene. They checked for him at his residence, just in case. He had not shown up.

But he did call. Karan rang home and spoke to his wife Nandini, finally. It was a very brief chat in which the meaningful remained unsaid. Nandini the brave lady sat down and cried. He asked her why. She said she was crying because he never did. "One day I will," he replied.

She had some parting words for him which she hoped would keep him alive: "Don't trust anyone." It was futile advice and she knew it because Evam had told her this when they met, when she complained that Karan was naive. "Trust comes naturally in the Aspie world," he said.

The department asked Parthasarathy for an explanation. He had none. The entire building was in shock. They were trained to routinely handle emergencies, but this was different. The description of the incident seemed a little fantastic. When the details emerged Partha shook his head and said, "This was not supposed to happen."

"Exactly what do you mean, sir?" they asked him.

"All of it," he replied.

Some people were puzzled that Karan got away unhurt. Others wondered at the fact that he could look into those bright lights, keep his eyes open, squeeze out shots between two moving cars, and be so accurate. What kind of man sits upright and stays calm when a meteor-like vehicle is hurtling into your face? And then he shoots only two bullets.

Rumbles were heard at the most senior levels. People were more concerned with who the perpetrators were who set this up. Was this an inside job? Two of those in the SUV were from a gang that was linked to Abbas. But this still looked like an inside job because only the *khabari* network could have tracked the jeep with Ranvir's team.

Partha was given the task of informing Ranvir. Ranvir, who was still on medical leave following his coronary scare, did not react immediately. Nobody expected him to show too much emotion yet he was expected to retaliate somehow. He asked to meet the chief of counterintelligence—alone. He was granted an immediate audience. The two men had a frank discussion and after an hour or so agreed that they would deal firmly with Karan. It was an informal agreement influenced by Mishra's view that the police force wasn't a family franchise. "Dons can be paternal," he said. "But we cannot. That would be repeating the mistakes of '83. But if you feel that Karan is 'special' and has some disability, then I can take a different view."

Ranvir thought that over and finally said, "He and the others are no different, and they are as good as any cops I have ever worked with. To give them 'special' dispensation would be a travesty."

Partha was asked to handle the Karan issue on his own. He was reluctant. "I fear he might disregard instructions again, in light of his recent behavior. There is a risk without Ranvir supervising."

"What's the risk?" asked the chief.

Partha tried to explain: "We're concerned because he's acting unpredictably. He attacked that man literally with his hands, remember?"

"But the doctor who did the postmortem said he died out of fear, from a sudden rush of blood to the head, correct?" said the chief.

Partha nodded. "A technicality. The doctor also said that the man who died had only one testicle."

"Oh shit," said Mishra. "Fucking shit. I know where that points."

Partha prattled on: "The meltdown we feared has happened. Karan is clearly under severe stress and needs to be reined in."

"So who's in his line of fire now?" asked the chief.

"Perhaps he's looking for a villain in all this. He is obsessive and compulsive and while people like him are supposed to be unemotional, how can we be so sure that what has happened to his team will not influence his actions? He must be confused. He needs closure."

"Could closure for him come from one last assignment?" asked the chief. "I don't see him coming in on his own otherwise, and honestly, I would hate to hunt him down. After all, he is still one of us."

"I spoke to Evam," said Partha. "I asked him if another encounter was the solution. And he said something interesting. He said, *If you consider routine to be a destination, then Aspies are habitues.* An encounter is Karan's comfort zone."

Mishra thought for a while. "I believe the gangs have put out a contract on Karan. Who is their shooter with the *supari*?"

"Atmaram Bhosle," replied Partha.

Mishra whistled when he heard the name. This was suddenly an opportunity to get even with a cop killer. "Let's suppose Bhosle learns about Karan's next move, and that Karan is told who is after him . . ."

"Are you thinking of staging a confrontation?" said Partha.

The chief drummed his fingers on the table.

"Shall we go ahead then?" asked Partha. "Perhaps in

Lonavla? Karan is comfortable there, and our people know the area well."

The chief nodded and left Partha sitting in his office. Down the corridor was a small room without a nameplate. He entered without knocking on the door. Seated inside, looking like a ghost of his former self, was Ranvir Pratap. Standing next to him was Pandey; his hands were folded in front of him.

"I expect hanky-panky from Tiwari in this assignment," said the chief. "There is going to be a classic showdown between two hunters: Karan and a sharpshooter from a gang. Mr. Desai, here's what you need to do . . ."

Encounter Thirty-Five

I blanked out. The only measure was time.

I realize I've been scrolling through photographs on my phone. Places, people, thoughts. Targets. Human stains. I can make sense of what happened. If I had time and someone to talk to I could calm myself.

I keep fiddling with my phone. Time yawns and I yawn. I should brush my teeth. There are two messages from Evam Bhaskar. *Urgent. Important.* I don't open them. Should I make a call? Who should I call? I'm surprised they haven't traced me yet. I have stopped zigzagging my way around Mumbai. If they want to come and get me they can. I have my Ruger and it's loaded.

I call Ranvir Pratap knowing he will not answer. My charge sheet is now long and infamous. I have shot a man I shouldn't have, I have disobeyed an order to execute someone, I have absconded, and now I have killed someone else who was unarmed, hopefully a gangster. In Ranvir Pratap's books I am guilty many times over. Yet my mind is at peace. I am just dog-tired.

My thoughts drift to the last conversation with Desai. It was a long, unconvincing monologue. They are setting me up, I think.

There is a pileup at the highway tollbooth. As if on cue, the phone rings again.

"This could be your last assignment," murmurs Desai. His tone is conspiratorial.

"Any assignment could be my last," I reply.

"You know what I mean, Karan. They are going to test you." He pauses. Desai rarely pauses so there must be advice on the way. "Just don't make a spectacle. I know people who make grand gestures. Or they do foolish things. We don't want that. Treat it like any assignment."

"Nothing you say will change me," I say.

He laughs. "I know that. You are special. You always were."

"That sounds like an epitaph. Anything else?" I ask.

"You did good, Karan." For a moment he seems less inscrutable.

The next stop is in the town of Khopoli. I order the local delicacy, a bun filled with hot potato mash. As I sit at a table the phone rings. This time Desai sounds unhurried, almost leisurely.

"Have you heard of a death wish?" he asks.

The snack is spicy, there's an ant climbing my plate, and a family next to me has a bawling kid with snot in her nose. I slap down hard on the ant, sending onions flying from the plate and onto the child. Her bawling stops momentarily in her amazement, then more tears. I walk to the counter and buy an ice cream for the kid. Her parents wave me away. I lick the sticky cream that runs down my fingers. The child bawls some more. And Desai rambles on.

"A death wish comes when you are driving endlessly and nothing is happening; you have passed thousands of vehicles and your leg feels wooden and your neck is stiff and your mind is idling toward the inevitable question of what would happen if I was a little slow on the uptake, what if I pulled out of the way of that huge trailer a little late? You need to see that gruesome image in your mind. You ask yourself: can this really happen to me?"

"Are you driving?" I ask him.

He hesitates and I suddenly realize he's following me. Now I know why he calls only when I have stopped.

He continues: "I don't want you to think—not when you drive, not when you are up against another with a gun in your hand. You have strange habits. You almost always face your quarry when you shoot. You give the other a chance. Why?"

"What if I cannot help it?" I say, as I brush crumbs off my shirt. "Sometimes things seem unreal because despite everything I do, nothing happens to me."

He pauses. This pause is unhappy.

"What is your real name, Desai?" I ask him suddenly.

He doesn't respond.

I enter the *ghats* and start the climb up the snaking road. Trucks and buses groan and belch smoke around the bends. The fumes make me cough. I am exposed to the elements in my open jeep. I sneak a glimpse behind to see if I'm being followed and I realize my tailpipe is spurting black puffs of smoke. I negotiate a bend too quickly and have to brake hard. Pulled over ahead is a recreational vehicle whose occupants have spilled out onto the road and broken into song. A few drops of rain arrive and that sets them off into a paroxysm of hip thrusts. The road farther up is blocked by an overturned truck. I settle down and wait and watch the revelry. Desai calls one last time.

"Any questions?" he asks.

"None that you will answer," I reply. But then I voice one anyway: "You've already written my epitaph—what am I missing?"

He remains quiet.

"Because the target's name is Bhosle?" I ask. "Is he that good?"

"Yes," he replies. "I have left some things for you. When you get there, pay attention. Pay attention to the plants."

Plants?

Tiwari knew Bhosle was a rogue who the *khabaris* needed to get rid off, an ace marksman who was in hiding. This was someone who the police hated because he had taken out a cop some years before and that wound had festered. Bhosle could shoot and pit a grape without squinting. His only weakness was disdain. Bhosle was told that if he were to be successful in this mission, he would be welcomed back into their fold. For Tiwari this was a dream scenario. By getting rid of Bhosle, Tiwari would regain lost ground with the *khabaris*. Pitting him against Karan was a master stroke. Either way he would win. He wasn't sure which loss would please him more. Bhosle was told that Karan would arrive at his hideout in Lonavla following the recent assignment in Mumbai.

"Is Atmaram battle-ready?" Tiwari asked of the *khabaris*. "Do you know who he'll be up against?"

The *khabaris* knew of Karan; everyone did.

"Bhosle can do it," they said. "He is possibly the only one. Just don't put the heat on him, that's all."

Atmaram Bhosle surfaced quietly, camping on the terrain and taking up a prime spot with a clear view of the lodge's entrance.

Tiwari had also planted a creature of the night in Lonavla for himself. She was someone with fight and he could hardly wait for the two days of role-play ahead with a busty woman. He would be the wanderer and she would play the waif. This would be thrilling in the cooler, wetter climate of Lonavla, a hill town that cultivated licentiousness.

"Are you going there directly?" asks Desai.

"Would I tell you if I were?"

"You could lie."

"I can never lie. But I can disappear."

And then Karan falls off the radar like a plane from the sky.

Tiwari is lost, but in the folds of a dress that is held up by pins and needles. Someone knocks, rudely interrupting his night of lust. He opens the door, bare-chested. Kamte and Pandey try not to look at him or beyond him. Their boss rants at the news till reason returns. He knows Karan will come. But he doesn't know when.

"Should we call in reinforcements for Karan?" asks Pandey.

Tiwari laughs, his pajamas hanging on him precariously. "Don't bother defending Karan. Where is Atmaram?" He leans heavily on a chair.

"In position, sir; I believe he's directly opposite the cottage on the first floor of a house slightly uphill. He has a clear view of the entrance, along with a scope rifle. His bullets can tear into armor. Karan will be a mess when he gets hit."

Tiwari drums his fingers against his legs. There is pent-up energy in him that has been deprived. The smell of cheap perfume fills the room.

"There's an undercover agent tracking Bhosle, sir," says Pandey, glancing toward the bed in the room. The blinds have been drawn and it's dark inside.

"He must be tired—it's been thirty-six hours of waiting. Who will keep him awake?"

Pandey laughs loudly and someone stirs in the bed under the sheets. "Sir, the agent is unlikely to fall sleep with Bhosle nearby."

The agent had wanted to call home. Upon learning that the job was a face-off between Atmaram and Karan, he thought it prudent to inform his family of his whereabouts.

Tiwari has a last-minute instruction. He looks at this young officer he has grown to like and puts a hand on his shoulder. "Pandey, are you carrying a gun? If so, keep it cocked and ready."

"Why do you ask, sir?" Pandey's voice shakes and he hates that it does.

"You and I will be in the vicinity. If Atmaram succeeds, then you have to be quick. Fire at him if you have a clear shot. But make no mistake—kill him. There should be no survivors."

Pandey stares at his fingers. He wraps them around his weapon but the cold metal gives no comfort. He has never killed a man, and a crack assassin is supposed to be his first victim? All he has to do is pull the trigger; at that range he would need more balls than accuracy.

"Sir," says Pandey, "why are we doing this?" It's obvious to him that the hierarchy has failed. The complex police machinery has derailed. This could easily turn into a botched operation and the participants know it; the problem is they don't care. All outcomes are acceptable.

I lie awake in the jeep at the edge of a precipice that defines a hill. There is condensation on my clothes, the seat, and the steering wheel. The windscreen has rivulets. Below me is a familiar cottage that awaits my arrival. I massage my temples to ease the pain. I need a coffee to clear my head. The remnants of a dream linger; last night's was a curiously serene one, bathed in a silver moon. It's time to rinse my face and get going.

I am hungry and if I don't eat I will wander. I abandon the jeep and descend toward the lodge, carefully observing every tree and its shadow. But then I invade a neighbor's home, setting off a mad dog. Soon the whole place echoes with barking, lights come on, and people emerge with flashlights and shout at each other. I set off two car alarms to drown out the sound. Amid the cacophony I ascend to a hidden approach along a side street.

I scale a low brick wall and vault over an iron fence. I land on my toes and wince as my weight comes down on my knees. My moon shadow drops down beside me and waits. There is no one around the bungalow. The watchman has gone for a cup of tea down the road. The car park is empty and I use the cover of a cloud to reach the fire escape. I climb the stairs sideways, chasing my shadow. My rubber soles soften my step but squeak over some water. I collapse like a shroud, crouch in a huddle, and scan the corridor. Nobody at this hour. The entrance is covered. I unlock the front door, three locks in sequence. The last is electronic and beeps before opening. I slip my right hand inside, bracing my left palm against the door. I find the alarm switch and a Post-it note. I slip inside, grab a flashlight, and read the note; it contains a code that I immediately feed into a keypad inside the door.

Desai has left me instructions, as usual. I take off my shoes and examine the soles out of habit. No debris. I step in carefully, survey the room end-to-end, and switch on a light. Bhosle will know I have entered. I turn around and kick the door shut. The second Post-it note is near the eyehole. Desai knew I would turn around and peer out.

Wash your feet first, then your hands and face.

Per routine, I amble into the washroom on the left. I scrub my hands with soap, then rinse my feet with hot water. I use a clean white towel and rub myself down hard. Next to the washroom mirror is a third note.

Sit at the table and empty your pockets.

I walk to the table in the living room and empty my pockets. Near the table is a small shredder. Stuck on it is a pink Post-it.

Paper trail goes here.

I had no ticket stubs this time so I dump the Post-its. I walk up to the kitchen counter. Placed on it is a tumbler with a full finger of amber liquid. I down the stuff in a single gulp and wait for the burn. I twirl the glass like I always do after draining the last drop.

Every time I visit here I stay for a week. Half an hour after I leave, my shadow will come in and check the sequence meticulously. He is a trained poacher, taught to track people like me. He will sweep the place like an anthropologist and if anything is amiss he will spot it and he will know what to do. If he feels I have made a run for it, he will hunt me down. Informers who have been sent here for safekeeping and have tried to flee have all been tracked and captured.

I would typically feed the Post-its into the shredder, bide my time as prescribed, and then leave just before daybreak. The door would shut behind me with a click and the electronics would kick in. There would be a slight breeze that ruffles the potted plants standing like sentries in the corridor. I would slip on my shoes and weave my way out.

Now what? I remember past instructions and move without thinking to the bedroom and look for a note under the alarm clock. This time the instructions are different. I half-expected what I read, but still, to see it in black-and-white and face the reality is difficult. I feel queasy and my stomach turns at what's in store. I am suddenly out of time.

There's a CD player beside the open window where I stand. A few minutes of eternal sound? Why not. Another drink? Why not. Something is happening. Something is welling up inside me and I cannot fight it. That last Post-it says, *Karan, this is your final encounter. Today you are the target.*

It happens in some kind of slow motion. Karan moves as if in a daze. He considers the glass, rolls it around, and tilts it to his mouth again. He shrugs his shoulders and walks up to the liquor cabinet. He has broken the chain of command. The last Post-it under the alarm clock should have said, *There is a change of plan. Take your things and leave immediately*. If he had done so then he would never have needed to return to Lonavla again. Atmaram would have drilled a hole in his head as he left.

Instead he pours himself another drink. He walks up to the CD player. He has never used it, ever. He shuffles through the discs on the rack above it and picks one.

He plays it. It starts slowly and some words are spoken. Karan waits for the music to build up and the sound swells gradually. They see him turn his back on them.

"Atmaram is shifting positions," says Pandey. "Because Karan hasn't left yet."

Pandey is on the phone with the undercover agent who has hurried toward the other side of the terrace. There he glimpses Atmaram looking around for a clear shot.

Tiwari shivers. "He can't see us, can he?"

I hope he can, thinks Pandey. He has been told of Tiwari's violent escapades at various brothels. News like this travels fast through the very network he created. Pandey has instructions from Mishra as well.

Suddenly Atmaram comes into view, his scope rifle waving dangerously in front of him. They watch Karan pour some more whiskey.

Karan downs the liquid and the sniper gets set. The drumbeats intensify, filling the bungalow.

"What is he up to?"

Karan walks up to the window and, seemingly counter to his instincts, stands directly in front of it with his hands on his hips. Atmaram isn't quite set yet. "Come on, *bhosadike*," he urges softly as he opens his scope and leans on the frame.

"I'm surprised nobody has taken a shot yet," says Tiwari.

Karan stretches out his arms, slowly steps back in front of the open window, then sticks his head out. The wind hits his face; he looks straight ahead.

Karan appears in Bhosle's scope camera. The auto focus zooms onto his face, blurs, and then adjusts. They can see his face clearly now in the corresponding video feed too. There, in full view, for the first time they see him cry.

"Wait," says Pandey, speaking out of turn. "This changes everything."

Tiwari looks at him in astonishment. Pandey speaks to the agent, who distracts Atmaram momentarily.

What on earth was Karan doing?

Somewhere across from the bungalow, up there in some house, somebody must be thinking that it probably took me enormous effort to step out into full view, unprotected. That goes completely against my training. I would never do that unless the place was secured. And to cry was even stranger. I was crying. I could feel all the tears that had never come before.

Why?

I had no idea. What I was going to do was new for me. I had no time to think through every step I was to take. Actually, I had no plan at all.

I step back into the room, just in time. Is it important that I survive this? There are three of them in that dark sky among the stars that matter to me. I should not let my team down and follow in their footsteps. Come on, shake off that memory.

I have to deal with this sniper. What caliber do they have in mind for me?

Karan?

I can hear Ranvir's voice in my head. My holster feels heavy and I slide my hand in and take my gun. The chamber is loaded. The gun has no sight but I can see well enough as I peek out through a corner of the window. I can see him across this divide, up there in the bay window where he is crouched, watching. I can pick him off in a fraction of a second. It would not take much time for the bullet to traverse and pierce that glass and what lays behind.

Stretch that ligature, Karan.

My boss Ranvir had called me before this assignment. He was brusque and told me I had to decide once and for all. Decide what? He said, *You are as good as you ever were.* Really? *Don't walk away*, he warned me. *Nobody can.*

Tense the finger, Karan. Trust the invisible armature when you aim.

I pace the length of the room and then head back toward the window. He is still there, I know, and this time he will be ready. I need him to be looking into the scope of his gun. I need his left eye.

Nobody shoots with their eyes wide open, Karan. Except you.

Tell me, Nandini, should I atone for all I have done, bear today the burden of it all? I would like to.

Second nature comes to natural-born killers.

I make my move, show myself as I whirl, crouch as I take aim and shoot. A fraction of a second before I fire, a bullet enters the side of my chest. It is a high-caliber bullet that leaves a gaping hole. As I recoil a second bullet catches me in the pit of my stomach, and after that I really cannot remember . . .

The Next Day

"Did you see what happened to him?"

"It's all there in high-definition. This camera has super-zoom."

"What were the seniors looking for? Why did they want all this on film?"

"They need to cover their backsides. They wanted evidence that this was not a setup where they killed one of their own."

"They fucked him."

"You can say that again."

There is the sound of evil laughter.

They wrap up their equipment. KK looks wistful. For once even DJ is moved by what they've seen. Over the past few days they had been tailing this guy and they felt like they were getting to know him.

DJ thinks aloud: "Was he just a pawn, a puppet? Will anyone remember him?"

KK is staring at a photograph from the man's final encounter. "I will. He was a fucking poet, the way he moved and the way he used a gun. He even had a lisp when he spoke."

"Did Pandey call you yet?" asks DJ. "He asked us to

show up tomorrow morning at a place called the Special Branch. We might have an official full-time job."

"Doing what?" asks KK. They are waiting to catch a bus that heads westward toward Versova. There, in the vicinity of a *paan* shop, is their source for good grass.

"No clue," replies his partner. "But he did say he had a new boss—Ranvir Pratap."

"So it seems like our friend Tiwari has been asked to take a long walk?"

They laugh together, loudly, both trying to visualize what happened when Pandey accidentally shot Tiwari in the thigh, right near his crotch.

"Do you think Pandey will miss him?"

"Yes and no."

They laugh some more.

"I wish our sharpshooter survived."

"Those who shoot first usually do, at least in the movies . . . Can you imagine their bullets crisscrossing?"

Life has been quiet in Karan's absence. My niece who attends a boarding school has come to Mumbai for her holidays. I often take her for long walks, doing things I haven't done in a while, like roaming parts of this city that are conducive to leisurely examination. It's a Saturday and we stand in Azad Maidan and an hour goes by. The vast open space teems with children playing cricket. The noise from the grounds is heartening. My niece picks up a stray ball and throws it back into play. She smiles when the boys cheer.

We head toward Churchgate Station skirting the Cross Maidan on the way. We reach the Oval Maidan, which is a smaller space, and we stand next to the Eros Cinema, sip a lemon drink, and enjoy the refined atmosphere. We take a leisurely stroll around the oval. One side is lined by art deco buildings where generations have resided. On the other side of the oval, buildings reflect the city's colonial history.

Near the Cooperage side of the oval, there's a small traffic island with a statue of the leader Ambedkar in the center, pointing to the sky as always. Behind his statue the road leads to the old business district. This is where Bombay intersects with Mumbai. It's not a peaceful coexistence.

"A Bombay state of mind," I say out loud, without thinking.

"Hello, Nandini," says a nearby voice. He emerges from the shadows of a semicircular building and steps to my side. He is young, younger than me, and looks nothing like what I had imagined.

I recognize his voice from the phone. "Mr. Pandey?"

He stands straight and his arms are folded across his chest. His eyes have a twinkle to them. We stay there for a moment avoiding the inevitable, but finally succumb to that posthumous discussion we were meant to have. We both start talking at the same time, then laugh awkwardly and begin again. He apologizes again for what happened.

"I was there," he says. "For the first time Desai got to see Karan at work."

How much will he tell me? I wonder. I make out that his apology is heartfelt.

It bothers him that he hasn't understood why Karan just stood in front of the window totally exposed. "When I replay the scene in my mind, all I remember is that it was like a fireworks display—the two flashes from Bhosle's rifle, the two puffs of smoke, and then the reverberations—and then suddenly Bhosle was thrown back as if a truck had hit him. And I saw a big hole. And I saw him struggle, trying to tell us something. Nobody was interested and we watched him die. In the chaos, I realized I had inadvertently let off a shot and Tiwari was rolling around and screaming, his hands bloody from the ooze coming from between his legs."

I state the obvious: "So he got his man yet again."

"Yes, but Karan was slow that day, a split-second slow that night, slow enough for—"

"Was it deliberate?" I ask him, hoping he will say no.

"We will never know. Maybe he was tired or confused. He had been through a lot. But Mr. Ranvir Pratap thinks differently."

As I press for more details, he says, "You will have to ask him yourself, Nandini. He's ready to meet you."

Pandey is wearing a jacket with a holster underneath; he inserts his right hand, pulls out a familiar gun, and offers it to me. "They've given me his Ruger. I have no use for it. Would you like to keep it?"

"Yes," I reply. What am I saying?

Acknowledgments

1. The phrase *Dans ce pays-ci il est bon de tuer de temps en temps un amiral pour encourager les autres* is taken from *Candide* by Voltaire.

2. The author owes a debt of gratitude to a growing list of people. Among them: Priya Doraswamy, a mentor in the guise of an agent; Ibrahim Ahmad, for his invaluable input; and the kind people who run residencies at Ledig House, New York, and Sangam House, Bangalore.

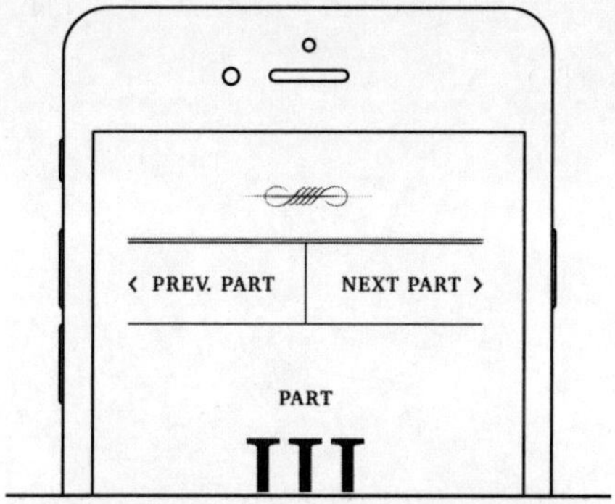

Beautiful Typography

The quality of print transferred to your mobile. Forget ugly PDFs.

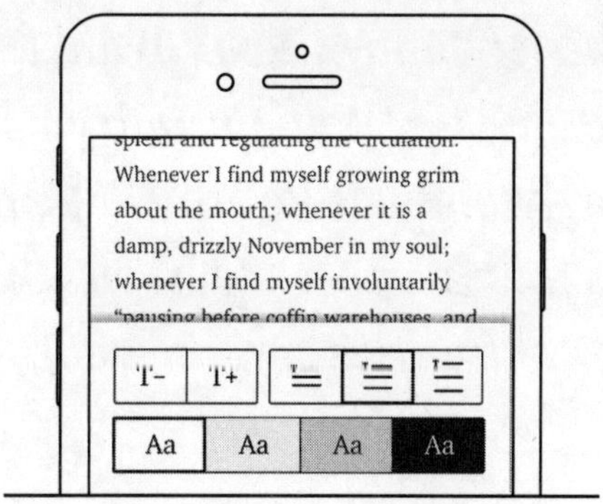

Customizable Reading

Read in the font size, spacing and background of your liking.

www.juggernaut.in

DON'T JUST READ; INTERACT

We're changing the reading experience from passive to active.

Ask authors questions

Get all your answers from the horse's mouth. Juggernaut authors actually reply to every question they can.

Rate and review

Let everyone know of your favourite reads or critique the finer points of a book – you will be heard in a community of like-minded readers.

Gift books to friends

For a book-lover, there's no nicer gift than a book personally picked. You can even do it anonymously if you like.

Enjoy new book formats

Discover serials released in parts over time, picture books including comics, and story-bundles at discounted rates.

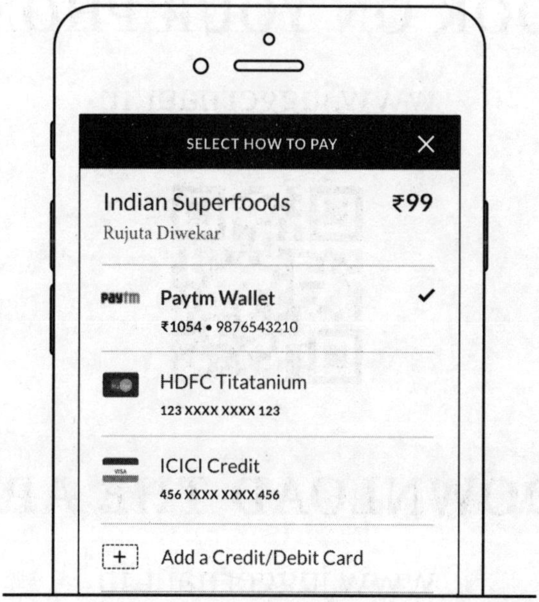

Paytm Wallet, Cards & Apple Payments

On Android, just add a Paytm Wallet once and buy any book with one tap. On iOS, pay with one tap with your iTunes-linked debit/credit card.